D1458165

As Young as This

As Young as This

ROXY DUNN

FIG TREE
an imprint of
PENGUIN BOOKS

FIG TREE

UK | USA | Canada | Ireland | Australia
India | New Zealand | South Africa

Fig Tree is part of the Penguin Random House group of companies
whose addresses can be found at global.penguinrandomhouse.com.

First published 2024
001

Copyright © Roxy Dunn, 2024

The moral right of the author has been asserted

The excerpt on p. 14 from *Murder in the Cathedral* by T. S. Eliot is copyright ©
Faber & Faber Ltd, 1935, 1936, 1937, 1938. Reproduced with permission
of Faber & Faber Ltd. Lines on p. 30 from *The Oresteia* by Tony Harrison.

This is a work of fiction. Names, characters, places and incidents are either the product
of the author's imagination or are used fictitiously. Any resemblance to actual persons,
living or dead, events or locales is entirely coincidental.

The author and publisher gratefully acknowledge the permission granted to re-produce
the copyright material in this book. Every effort has been made to trace copyright holders
and to obtain their permission. The publisher apologizes for any errors or omissions and, if notified
of any corrections, will make suitable acknowledgement in future reprints or editions of this book.

Set in 12/14.8pt Bembo Book MT Pro
Typeset by Jouve (UK), Milton Keynes
Printed and bound in Great Britain by Clays Ltd, Elcograf S.p.A.

The authorized representative in the EEA is Penguin Random House Ireland,
Morrison Chambers, 32 Nassau Street, Dublin D02 YH68

A CIP catalogue record for this book is available from the British Library

Hardback ISBN: 978–0–241–63269–7
Trade paperback ISBN: 978–0–241–63271–0

www.greenpenguin.co.uk

MIX
Paper | Supporting
responsible forestry
FSC® C018179

Penguin Random House is committed to a
sustainable future for our business, our readers
and our planet. This book is made from Forest
Stewardship Council® certified paper.

For Ceri, David, Gemma

The Men

You press your phone to your ear to hear Lillie over the noise of the restaurant.

'I maybe definitely shouldn't ask this,' she says.

'But obviously you're going to anyway.'

You smile as she pauses and think she's probably smiling too. 'Do you regret any of them?'

You've been asking yourself this same question. Until now you'd always pictured them like stepping stones: each man since you were seventeen leading you closer to your ultimate endpoint. So how did you get here? It's almost funny, given your strategic approach to finding someone you want to do this with.

'Weirdly, I don't think I do.' You lean your head back against the padded leather booth as you glance at the clock and count fourteen hours and sixteen minutes until tomorrow's appointment. 'I probably should but it's just, well, it feels kind of hard to regret love.'

'What about the ones you weren't in love with, though?'

'OK, are you goading me into regret?'

Lillie laughs and then says quickly, 'I'm just curious. I actually think it's great you don't regret them.'

'It's hard to know which of them to regret.' As you say this, a couple of candidates immediately spring to mind. 'Even if I took one out, would it have changed anything, or would I still be in this same place?'

'Juicy hypothetical. I got a fish bone stuck in my throat the other day and it made me think about that medic I used to date—'

'Luke?'

'Good memory. And how much more useful it would be if I'd ended up with a doctor instead of a product marketing manager.'

'George is better, though. Even if you do end up choking to death.'

'Sweet. Speaking of which, this is precisely the worst timing but he's just walked through the door with dinner. Can I call you back once we've eaten?'

'Don't worry, the locksmith should be calling any minute.' But that's not the call you're waiting for, not really.

'You know you can stay here tonight, right?'

'Thanks but I think I need to be by myself.'

'All right, but don't go having one of those dark nights of the soul. Or actually, maybe this merits one.'

'I promise to indulge in moderation.'

As you hang up, you check your phone for any missed calls. It's still not too late for Noah to ring. This thought has been playing on a loop since Friday like a lyric or a jingle designed to sell you hope. It wouldn't need to be dramatic; you'd rather it wasn't. You wish you could insert yourself into his body and make the moves for him, open his pronounced bow lips to say the words, 'You don't actually need to do this because I want to do it with you.'

At the table opposite, a little girl in a chequered pinafore dress and gold hoop earrings is staring admiringly at you, her dark eyes large and doll-like. You've done nothing other than misplace your door key and drink sugared tea these last couple of minutes, making you nervous and undeserving of the attention.

It's not even as though your situation is all that rare or unusual. Countless women make this choice every day. So why does it feel so surprising? Like stepping out of a cool dry plane and being hit by a cloud of hot humid air.

The little girl is still staring at you as her parents photograph themselves posing with their drinks. Shutting your eyes, you hear the grill from the open kitchen hiss as meat touches it; the scraping of chairs on the mosaic tiled floor makes your spine momentarily judder. It still doesn't make sense to you. This wasn't meant to be part of your story.

1. Elliot

You have kissed boys before and been out with them for several weeks at a time during which you have texted and held hands at the cinema but have never felt anything close to the teenage infatuation presented in *Dawson's Creek* which has set the bar high and is what you are aspiring to. Ideally you want a love that involves climbing in and out of each other's bedroom windows with ladders, but the impracticality of this means you will settle for long phone calls from the bay windowsill of your Victorian house in residential Norwich, and a complete desire to be with the other at all times. You aren't looking for sex or even romance per se; what you want is a soulmate, someone you cannot live without, who will join up the dots inside your torso so that you glow like the tiny bulb in a circuit board.

It is inside your sixth-form college library, midway through annotating notes on Edward Gordon Craig's set design for your approaching AS Theatre Studies exam, that you have the sudden realization – you want Elliot to be your boyfriend. This discovery is so obvious and simple that it makes you feel soft and dense as though your body is made of dough.

Elliot is a peripheral friend of yours, in the same circle of drama students who all hang out together and, although you don't know each other hugely well, you always seem pleased by the other's presence. You make a pact with yourself that if you focus solely on revision for the next two weeks, the moment your exams are over you will tell him how you feel. You are studious, not by nature but because you understand that good grades will give you opportunities and you are obsessed with the notion of keeping your future as open as possible, of not cutting off options you might later regret. Currently life feels as infinite as an unpolluted sky littered with stars, all and any of which might make up the constellation of adulthood.

And so you work diligently, using your self-imposed five-minute breaks to daydream about him, to foster your image of the two of you together, so that by the time you put your pen down in the final minute of your English Lit paper on *Hamlet*, all you can think about is being with him: whether the rust-coloured curls of his hair will immediately bounce back after running your fingers through them, if you will hold hands with your fingers intertwined or palm to palm, will you walk his family's springer spaniel together? In truth, you get nervous around dogs but will make an exception to adhere to this image of perfect coupledom.

Two nights later in the house of your mutual friend Holly whose parents are on a Bermuda cruise, you and Elliot get together. With your permission, Holly has told Elliot about your feelings for him and has reported back that he is 'surprised but up for it'.

'Hey,' you say, walking into the kitchen where Elliot is sitting on the counter taking Beechams tablets out of their packaging.

'Hey. Want one?'

'I'm all right, thanks. Have you got a cold or something?'

'No. It just gets you more drunk.'

'Oh. I didn't know that.'

He tips back his head and swallows a couple with the large Smirnoff Ice bottle squeezed between his thighs. He offers you the packet again and instead you take the bottle from his legs and swig from it.

'Have you ever counted all your freckles?' you ask, lightly tugging your earlobe as you have seen girls do in films.

'Maybe like when I was ten. Why, have you counted yours?'

'Yeah, but I've only got sixteen.'

'Sixteen's ideal, I reckon. A smattering.' For some reason, 'smattering' makes you both laugh. 'Shall we have a cigarette?' he says.

'I don't smoke.' Your natural earnestness means it only occurs to you afterwards that you could have lied about this. 'I could watch you, though?' you say, keen to salvage the moment.

'It's fine, I'll just wait.'

You stay drinking together, passing the bottle back and forth between his legs until Holly comes in to be sick in the sink.

Later that night, after substantially more Smirnoff Ice, you summon the courage to climb into his sleeping bag and make the first move to kiss him. His dark grey T-shirt smells of laundry detergent and reassures you of his hygiene, unlike most of the boys you know whose primary odour is sweat or Lynx from an aerosol which they spray without restraint. You lift up his T-shirt to stroke his shoulder blades, deliberating whether it would be romantic or corny to refer to them as wings, in the end whispering it and hoping he hasn't heard. The next morning it is settled without discussion: you are boyfriend and girlfriend, and you are as happy as you can ever remember being.

It's the look and feel of everything you see and touch being sherbet yellow, happiness that's young and uncomplicated and lasts for three whole weeks. You only see him a couple of times during this interim but that's not a problem, at least not yet. Without him there you can feed off the night you got together, slowly peeling the images on to your memory like transfer tattoos, rather than having to overlay them with new ones.

You continue not to see each other much; he's always busy with college work, rehearsals with his youth theatre and hanging out with the circle of drama students, of which he's at the centre. Although he invites you along, what you crave is time with just the two of you so that he can come to understand absolutely

7

every part of you in the way that your parents and sister and best friends inexplicably fail to – a failure that makes you feel irrationally alone. For every sting of prior misinterpretation, you believe Elliot will be the balm, the cure.

The few occasions the two of you spend alone together you do a lot of kissing – never more than this even though you'd like to do more but his hands never stray – and laugh a lot. It feels comparable to hanging out with a best friend except for how much time is spent rolling your tongues around in each other's mouths.

The album of that summer is *Twelve Stops and Home* by The Feeling and it becomes the soundtrack to your longing. In particular, the song 'Fill My Little World' seems to perfectly articulate not only your desire for Elliot to want you but your desire to assist him in wanting you. This striving for equal affection will be a recurring feature of your romantic relationships, but of course at seventeen, you cannot know this yet.

You wish you could talk to your sister, Romily, who – at twenty-one – would surely be able to tell you whether Elliot's lukewarm conduct is anything to be concerned about, but she is Interrailing around Europe that summer with her university boyfriend, Doug. Although you get regular postcard updates on the various cities she's visited and descriptions of gelato that make the Cornetto in your home freezer taste vastly inferior, she has no fixed address to reply to.

Ciao from scorching Rome! Everything is SO OLD here it feels like walking around inside a BC computer game (minus the togas). Yesterday we visited the Sistine Chapel which was pretty whelming. The food lives up to the hype, though! Even their pizza WITHOUT cheese is insanely delish. Love you long time, Romy xxx

A couple of times you try drafting responses anyway.

Ciao from thunderstormy Norwich! Rome sounds . . . ancient! V jel of the food (even though I still think pizza without cheese is criminal). Guess what . . . I've got a boyfriend! His name's Elliot and he's a thesp *like me *ignoring your eye roll*. We haven't done stuff yet but I think maybe he just wants to take things slow? What do you think?? Loadsa love, Marg xxx PS Are you saying you were only moderately impressed by the Sistine Chapel? If so, Mum says your use of 'whelming' is incorrect. The grammar lessons continue ;-)*

But you're so mortified when you read your replies that you rip them into confetti pieces and scatter them in your waste-paper bin.

One afternoon at your house, you and Elliot go on Myspace and review each other's profile photos. He tells you that your best physical feature is your straight white teeth and, when you look disheartened, says, 'What I mean is your smile.'

'Yours is your curls,' you tell him, which are red and wild and vivid next to your own hair which is flat and a nondescript shade of brown, but in actual fact, it's not his appearance you're particularly drawn to. While you by no means find him unattractive, it's his personality that has caused you to feel this connection to him. But you think that listing his personality as his best physical feature would be more insulting than him listing your teeth.

It's difficult to pinpoint the exact details of how or why you break up; it just fizzles out, instigated by his lack of interest in seeing you, and you are pleased to feel a twinge of the heartache you have read about in magazines, although there is something undermining about the proximity of these break-up articles to sample sachets of lip gloss.

Later that summer you encounter Elliot at a party hosted by one of the drama circle. Everything is still amicable but for some reason he has been acting strangely all night, avoiding eye contact and finding excuses to leave the conversation you're in. You can't understand the reason for his aloofness when he's the one who essentially ended the relationship, but are about to find out.

You are standing in the living room next to a circular coffee table on which there is a bowl of Jelly Babies; disappointingly, only green and orange ones remain. There is the distinct smell of Doritos ground into the carpet combined with the smell of grass that people are bringing on their bare feet through the open conservatory doors. Outside, Elliot is lying flat on his back while your friend Simon bounces him on the trampoline. You watch Elliot's legs hitting the mesh seconds before his back does so that his torso jerks as it lands as though he is briefly sitting upright inside a coffin. He is wearing the same grey T-shirt he wore the night you first got together, making it hard to decipher whether the flapping in your ribcage is owing to nostalgia or attraction.

'Why is Elliot acting off with me?' you ask Holly who has just swayed over holding a bottle of Malibu by its neck.

'I dunno.' But she leaves a deliberate pause before she says this, prompting you to ask again.

'What is it? What are you not saying?'

Her eyes have gone bright and narrow, the way your cat's go when it skulks towards a bird.

'OK, there's something you should know.' She's trying not to smile but cannot suppress her relish in being Elliot's emissary. 'Simon and Elliot are more than friends.'

'As in . . .'

'They've been sleeping together and now they're boyfriend and boyfriend.'

You could have done with more breathing space between these pieces of information. Oddly, the bit that's most important to you is saving face. You can show you're shocked but won't permit yourself to show you're hurting.

'No way, are you serious?' you ask, as if receiving a piece of gossip unrelated to you.

'It's crazy, right? I only found out like a week ago.'

You nod, trying to disregard the nausea currently permeating your stomach. It occurs to you, with both regret and irritation, that you will never again want to wear your white ruffle mini-skirt and favourite jade tank top you are currently dressed in.

'So, you're OK with it, then?'

'Sure, I mean it's not like we're together any more; I'm just, you know, surprised.'

'Totally.'

You can't recall at what point in the night this conversation happens or what immediately follows it. What you do recall is that it's only later, when a girl throws up inside your suede bag and you're confronted with the acidic scent of vomit you feel inside your own mouth, that you call your mother and ask to be picked up, promising to explain when she gets there.

Dressed in her Berghaus waterproof and tartan pyjama trousers, she drives all the way out to the village where the party is being held, in the middle of the night. Too stunned and upset at this point to care about the embarrassment you also feel, you tell her that Elliot is probably gay. As she briefly removes one hand from the steering wheel – something she never does and objects to other people doing – and places it on your shoulder, you're unsure whether the pain you feel is for the loss of what you thought you'd shared with Elliot or the humiliation of having been profoundly fooled.

The next morning, leafing through the week's backlog of *Guardian*s scattered across the kitchen table, your mother declares, 'I've been thinking hard about this since last night and I think he must have decided that if he didn't want to be with you then he didn't want to be with any woman.' She has firmly fixed on this conclusion to prevent you feeling rejected, and in doing so turns an awkward and painful first break-up experience into one in which you can go forth with confidence in your abilities to find a future partner – if you choose to latch on to the narrative she's offering, which you do, gratefully replying,

'Really? I guess maybe you're right.' You can see already that no irrevocable harm has been done. You're relieved you and Elliot never slept together but are also critical of your own judgement, as if his lack of interest in having sex with you should have been a strong enough indication of his interest in men.

Whenever you see Elliot at points over the years, you're struck by his extravagant gestures, by how much more at ease in his skin he seems, compared to when the two of you went out. The last time you bumped into him was a few summers ago on Hampstead Heath, at the intersection of two gravel paths. You congratulated him on his queer theatre company you knew about from Twitter and he told you how pleased he was to see you pop up in a BBC sitcom last year.

Heading away, you said to Noah, 'We went out when I was seventeen. He was technically my first proper boyfriend, even though we never slept together. But emotionally he was the first person I ever felt anything for.'

'He seems nice,' said Noah, wiping sweat from his forehead with the back of his hand. 'Kind.'

As you take in Noah's energized strides, the damp patches under his arms, you feel grateful for his enthusiasm for walking, despite the heat.

'Obviously his body language was different back then,' you add, as if to reassure yourself you weren't completely deluded to have fallen for Elliot – not that you harbour any resentment. Your discovery of his sexual orientation was presumably easier and less complicated than his own discovery and reveal of this.

Noah nods and smiles, hooking his arm around your shoulders. Placing your palm on his back, you stroke the wet cotton of his shirt, feel stifled with love, thick and un-budging. It's so easy to wish happiness for Elliot and for all the men you've been with, believing that collectively they've led you to this moment, treading with Noah in the relentless sun.

2. Joe

You meet Joe the month you turn nineteen and are determined to lose your virginity. Each of your closest female friends has lost it by this point, while you are not only still a virgin but haven't even fooled around with guys. You still recollect, with excruciating detail, a morning during the first few weeks of sixth-form college when Rosie and Amber – two of your oldest childhood friends – had turned to you inside the cafeteria and, with a coyness that struck you as artificial, revealed they'd gone to third base at a party you weren't at. You'd been invited but had chosen not to go because you often get bored around the midpoint of parties and crave being at home, and so of course this was the party when they had taken it in turns to go into the bathroom and suck off two guys from their biology class.

Listening to them deliver this breaking news while trying to swallow the piece of cinnamon swirl currently lodged inside your mouth, you feel panic – confirmation that you are too far behind to catch up and will lack integrity if you suddenly adopt your friends' loose approach you've shunned until now – deciding that the only way you can stay true to yourself while not staying a virgin is by getting another boyfriend, and fast. But in the months that follow, this proves to be more challenging than anticipated.

It's not that you couldn't get any boyfriend or that you're being picky. At this stage, you have no set criteria in terms of what you're looking for; your only requirement is a feeling of connection between yourself and a member of the opposite sex – something you don't know how to fabricate, and without which can't bring yourself to commit to someone, even temporarily.

'I just don't find the stuff boys my age talk about very interesting,' you confide in Romily that Easter, observing her in the mirror as she contours her already prominent cheekbones.

'Then try talking to them about the stuff you do find interesting.'

'I think they find that a bit weird and intense,' you say, wincing at the memory of quoting T. S. Eliot's *This is one moment/But know that another/shall pierce you with a sudden painful joy* to the injured college rugby captain as you'd queued behind him at the vending machine. His expression of confusion, and stiff posture as he slowly turned in his neck brace to look at you, further heightening the discord of the exchange.

'You're not signing up to a marriage,' says Romily, attempting to roll her eyes while applying mascara. 'Just go for someone you're attracted to and see if the other stuff follows.'

'Is that what you did with Doug?'

'Pretty much. We just kept getting together on nights out and then figured we also had good breakfast chat,' she says, pulling at her lashes to separate them. 'I doubt we even had a sober conversation for at least the first six months.'

From this moment on, the finding of someone who you want to both kiss and converse with over breakfast – and who shares this twofold desire – becomes your sole aim and deepest aspiration, but one that continues to remain unrealized. Since this discussion, more than two years have passed in which you've stayed chronically single and inexperienced.

It's currently your gap year, and despite a six-month stint in Bordeaux where you go on dates with guys (including an Erasmus student who you share a dozen oysters with on the quayside, attempting to enjoy their gelatinous texture so you can feel sophisticated), you've still, to your shame, never had sex. Already the middle of June, there are now only a couple of months to rectify this before you leave Norwich to go to drama school on the outskirts of London.

You are working as a barmaid in a pub near the university campus when Joe comes in one night wearing a Rip Curl hoodie and Vans trainers. Immediately apparent is his defined bone structure and surfer hair which sweeps across his forehead resting just below his left eye, partially obscuring his vision; you're at an age where aesthetics trump practicality.

Pulling him a pint of Kronenbourg, you get chatting and he mentions he's a student at the university, has just finished his exams, but is staying in Norwich for another month until the lease on his house-share runs out. You're surprised when he says he's studying Computing Science because he defies the stereotype in that he's talkative and asks questions, is viscerally drawn to the football score on the television in the corner, and proves comfortable conversing with sustained eye contact. You find it remarkable that he not only reveals he's single but also appears to be attracted to you when he joins a game of pool with some other students and you catch him looking at you on several occasions while he chalks his cue. At the end of the night as you collect up glasses, you pretend not to notice him lingering by the bar, even though you can see his reflection in the large rectangular mirror above the fireplace.

'Hey, so a few of us are going to Chicago's tomorrow night if you're up for it?' he asks, drumming the tips of his fingers against the wooden counter.

'Sure, I'm always up for some Ricky Martin.'

'That's good cause "Livin' La Vida Loca" is pretty much guaranteed.'

'Obviously now I'll have to hold you to that.'

'Pressure,' he says, smiling out of the side of his mouth so that you think of one half of a skateboard lifting off the ground. 'We'll probably end up pre-drinking at mine if you want to join?'

'I'm working till close but maybe you can take my number and let me know where you're at?'

As he retrieves his Motorola flip phone from the pocket of his baggy jeans, you can't help feeling hopeful this might be the chance you've been waiting for.

The following evening you arrive at Chicago's shortly after midnight and push through the dance floor until you find Joe energetically flailing in a circle with four others. He puts his arm around you while his friends wave in your direction as they mouth the lyrics to 'Mambo No. 5'.

'Here. I'm guessing you've got some catching up to do,' he says, placing his blue WKD in your hand. You don't mention you've been drinking vodka lemonade behind the bar during the final hour of your shift, just finish the rest of the bottle and join in dancing and lip-syncing. Your first kiss is during The Cardigans' 'Lovefool', and although the feeling you get is closer to pleasure than indifference, it's still notably far from arousal. But objectively he's attractive, intelligent and kind. Over the next decade and a half, you will experiment in dating men with a host of varying attributes, but at least two of these three traits, in various combinations, will always be present.

Together you and Joe go on nights out and drink snakebites until your head throbs. One afternoon you help him bake a birthday cake for his housemate during which your mother makes repeated excuses to enter the kitchen, curious to see the sort of man you have chosen as your next boyfriend.

'Perhaps I ought to top up the birdfeed,' she says, peering through the window at the feeder full of nuts, less than twenty minutes since her last appearance.

Ignoring her remark, you pass Joe the bowl of flour. 'Do you want to sieve?'

'So, Joe,' she says, turning to face him with her back to the sink. 'Margot says you're studying Computing.'

'Yeah.'

'Well, with the exception of Romily, we're a Humanities household, so you're a welcome addition.'

'And by that she means your role as my boyfriend is to assist with her crosswords.'

'I'm sure Joe can handle a bit of dual functionality,' says your mother, looking pleased with her remark.

He pulls at the bottom of his T-shirt and laughs in a way that implies agreement.

'Now. Big O notation. Can you give it to me in layman's terms? Ideally in the time it takes this kettle to boil.'

'Er. I can try.'

'Correct answer.' Your mother believes that even the most complex technical concepts should not be beyond her basic understanding. 'I warn you now, it's a fast boiler,' she adds, as your father enters through the French garden doors dressed in samurai armour and carrying a sword.

'Ah, you must be my daughter's latest suitor. I suppose I ought to propose a quick duel?'

'Just ignore him,' you say to Joe who looks caught between alarm and confusion.

'It's, er, nice to meet you, Mr Wilkes.'

'Oh please, call me Michael. I don't go in for formalities.'

'Great costume,' says Joe, looking more relaxed. 'What's the theme?'

'Theme?'

'For the fancy dress.'

'There is no fancy dress.'

'Oh. I just assumed . . .'

'He just wears weird things and says weird stuff,' you say without emotion as you cut into the butter.

'One shouldn't require an occasion to don one's finest attire. Don't you agree, Joe?'

'Yeah. I mean, yes. I mean, one should not.'

Pained by Joe's awkwardness, you glare at your mother and father and gesture towards the door.

'You can both leave now.'

Three weeks in, Joe suggests catching the train to Great Yarmouth for the day where your shoulders go pink from sunbathing. You eat battered haddock and chips on the beach, the grease lingering on your fingers after cleaning them with a square lemon wet wipe, leaving your hands smelling of fried citrus. Lying on the sand, watching the encroaching tide, you feel full and expansive like a parachute opening in flight. *Tonight is the night*. The decision makes you curiously bound as well as liberated, as though you have willingly handcuffed yourself and given him the key when, in fact, he has no idea that this evening you intend to lose your virginity to him.

Five hours later you perch on the edge of Joe's bed studying the Watford FC poster on the wall above his headboard while you wait for him to come back from the kitchen. Sitting down next to you, he hands you a wet bottle of Heineken which you take a couple of malty sips of before placing it on the floor and pulling down the straps of your top expectantly. He looks hesitant but, when you nod, quickly changes his expression to casual acceptance as though not wanting to make a big deal out of the moment in case it triggers you to change your mind. As he starts to undress you, he gets stuck unhooking your bra and so you switch to undressing yourselves which makes more sense to you anyway. Looking at him, you wonder what he makes of your naked chest. You find your breasts cumbersome and ugly but will just have to trust the magazines you read that men will consider them sexy, in the way that you personally dislike the taste of watermelon but appreciate it has mass appeal.

You bleed only a small amount and he is very considerate

throughout, checking you're OK as he gently thrusts into you under the thin navy duvet that's cool against your skin. Afterwards, it's relief you feel more than anything – that you have got it over with, that you will no longer feel like an imposter when sex enters the conversation among your friends.

At the end of July, you go to stay with him at his family home in Watford and, at his mother's suggestion, he takes you on a walk around the local nature reserve to see the herons. At nineteen, you have no interest in any kind of bird, and are convinced that the moment any develops, you will be decidedly old.

You like being able to hold Joe's hand and be a girlfriend but don't think you feel the things you're meant to and still get slightly anxious before each time you have sex. While it no longer hurts, you have no desire to have him inside you; the most you can muster in terms of excitement is when you close your eyes and picture your naked bodies entwined – an image that makes you feel suave and worldly.

His parents make a fuss of you, topping up your wine glass with sweet, warm Chardonnay while referencing your 'posh background' which makes you uncomfortable because you aren't posh, just more well-off than them. To compensate for this, you compliment his mother on the tidiness of their cream living room and glass-topped dining table, empty except for a silver vase of artificial orchids.

'My parents' house is a tip compared to yours. There are literally no surfaces not covered in newspaper.'

'Your parents sound very clever. Joe says they're both doctors.'

'Mum,' says Joe, looking embarrassed as though he has disclosed a piece of confidential information.

'Not really. I mean, not the proper kind. They just teach at the university.'

'Gosh, well, Joe's the brains in our family.' She laughs and you laugh with her, not wanting to cause offence, although it occurs to you too late that your laughter may be offensive. At points throughout your stay you wonder whether you ought to be more reserved, to not imply you necessarily see a future with Joe, but can't help responding to his parents' eagerness with enthusiasm and, when you leave, tell them you hope to see them again soon.

For the final month of the summer, you go travelling in Indonesia with Romily, who will shortly return to Bristol to begin the fourth year of her Biochemistry degree. Although you don't miss Joe, you enjoy trying to as you gaze at paddy fields while listening to John Mayer on your MP3 player. One afternoon you ride fast on the back of a tour guide's motorbike, clutching his ribs and taut waist as he bends into the mountainous curves, convinced any second you might die, promising someone or perhaps just the air that if you survive you'll never do this again. A lot of life for you is about ticking boxes but not so that you can brag to others, only in the sense that you want to experience as much of it as possible.

'So, do you think you'll end up marrying Doug?' you ask, lying on your stomach on Kuta beach, propped on your forearms watching a surfer catch a wave before falling off his board.

'Probably not,' says Romily, resting the open pages of her book against her torso like a tent. You envy her flat chest and athletic physique next to your own sizeable bikini cups and fleshy thighs which make you feel self-conscious, as if there is too much of you by comparison.

'Why not?' Having grown accustomed to Doug's background presence in your life, you feel nostalgic about the potential loss of him.

'He just feels increasingly brotherly.'

'But I like that about him.'

'You're not the one going out with him,' she says, repositioning her sunglasses on top of her head.

'He's so sweet and fun, though.'

'So are Labradors.'

'Yeah, but he smells better.'

'He does smell great.' She pauses and you sense her slight reluctance to fully engage in the conversation, a hesitancy as she teeters between the role of older sister and friend. 'I just think it would be weird if this was it for me now in terms of partners. I mean, it would be like you marrying Joe. I take it you're not planning on doing that.'

'No way.' Your tone is both flippant and emphatic. 'Joe's nice, I mean he's really nice, but he's not the one.'

'I hate that expression. There's no one person for every person, how could there be? I mean, statistically you just wouldn't find them.' You're used to her employing pragmatism to win arguments, a skill she has acquired from your parents.

'All right, fine, I mean the one as in the one you choose to marry.'

'I don't know if I even want to get married,' she says, flexing her feet.

'I kind of know what you mean, actually.'

Growing up, while your friends designed bridal gowns on their exercise books at school and described at sleepovers their dream weddings, it has always made you feel deeply awkward to visualize yourself dressed in white next to a full-grown man at an altar. Instead, with meticulous detail, you have privately fantasized about motherhood, attempting to conceal the level of your longing, for fear of sounding strange and matronly. Throughout your teenage years you keep a list of potential baby names on a scrap of paper inside an old tin in your bedroom cupboard which you routinely revise, crossing out and adding new ones. You take a keen interest in Rosie's younger siblings who you offer to babysit for free, and when your parents' colleagues descend on your garden for the annual departmental BBQ you cannot help remembering the names and ages of their accompanying children, which becomes so embarrassing that one year you pretend to have forgotten this information, causing your mother to regard you dubiously, although thankfully without comment. Your mother will indulge your fascination with other people's children, providing you yourself do not become a teen-pregnancy – the most egregious waste of your education. At present, your own imagined future offspring (identical twin girls) are full of your own ego; they are the prettiest, sportiest and most popular in their class. They are the version of yourself you wish you'd been.

'As in I definitely care more about having kids,' you say, picking up a pile of soft dry sand and letting it fall through the slots between your fingers like water from a showerhead.

'It's not like it's an either/or scenario,' says Romily, rotating her wrists before adjusting her ponytail; her chestnut waves look particularly rich in the sun. 'We've got ages before we need to think about this stuff anyway.'

'Sure, I'm not in any rush. We've still got time.'

'Tons of time.'

You look down at the tiny hairs on your arm which have risen upright like millipede legs despite the heat. 'I'm going to swim again. Coming?'

'Just let me finish this chapter. I think someone's about to get murdered.'

'Nice.'

Landing at Luton, pleasingly tanned (in so much as you have visible bikini marks), you take a coach to Watford where Joe is waiting outside the station. You present him with a shell necklace and a pair of Havaianas flip-flops which precipitates the conversation in which you agree to stay together when you leave for drama school next month and he goes back to Norwich for the start of his final year. In actual fact, that weekend you spend with him at his parents' house will be the last time you ever see each other but neither of you know this yet.

Ten days later, your father drives you to your student halls in Eltham, situated half an hour's walk from the campus where you will spend the next three years.

'Are you going to miss me?' you ask, pressing your feet against the dashboard.

'Not particularly, no.' Despite his lightness, there's a truth to the remark that saddens you.

'You could at least try getting to know me,' you say, splaying your hand against the hot glass of the window. 'You socialize with your post-grads and they're not that much older than me and Romy.' As far as you're aware, your father's dynamic with his students has never preoccupied your mother or sister beyond the odd remark, but for you it is a source of prolonged intrigue and envy.

'I socialize with a select few, the ones I find stimulating. And the fact is, you and your sister don't interest me enough yet as people.' His casual dismissal of your character stings in a way that is both painful and enticing.

'Dad, that's quite brutal.'

'Brutal? Nothing about your life is brutal. You've led an entirely sheltered upbringing from what I can see.'

'That's not my fault. If anything, that's your fault,' you say, annoyed by his glib accuracy.

'Margot, listen to yourself. Trying to cast blame for your privilege is the sort of thing I'm talking about in terms of why I don't yet feel I can relate to you.'

'How about the fact I'm your daughter? How about the fact we share the same blood?'

'Remind me why I'm paying for you to become more dramatic?'

Attempting to take the moral high ground, you reply coolly, 'I don't think we should continue this conversation. It's just weird and I can't work out how serious you're being.'

'I'm entirely serious.' He glances across at you before continuing. 'Look, your mother and I adore you both but we've made things very comfortable for you and your sister and as a result I don't find either one of your life experiences suitably engaging.'

'Normal dads don't say things like that. They just love their children unconditionally.'

'I love you immensely but we're talking about liking not loving.'

'What, so now you're saying you don't like me?' You feel torn between defensiveness and curiosity.

'I'm saying there are aspects of fathering you I find problematic.'

Hugging your knees to your chest, your scrunched-up legs feel compressed like a coiled spring. You are out of your depth – vastly unprepared and ill-equipped for the way in which the conversation has spiralled.

'The rub of parenthood is that you can't predict the ways in which it's going to fulfil and disappoint you and by that point you've already committed to it. It's too late.'

'Yeah? Well, that's why I'm not having my kids till I'm at least thirty,' you say petulantly, angling yourself away from him and watching as two children begin hitting each other in the back seat of a red people carrier.

He shakes his head in your peripheral vision as he exhales. 'You don't stop wanting irresponsible or conflicting things just because you turn thirty.'

'I reckon Mum did,' you say, unable to resist glancing at him as he smiles in acknowledgement of your mother's flawless parental record.

'Yes, well, as we know, your mother's exemplary. She'd dismiss my claims entirely. Although, arguably, she never wanted irresponsible or conflicting things in the first place.'

'Well, that must have suited you to some extent otherwise you wouldn't have married her. Or do you regret that too?'

'Margot, I don't regret any of you,' he says sharply. 'Not your mother, you, or your sister. You're all immeasurably good.'

'Why do you say that like it's an insult?'

'That wasn't my intention. I'll work on my delivery.' He sounds sad and suddenly tired of the discussion.

'You should do that. And just so you know, I'm going to do so much living before I have my children that I won't be able to resent them, not even a bit.'

'I wish you every success with that.'

'You're patronizing me.'

'I'm admiring your certainty. I wish I could share in it.'

'I don't want to talk any more.'

'I'm sorry if I've upset you. I thought you wanted us to connect as people, outside of our roles. That's something I wish I'd done more of with my own father.' You stare at his tanned forearms, at your grandfather's leather watch strap on his wrist, and feel a stab of guilt and frustration that you are running out of time to get to know each other, and that this latest attempt has not gone the way you intended.

'I said I don't want to talk.'

'In that case I'm going to turn up Janis Joplin.'

'Presumably if I overdosed I might also be of interest to you.'

He bellows with laughter, gripping the steering wheel, and you try not to smile but the sound of it feels like a victory.

'Now, if you can come up with more lines like that,' he says, twisting the volume knob, 'there's hope for us yet.'

As he winds down the window, he begins singing along to 'Me and Bobby McGee'. When he gets to the chorus of *la da* *da*s you join in and when you look across at him you see his eyes are wet.

To your chagrin, the drama school itself technically sits within the boundary of Kent, within the salubrious grounds of a former stately home overlooking a lake. Nevertheless, you are on the cusp of London, edging towards it. Occasionally you get irrational bursts of panic that the city will announce it is too full and you will be denied entry before you've had a chance to fully experience it, but reassure yourself that you don't live in a dystopian universe where this scenario is presently feasible.

On arrival inside the communal kitchen you are greeted by a willowy girl with an angular jawline who you recognize from your recall audition. Her monologue had been unequivocally strong and you'd felt a hot burn watching her, a small dial inside your throat fluctuating between envy and admiration.

'I'm Lillie,' she says, twiddling a strand of her ash-blonde hair. 'With an ie, not a y.' You're struck by how well she suits the name – the light ethereal quality both to it and her.

'Margot,' you say, feeling weighty next to her.

'I remember you. You did that Hermione speech, I knew you'd get in.'

'Yeah, well, I thought the same about you when you did your Portia.'

To your mind, there is a split second where you size each other up, wondering whether you ought to retain a competitive distance, before she picks up a mug from the counter and asks, 'Tea?'

'Sure.'

You'll quickly come to learn the abundance with which she drinks this, will find endless unfinished mugs of it in her room while she obliviously wanders into the kitchen to make another cup.

Waiting for the kettle to boil, she pulls an open packet of custard creams down from the shelf, offering it out to you.

'I'm OK, thanks.'

As she takes a biscuit and bites into it, you notice a half-eaten one on the counter next to her. You will soon discover that her thinness is not a result of temperance but of her genetics and a tendency to forget about whatever she's eating before she's finished it.

'Is that your boyfriend?' she asks, pointing at the screensaver on your phone as you place it on the white plastic table and take a seat on one of the six lime-green metallic chairs.

You nod. 'We haven't been together very long, though.' Do you add this defence in anticipation of the relationship's imminent ending? Or is this just how you interpret the line in hindsight?

'He's hot,' she says, delivering the statement as though it's fact, making you pulse with pride.

While she retrieves a carton of milk from the fridge with the fluidity of a contemporary dance move, you send Joe a blank text message with three kisses. You do this throughout the week when you remember you haven't spoken to him, or realize with guilt that he has not even entered your mind – too preoccupied with the intensive timetable of induction classes and socials.

At the end of Freshers' Week you text him asking if he's around to speak. You can see already that this new world of yours is going to be intoxicating and all-consuming; even with someone you feel a deep connection to, it would be hard to stay together, let alone with Joe who you are fond of and grateful to but have never felt anything close to infatuation for. He's been your first consummated relationship but not your first love. This is still to come.

I've been doing some thinking . . . wondering if you're around for a chat? You're hopeful the tone of your message will lay the groundwork for what you're about to tell him, and sure enough, when he picks up the phone, he says, 'I think I know what's coming.' You've written out on a slip of paper what you're going to say: *I liked you so much that I wanted to at least try to make it work but I think staying together will be unfair on both of us.* You worry about sounding clichéd or overly sincere but are more concerned about ensuring you are kind and honest; you want to be these two things always, although will learn as you age that at times they will present themselves in opposition.

It's difficult to tell whether he feels sadness at the break-up. You can't hear any emotion in his voice so can only assume he's either hiding it, unable to access it or genuinely not too bothered and you suspect the last. He's very understanding in any case, wishing you the best of luck and saying, 'Take care,' as he ends the call. You feel pleased as you put the phone down, impressed with the way the two of you handled it and thankful that your first time was with someone as caring and conscientious as Joe.

Sensing you ought to mark the occasion, you message Romily, adding reference to your sadness only as an afterthought, not because you feel much but because it feels expected.

I've ended things with Joe. Bit sad but def for the best xxx

Ouch & well done! Just finishing in the lab, call you in 15 Xxx PS Look out London, here she comes . . .

Technically Kent but thanks!

With Joe now out of the picture you feel free, free to begin finding out what sex and love are meant to feel like. Lying on your bed you rest your hand on your pubic bone and try to summon the face of a stranger but all you can see is a flock of swifts, how they never land.

3. Tommy

He singles you out in the first fortnight of term, pointing and declaring, 'You're beautiful, look how beautiful she is,' to his friends as he passes you in the corridor, keeping this up in the days that follow. You are flattered but confused by Tommy's behaviour. Firstly, you are not beautiful – reasonably pretty but resolutely not beautiful – and secondly, you have no idea how to react to this level of attention which has never been displayed to you until now.

He's a third-year Acting student, two years above you, giving him an automatic status. His lilting Irish accent and objectively good looks only add to your distrust regarding what he sees in you. It's embarrassing, your lack of craft in dealing with it. Presumably he'll soon go off you if you prove to be inept at witty responses and devoid of personality? You do have a personality, an assertive one by your friends' and family's definition, but this focus based entirely on your looks has temporarily misplaced it, so you find yourself smiling awkwardly and rebuking his advances with a dainty laugh that doesn't sound like yours.

It's the second week of teaching on your course, and you and your fifteen classmates are all still getting to know each other, although you suspect the fact that you are drama students, and are therefore expected to roll around on the floor together and bark, somewhat accelerates this process. Already you have had to request alone time to Lillie who, having boarded throughout her school years, had adopted the habit of wandering into your room without knocking. Thankfully she looked amused rather than offended when you explained your need for 'a window of solitude each day', and had happily started stationing herself in the kitchen to strike up conversation with whoever appeared.

'Knock knock,' she says, outside your bedroom door, early Wednesday evening.

You look up from *The Oresteia* on your desk as she enters. 'You know you can just do the knock without saying the words, right?'

'Ah but then I wouldn't be simultaneously mocking you,' she says, smiling. 'What time do you want to leave?' she asks, as she lifts one of your gold-leaf earrings from the top of your dresser and holds it up to her ear in front of the mirror.

'I don't think I'm coming. I've still got eight sections of this to learn. It's just not going in for me.'

'Same for everyone. We can all test each other in the pub.'

'Yeah, see "testing" implies some level of knowing. It's literally like I'm still reading it for the first time.'

'I bet you know more than you think. Let's recite some together now,' she says, picking up the book and tossing it on to your bed. '*Two preybirds came as prophecy/blackwing and silverhue/ came for our—* Go on.'

'Something about blue twin kings?'

'Yeek. You really don't know it. I reckon you can wing it, just come anyway.'

You feel exasperated by her ease and capability, that somehow with the same timetable as you she's managed to succeed in learning what will take you the entire evening and well into the early hours of the morning to memorize.

'Greek verse is way beyond my blagging skills. Definitely go without me.'

'Who's Tommy going to obsess over if you're not there?'

'I'm sure he'll find someone else.'

'You're not interested in him, then?'

'Maybe. But I'm more suspicious of his interest in me.'

'So modest. Can I borrow these?'

'I thought earrings were like razors. As in people don't share them.'

'Girls shared toothbrushes at our school, but sure, whatever. I'll borrow this instead,' she says, picking up your grandmother's gold chain necklace and watching you wince.

'It's my grandmother's.'

'I'm not going to trash it or lose it. No? OK. Not a successful visit to your room on any front.'

'Just take the earrings, it's fine,' you say, picking up *The Oresteia* from your bed and sitting back down at your desk. 'I need to get back to this.'

'I'll tell people they're yours if they get compliments.'

'Don't bother. Compliments belong to the wearer, not the owner.'

'Ooh, who said that?'

'I just did.'

'Very Wildean.'

The BA Acting students form an exclusive and tight-knit community, meaning Tommy quickly ascertains that you arrived with a boyfriend (a detail which seems to have intensified your attractiveness) and that you are no longer with this boyfriend – a decision which was led by you and, as a result, you are not particularly sad about. In return for your relationship status, he offers up that he has a twin brother who is training to be a musician at a performing arts institute in Liverpool, and that prior to leaving Dublin the two of them were represented by a top commercial agent and regularly appeared in Irish television adverts. Tommy's bright blue eyes and dark messy quiff make it easy to imagine him as a heart-throb in a teenage vampire franchise, and it is widely accepted – and resented – among the other students in his year that, thanks to his marketable look, he will likely find immediate work on graduating, despite his 'one-trick' acting style that you have frequently heard referenced behind his back.

He is staggeringly self-assured in his pursuit of you, and you're not sure if it's his flattery or persistence (suspecting both) that means four weeks into term, inside a notorious bar next to Sidcup station, you give in to his attempts to kiss you; your tongues taste of apple VK and wriggle like tadpoles emerging from frogspawn. Half an hour later he tails you back to your halls where the neatness of your room leaves you feeling self-conscious and wishing you'd left some clothes littered across the floor. He smirks as he lies back on the bed, pointing to the large *Breakfast at Tiffany's* poster Blu-Tacked on the wall.

'Jesus, why do all girls love that film?' The question makes you feel parochial, heightened by your realization that you've never considered the answer. 'Is it literally that you all just want to be Audrey Hepburn?'

Now that he's said it, you suspect this is in fact the appeal but in your desire to sound unique, you say, 'No, and anyway, I'm not *all girls*,' as you move to lie next to him and put your hand on his crotch. Hesitantly, you take out his penis, discovering it to be surprisingly wide. Now you're holding it you're not sure what to do and wish you'd experimented with Joe's when you'd had the chance but, seeing as he was the one out of the two of you who came during sex, had never bothered. You feel flustered and indignant that your ineptitude has remained unchallenged until now.

Perceiving your incompetence, Tommy takes hold of it himself in the end and rubs it vigorously, gets come in your eye as you place your head down by his torso, watching, trying to learn. You blink from the sting of it and feel your mascara watering, confirmed by the grey smear on your knuckles when you wipe your cheekbone. Hiding your face with your hair, you pad on the balls of your feet to the bathroom, too ashamed to even be heard walking.

'So? Was he worth the wait?' Lillie asks the following morning as you enter the kitchen, a neglected bowl of cornflakes pulpifying next to her.

You squat on the floor and rummage inside your cupboard, pretending to have misplaced the peanut butter in order to avoid looking at her.

'We were pretty drunk, to be honest. We didn't really get that far.'

'Watch out. He's going to want you even more now.'

'I doubt that. I'm pretty sure the allure's been broken.'

'Oh sure, cause that's how men work.'

You want to ask her more on this subject but don't want to disrupt the image she has of you as someone who is knowledgeable and accomplished in this field. You have just left behind your schoolfriends who knew your flaws and insecurities, and this is a new beginning – a chance to reinvent yourself in an environment in which you are no longer the novice.

'What about you? You've been impressively restrained since we arrived.'

'It's not restraint, it's just lack of attraction. I'm not really into artistic types.'

'Too much ego?'

'Exactly. Not enough room for mine.'

Sure enough, Tommy quickly loses interest in you after that night and becomes fixated on another girl in your class, leading you to assume that he has already exhausted the supply of girls in both his own year and the year below.

Unlike you, your classmate is experienced in sexual conduct, announcing to the rest of the girls in the group one day while warming up for your mid-term vocal assessment that Tommy proclaimed her blowjob to be the 'best he'd ever had'. You feel frigid and rejected listening to her. It's not only expertise in performing sexual acts that she possesses; she also understands how to maintain an emotional power over Tommy – firmly and repeatedly stating that she has no interest in the label of 'girl-friend' so that in the end the challenge for him becomes persuading her to accept this title, which she does with a reluc-tance that to you appears feigned but skilful.

It's your first realization that other women know how to play games and you don't. After all, you'd had the natural advantage; Tommy had liked you most initially but you'd lost your lead. This experience teaches you that it's not enough to be earnest and rela-tively attractive but that tactics are also necessary if you're to be successful with the opposite sex. In acknowledging this you have grasped a valuable lesson, but there's a bleak discomfort to the dis-covery that sex and affection should be gained not through honesty and directness but through calculated advances and retreats.

Returning home for Reading Week at the start of November, you crave the stability and familiar comfort of home, but find your parents oddly withdrawn and sleeping in separate rooms.

'Is Dad not eating with us?' you ask your mother as the two of you sit down to lunch.

'He's marking.' She glances absently at the draining board before turning back to look at you and brusquely instructing, 'Tell me about your term, then.'

'Fine. Good. Tiring. He seems off.'

'Who does?'

'Dad.'

'He's not been feeling well.'

'What kind of not well? It's not cancer, is it?'

'It's just a lingering cold your visit happens to be coinciding with,' she says, pressing her palm firmly on to the top of her sandwich.

'So, that's why he's sleeping in the guest room?'

'Exactly.'

But you observe him over the days that follow and can't detect any physical signs of illness, more just a mental weariness and general detachment from the conversations going on around him. Although never hugely tactile, you notice the sparsity of touch between your parents and, having observed this, can't help fixating on its absence.

Whereas before you enjoyed mocking them in the other one's company, you now find yourself openly endorsing them, concluding from your internet search – *back from uni parents acting weird* – that they are likely experiencing a transition period in their marriage caused by your leaving home, taking it upon yourself to personally hold them together.

'I'm enjoying your beard that length,' you say to your father on the staircase in deliberate earshot of your mother.

'It needs trimming,' she says curtly, as she crosses the landing on her way to the bathroom and closes the door.

'At least you can rely on her for an honest appraisal,' you say to him with false cheeriness. 'Some wives would just lie and say they liked it.'

'It might be preferable to have a lying wife.'

'You don't really mean that, do you?' you ask, alarmed.

'No man's knowledge can go beyond his experience,' mutters your father as he pointedly shuts the door to his study.

Agitated by his lack of assurance, you stride into the bathroom without knocking and blurt out, 'I demand to know if you're getting divorced.'

Unruffled by your request, your mother calmly removes her dressing gown and steps into the shower. 'And incidentally,' you say, gathering momentum, 'I don't think you should bother because, to be honest, there's barely any point at your age anyway, but I still want to know if it's on the table. Even as an option. As your daughter, it's my right.' You stubbornly stand your ground, feeling the fast thud of your heartbeat.

'Margot, no one is getting divorced,' she says, lifting her feet in turn to inspect the dried skin on her soles. 'Or rather, numerous couples across the country are getting divorced but your father and I aren't currently one of them.'

'Define currently,' you say, crossing your arms over your chest.

'No immediate or future plans,' she says, firmly and with eye contact.

You feel relieved but also concerned that there is no concrete cause to account for their change in mood towards each other.

'That said, I resent the implication that our lives are essentially over,' she says, reaching for the pumice stone. 'Now could you either close the door or leave. You're wasting thermal energy.'

'They just don't seem that happy,' you say to Romily on the phone that evening.

'It's a marriage, isn't it,' she says, yawning. 'It's not going to be great all the time.' Her casual tone prompts you to double-down on your argument.

'I've been reading up on it and apparently when the youngest offspring leaves home it's a common time for couples to separate. On the plus side, if they make it through this transition then they've only got retirement left as a final hurdle and most people just decide to hold on till death at that point.'

'Marg, do yourself a favour and get off Google. This is like the time you thought you had prostate cancer.'

'I had all the symptoms!'

'Yeah, you were just missing a prostate,' she says drily.

You feel embarrassed but also affronted, aggrieved by the implication that you are being unduly paranoid.

'You're not here in the house observing their energy.'

'Even if I was, I probably wouldn't be picking up on it. You're weirdly sens— I mean, perceptive when it comes to stuff like that. I'm sure they're fine and this is just some minor blip.'

You pause, deliberating whether to concede, and Romily takes the opportunity to move the conversation on.

'Anyway, enough about their relationship. What's going on with you? Are you still enjoying your singledom?'

'Kind of.' You consider recounting the incident with Tommy but, despite yours and Romily's closeness, soliciting fellatio technique from her is beyond the level of intimacy you share. You imagine her rolling her eyes on the other end of the phone and replying, 'Oh god, this makes me really awkward, can't you ask one of your friends?' But you haven't spoken in-depth to Rosie or Amber or Holly since the start of September, and your relationship with Lillie has remained on equal footing, making you too embarrassed to admit to her your sexual shortcomings.

'You don't sound very inspired.'

'I'm just more focused on work right now.'

'All right but don't become a martyr. It's drama school, not medical school.'

That night you wait until your parents have retired to their separate rooms and open up your laptop where you type into YouTube *how to give a blowjob* as you towel-dry your hair. A computerized voice tells you that the key to him loving it is you loving it, while water drops on to your neck and leaves a blotch on your collar.

4. Nathanael

The final week of the autumn term, the second- and third-years are invited to watch the first-years perform in their first major assessment. It's a devised piece inspired by the theme of *the fairy tale*, and you and your classmates are keen to impress both the staff and other students, each wanting to stand out as talented and most likely to succeed when the time comes to graduate into a saturated industry of actors and theatre-makers.

Knowing that Tommy will likely be in the audience, you are determined not to let your desire to remain attractive to him jeopardize your performance. To ensure this doesn't happen, you decide halfway through the devising process to give your character a limping gait and vacant expression which inspires the group's decision that you should morph into an orang-utan by the end.

After the showing, several students approach to congratulate you on this 'lifelike transformation' but Nathanael isn't one of them. It isn't until the two of you pass each other inside the school foyer on the first day back after the Christmas holidays that you exchange words for the first time and he references your performance.

Nathanael's in his second year, on the Actor Musician course, and although you've never spoken, you're aware of him – how muscular his thighs are in the leggings he wears for movement class, the small tattoo on his left biceps that looks like an *H* but when you start going out will learn is the symbol for Pisces, his star sign. That you should be attracted to someone who believes in star signs, and ardently enough to have one inked permanently on his skin, is uncharacteristic. You've already got a reputation among the staff and your classmates for being cerebral, or as one faculty member bluntly put it, 'a talking head', triggering a collective titter from the room.

'Nice orang-utan,' he says, nodding, his beige canvas rucksack slung over one shoulder.

'Thanks. It came pretty naturally.'

He doesn't laugh at your comment or even smile; he's surprisingly serious.

'So, how are you finding it? Second term now, things are gonna start heating up.'

You want to answer as sincerely as possible, discerning his preference for directness.

'Yeah, it's quite full-on.'

'Believe me, it only gets tougher.'

'Thanks for the tip-off.'

'Well, let me know if you want to get a drink sometime, chat about stuff some more.'

'OK. I mean, yeah, sounds good.' You're cautious of saying anything else, anything that might make him go off the idea.

'Let me take your number, then.'

After you've given it to him he walks off and you think about his thighs for most of your seminar on nineteenth-century European dramatists, surprised to discover when you come out of the lecture theatre and check your phone he's messaged already. *How about tonight?* He suggests a pub off campus, *somewhere away from prying eyes.* You'll come to learn that, like you, he shares a simultaneous disdain and respect for the institution you both attend.

He's standing waiting by the bar when you arrive, wearing a wool-knit beanie which he takes off when he sees you approaching but which you think looks excellent. The conversation that follows is largely course-related: the work itself, the other students. He does an appraisal of the staff, telling you who to look out for and who will soften in time. At the end of the night he walks you back to your halls and pulls you in for a kiss at the door, making your groin flutter as though it possesses wings. You kiss for some time and, when he breaks away, this time it's you who goes in for a second one, grinning in the cold night as his hands roam over your red winter coat.

'Let's do this again then, yeah?'

You nod, want to reply you're free tomorrow but, remembering your recent lesson from your experience with Tommy, are cautious of sounding too available in case it weakens Nathanael's interest in you.

'Text me,' you say instead, before turning to go inside.

Things develop quickly so that within weeks you are officially a couple. The teachers and other students, including Lillie – by now established as your closest ally – don't hide their intrigue, one teacher even bringing it up at the end of class. 'So you and Nathanael? Not the most obvious pairing,' she says, clearly hoping you'll expound on this, but you just shrug and say, 'I suppose not.'

You know how different the two of you are, that in many ways you aren't compatible. He often looks puzzled when you talk, leaving you to wonder whether you're being inarticulate in explaining yourself or if he simply doesn't connect to what you're thinking and feeling in these moments. Similarly, you can sense his disappointment that you don't share his reverence for jazz piano or the supernatural – 'Who doesn't believe in ghosts?' he asks, confounded.

'I've just never seen one,' you say, embarrassed by your bland logic.

'That's because you don't believe in them.' But you would need to see one in order to believe in them, and so the discussion remains deadlocked by this paradox.

However, your physical attraction to each other and the common ground you share in being students on the same course are enough at this early stage of the relationship.

As a second year he no longer lives in halls but shares a flat with two guys on his course where he cooks kedjenou with attiéké for you and calls you 'babe'. Before you have sex he massages you with oils and teaches you to do the same to him, guiding you in sourcing and responding to pleasure. It's thanks to him that you buy your first set of underwear from Ann Summers and Kama Sutra playing cards that you use to experiment with different positions, including a viscous night involving a jar of Manuka honey, originally purchased under the instruction of your singing teacher due to its vocal lubricating properties. He's also the first man to ever put his tongue between your legs, allowing you to make the obvious link between your new-found enjoyment of sex and the discovery of an orgasm. Although the sex is a defining factor, he's also romantic and affectionate, gives you a Valentine's card in which he's copied in cursive handwriting all sixteen lines of 'Sonnet 18', making you swoon. When you think of this card in the years that follow you will cringe and then feel a pang of envy and nostalgia for the nineteen-year-old version of you who could buy into such ardency without a trace of irony.

The further you fall for him, the more removed you feel from other people and activities, as though you are walking around inside a layer of film, so that comments from your teachers and classmates bounce off your skin rather than penetrate it.

When you begin your Tuesday morning vocal class with the routine exercise in which you stand in a circle and attempt to make each other laugh with comic noises and goofy faces, as usual, you are the last one to remain straight-faced. As your teacher declares you 'the winner once again' in a tone that makes it clear this ought to evoke shame, and you overhear one of your classmates say, 'It's like she's made of stone,' while the remark still bothers you, it bothers you less than it would have done before.

'Are you never tempted just to fake laughter?' says Lillie as you refill your water flasks from the drinking fountain in the corridor.

'Why would I do that?'

'Just so people think you're less serious. But maybe you don't care what the class think?'

'I do care a bit but not enough to fake it.'

'Winning at integrity too,' she says, taking a slug of water from her flask. 'Do you want to cook together tonight? I've got some ravioli that needs eating.'

'I told Nathanael I'd run through his satirical prose speech with him. It's his assessment next week and he's still tripping up on his diphthongs.'

'You could do it at ours? I feel like I barely see you any more.'

'I see you all the time. We live together and spend all day in class together.'

'That's not the same as hanging out. I'm basically a total loner these days.' Although she says this light-heartedly, you feel a sense of confinement on hearing it – the underlying expectation that you owe her your time and attention which makes you feel both guilty and resentful.

'Why don't you try making more effort with the rest of the class if you're lonely? I think they're going for pizza at the Alma tonight.'

'I didn't say I was lonely,' she snaps. 'I just said it would be nice to see you, but if it's not reciprocated then don't worry about it.' You are caught off-guard by this sudden gear-shift in the conversation, but before you have a chance to make amends, she walks off, her expression of defiance trying to mask her hurt.

Later that evening, you leave your bedroom door open and wait until you hear her inside the kitchen, humming Laura Marling.

'Sorry about earlier,' you say as you enter, pressing your palms against the wall behind your back.

'It's fine,' she says, not looking at you as she surveys the interior of her cupboard.

'I'm not someone who drops their friends for their boyfriend, like I really actively dislike people who do that.'

'Sure.' She pulls herself up on to the counter, swinging her legs so that they kick against the cabinet.

'But I'm also not very good at having one "best friend", like I start to feel a bit trapped in that dynamic. And that's got nothing to do with Nathanael, or you. It's just the way I'm wired. But I'm sorry if it feels like a reflection on you. It's totally not.'

'It's funny,' she says, shrugging. 'I thought I'd meet like-minded people here but, other than you, it's like being back at school where the cool girls are still the ones who wear loads of make-up and don't read.'

You nod and smile weakly in recognition.

'I mean, you've got your sister and Amber and Rosie and now Nathanael but I've never really had that close-friendship thing with anyone. I guess I just don't really click with people that easily.' You frown, wanting to object to this without dismissing her feelings. 'I've always told myself it's because I'm an only child and that we moved around a lot when I was younger, but I think the truth is I'm probably an acquired taste.'

'Well, you're very much to my liking.'

'Cute and a bit creepy.'

You laugh and rise up on your toes, your heels sliding against the skirting board. 'So, we're good?'

'You're good. I'm still exceptional.'

Smiling, you open the fridge door. 'Do you want some of this?' you ask, holding out a bowl of leftover couscous.

'What about Nathanael and his diphthongs?'

'That sounds like the title of a porno.'

'OK, you clearly don't watch porn.'

You laugh and say, 'True. They can wait until tomorrow in any case.'

'Well, in that case, when have I ever said no to food?'

But for the rest of that week, she doesn't knock on your door, even though you make a concerted effort to be at home more evenings. You consider knocking on hers but are stopped by the fact it might confuse her and indicate a desire to return to the closeness you had before, which you found claustrophobic and diluting of your individual identity, and so you allow a distance to form between you, feeling both relief and guilt about this.

That Easter you visit Nathanael's mother and grandmother in Lyon, enthralled and enlarged by everything about the trip – the local food market by the river teeming with grocery carts where you sample an assortment of cheeses and fresh peaches, the rose and ochre facades of the Renaissance old town with its network of narrow passageways that Nathanael leads you down, explaining the stone tunnels were originally used to transport medieval silks.

You delight in the stories his mother tells you about him coming to stay as a boy and later as a teenager, feel as though you're getting a sped-up slideshow of his life, allowing you to glimpse into all the years you've missed out on having only known him a few months. His grandmother doesn't speak English and, despite your A-level French, you struggle to keep up with the pace of their conversation and interwoven Baoulé dialect but smile and nod until your face aches to try to convey your happiness at being there.

On the afternoon of the final day, you lie down next to each other on the grass inside the Jardin des Plantes, so aroused by this point from sleeping in separate rooms that you slip into a nearby rustic public toilet and make each other come with urgency. Years from now you'll continue to recall the coolness of the cracked stone wall against your back, the earthy smell of damp as you'd cried out and felt Nathanael's other hand over your mouth, panicked someone might hear.

Landing back at Gatwick, he takes you to stay at his dad's house in South London where later that night you go for dinner at a Lebanese restaurant with his old schoolfriends. The place is warmly lit, full of ramshackle furniture and an old wooden piano in the corner. At one point in the evening, Nathanael gets up to play it, the room filling with melancholic and discordant notes that build and fall seemingly at random. The restaurant stills as people stop talking and eating to watch. He keeps his head down, looking at his hands, but every so often glances up and catches your gaze so that you feel your chest expanding. It's haunting and beautiful, not only listening to him but finding yourself in this new place with these new people because of him. That's what makes relationships different to friendships, you decide; no one friend ordinarily uproots and transforms another's life so completely in the way a romantic partner does.

That night the two of you go to sleep on the top bunk inside his childhood room, the faded remains of Teenage Mutant Ninja Turtles stuck to the pine bedframe. As you lie under the soft green glow of the stars on his ceiling, you feel a closeness to him you haven't felt until now. Having thought you might love him, after tonight and the last few days in Lyon, you're sure of it. The knowledge sits inside you like a solid chocolate egg, sweet and robust. It's the first time you've ever said the words to anyone other than your parents and Romily, and you choke on the *I* slightly so that it ends up sounding more like 'love you'. Pulling

45

you into him, he tells you he loves you too and you hold each other with no space between your bodies.

Waking early from thirst, you see Nathanael already awake next to you. It's barely light outside; neither of you have slept well on the narrow boxed-in mattress and so decide, rather than trying to fall asleep again, to catch the train back to his flat in Sidcup. His dad and step-mum are still asleep as you let yourselves out and walk hand in hand down the streets of Lambeth which are empty and still at this hour on a Sunday. A fox passes you on the other side of the road, not trying to hide, just brazenly strolling down the pavement, and you start to laugh.

'Don't you have foxes in Norwich?' Nathanael asks, confused.

'No, we do, I've just never seen one so . . . sure of itself.'

The love you feel for him and the love you feel for this new and exhilarating city that belongs to him are intertwined and impossible to separate.

It's hard to determine at what point it changes. You just know that by the summer term you see each other less and less and that when you do, you often get annoyed — that your differences which had seemed attractive and insignificant at the start now grate and feel insurmountable.

One week when you haven't seen each other for five nights because he's been too busy with coursework, he messages asking if you're free that evening, saying he'll cook for you, but when you arrive at his flat he's stoned. You wish you could be relaxed about it but had wanted to spend the evening reconnecting with him and now he's slumped on the sofa, laughing uncontrollably at a YouTube clip with his flatmates.

Leaning against the kitchen counter stacked with dirty plates, you resist the urge to wash up in the hope it might prompt him to start cooking and, after a few more minutes of being ignored, announce your intention to leave.

'Babe, just have some weed,' he says. But the two times in

your life you've smoked it you've hated the feeling of it, the panic you'd experienced at not being in control.

'I'm just going to go, OK.' You put your jacket on slowly, giving him time to object, but he only runs his hands over his stubbled head and goes back to looking at his phone. You try to slam the door on your way out but its stiffness prevents this and so you use your other hand to clang the letterbox as you pull it shut which makes you feel petty, as though you have needlessly undermined your position. As you begin walking home, you look back, hoping he might be following, but he isn't, and the gap between you expands further like cubes of stuck-together ice separating.

You have also been steadily and subtly drifting from Lillie since the middle of last year so it's of little surprise but still hurts when she knocks on your door the following week to announce she's planning to move into a house-share from September with two girls on the American Theatre Arts course.

'That's OK, right? I kind of assumed you wouldn't want to live together next year.'

'Sure. I mean, I don't not want to, but I also get if you want to live with people who are more, you know, social.'

'Cool, I just wanted to check before we sign anything.'

'Sign away, friend.' You try to sound casual but feel irrationally jealous that your position as her housemate is being usurped, despite your half-hearted investment in it.

'I haven't been in here for ages,' she says, looking around. 'You've moved the furniture.'

'It's just a thing I do. When I get bored.'

'Looks good.' She hovers by the chest of drawers and points to a photo of the two of you from Freshers' Week stuck to the corner of the mirror. 'Dare I say it, I think we've enhanced with age.' You smile, not realizing until now how much you've missed her musings.

47

'I wonder when our tipping point will hit.'

'Hopefully we'll have husbands by that point and it won't matter.' She frowns and jerks her head. 'Ew. That was horribly unfeminist.'

'Fair, though. It's also just the world we live in.'

She pauses for a moment. 'I tell myself that looks aren't part of my currency with men but I don't actually believe that. It's more just that I want to believe it.'

'What, cause it's more in line with a societal ideal?'

'That. And cause it would be a huge endorsement of my personality.'

You laugh and smile at each other, and as she goes to leave your room you feel regret that you have pushed her away, and are compelled in that moment to lean in and make an effort to restore your friendship.

'You should come and stay with me this summer.'

'Really?' Hopefulness flashes across her face, and you catch a glimpse of her vulnerability, silently vowing to treat her with more care going forwards.

'Yeah. I mean, you'll have to tolerate my mum dragging you on a walking tour of Medieval Norwich, and my dad's unorthodox comments, but it'd be nice to hang out, you know, outside of this place.'

'History and eccentricity,' she says, cocking her head, her air of confidence returned. 'I'm in.'

Your parents excel in conforming to the image of them that you have painted in advance, so that Lillie whispers, 'It's like they're a pastiche of themselves,' as your mother strides along King Street in her Birkenstock sandals and corduroy dungarees, providing a live audio tour en route.

'Now to your left you'll see Dragon Hall, built by the merchant Robert Toppes in the early fifteenth century. It was used as a meeting place to trade goods – most commonly wool, due to the large number of weavers who arrived from Belgium and Holland, and who famously brought their canaries with them, hence the canary crest used by Norwich Football Club.'

'Canary copulation fact for you,' says your father, turning to Lillie. 'The males use two-note syllable tunes to arouse the females who, like us humans, are turned on by song complexity.'

'Not me,' says Lillie. 'I prefer my men to be one-note.'

Your father laughs delightedly. 'You,' he says, pointing at her, 'can come again.'

Although you cringe at this exchange, you are pleased to see him returned to his extroverted character, and that your mother, too, is on formidable form. Whatever rift you'd witnessed between them at the end of last year, to your relief, appears to have been resolved.

That night the four of you eat Thai takeaway out of plastic containers around the dining-room table. Your father insists on repeatedly topping up everyone's wine glasses so that you feel yourself becoming drunk and performative, interrupting your mother's tutorial on morphology to announce, 'Basically, Lillie, the success of your visit hinges on its educational value.'

'Excuse me, that grossly undermines my contribution to this weekend,' says your father, throwing out his arms in pantomimic outrage.

'Which is what? Deliberate provocation?' you ask, trying to sound dismissive, but feel a smile seeping from the edges of your mouth, as Lillie laughs in response to this improvised routine the three of you are enacting for her.

'That and ensuring us all a hangover,' adds your mother, with false sternness, holding her hand over the top of her glass as your father, yet again, reaches for the wine bottle.

★

'I can see where you get your groundedness from,' says Lillie as you draw the curtains in the guest bedroom for her that night. 'Your parents are so solid.'

'Yeah, I guess their marriage is strong. Not that they'd tell me if it wasn't.' You pause, wondering whether to divulge the distance you'd observed between them back in the autumn.

'No, but just in themselves. Like, they don't really have any complexes or insecurities. At least not visible ones.'

'Not unless you count their entire personalities.'

'You're really lucky.'

In spite of your father's somewhat painful bluntness, you agree. But, not wanting to sound smug, reply, 'You've really charmed them.'

'Standard. Parents and pets go wild for me. It's just my peers I struggle to woo.'

'Well, you've won me over.'

'Finally.'

You smile at her, acknowledging the journey the two of you have been on to get to this point where she is sleeping inside your family home. She smiles back, and suddenly the moment feels awkwardly sentimental.

'I'm going to leave this paracetamol by your bed for when the hangover kicks in.'

'Fun.'

You touch her shoulder as you say goodnight and feel grateful for her lack of a grudge, that she has given you another chance at her friendship.

You don't see Nathanael all summer, and when September arrives – reluctantly greeting each other outside the school's reception for the start of another year – you agree that the relationship is over, taking your joint dearth of communication as a sign that whatever you'd felt for each other no longer exists.

You do mourn in the form of purchasing an Oscar Peterson album on iTunes and crying to the backdrop of 'Georgia on my Mind', but acknowledge that it's being in a relationship more than Nathanael specifically that you miss.

Your new housemates are two European Theatre Arts students who you have selected because you know them only vaguely and can therefore adopt a degree of distance without offending them. The woman, Leonie, is from Vienna, and rarely leaves her room except to sign for endless packages which you assume must contain food as, to your knowledge, she doesn't ever use the kitchen. By contrast, your Polish housemate, Lukasz, spends hours cooking meaty stews while you try not to stare at his exceptionally long thumbnail. In truth, you feel lonely without Lillie and Nathanael but remind yourself that this is what you have chosen – albeit inadvertently – and find comfort in the fact that the choices you've made, at least at this stage in your life, are only temporary. Besides, you are not resistant to loneliness, have always considered it as valid an emotion as happiness; in some ways you find it easier than happiness which comes laced with the anxiety of losing it.

That October you visit Romily in Oxford where she has recently begun her PhD involving something to do with proteins in fruit flies, which she explains 'may or may not be used in cancer research' as she mounds clotted cream on to a scone inside a tearoom. 'So the next four years could ultimately be pointless. Watch this space.'

'Either way, you'll have a PhD and I'll be the leper of the family.'

'An entertaining one at least.' Her phone pings and she picks it up and begins typing. 'It's Sami. He's finished early in the lab. I'll tell him to come and meet us.'

'But we've hardly had any sister time.' You hear the whine in your voice, feel petty frustration that your company alone is not adequate.

'You literally sound five,' she says breezily. 'I'll tell him to join us later for dinner?'

'Sure,' you say, trying not to sulk while taking a deliberately small bite of your scone. Romily's propulsive energy has always made you feel slightly rushed, as though you are fighting for her time and attention. But despite aspiring to her tempo, something stubborn and defeatist in you insists on attempting to slow her down, rather than speed yourself up.

'Hopefully he'll be able to get us into Le Kesh. It's normally rammed on a Saturday but he's made friends with the owner. They speak this mix of Arabic and French together. I told you Sami's trilingual, right?' You nod, recalling the lengthy phone call in which Romily had spoken fervently about his early childhood in Morocco and the international school in Geneva he'd been sent to as a teenager.

'I'm meeting his dad in a few weeks. He's practically a celebrity within epigenetics.'

'What's epigenetics?'

'Basically the way behaviour and environment affect your genes without affecting your DNA. He's published a whole ton of papers on it.'

'Nice to know nepotism's alive and kicking,' you say, raising your eyebrows as you lick jam from your little finger.

'How do you mean?' she asks, her tone unexpectedly sharp.

'His dad's a research scientist and now his son's doing a post-doc at Oxford?'

'On his own merit. They're in completely different fields, and anyway, Sami's insanely clever. I feel like I know nothing when I'm next to him.'

'Why would you want to go out with someone who makes

you feel you don't know anything?' You sit back in your chair, pleased to have momentarily gained the upper hand.

'You're twisting my words,' she says, shaking her head and looking annoyed. 'I just mean I know less than him by comparison.'

'You know loads, though.'

'Margot, it's not a competition. When you love someone you're a team—'

'Love? You've only been going out a month. It took ages before you and Doug said you loved each other.'

'What I had with Doug was totally different. We were teenagers when we got together.' Her voice is light and dismissive again, making you feel obliged to offset it with sincerity.

'That doesn't mean you have to undermine it in hindsight.'

'I'm not undermining it, I'm just saying it was different. Also, in case you've forgotten, you weren't a massive fan of Doug at the beginning either.'

'That's not true. I always liked Doug.'

Romily is right, though. Initially you had resented the partial loss of her due to him, and he had worked hard to gain your approval.

Once again, it's tricky to discern whether your reservations towards Sami stem from Romily's veneration of him, or your jealousy – that her identity as your sister feels of secondary importance to her identity as his girlfriend.

'Everything's back to normal with Mum and Dad, then?' she asks, leaning her elbow on the table and resting one half of her face in her palm.

'Seems to be, yeah.'

'I reckon they're too rational to get divorced, even if they wanted to.'

'Isn't that the opposite of rational?' you ask, confused.

'I just mean in terms of time and money. Like knowing them, they'd do the maths and come to some equation it's not cost-beneficial.'

You find her reasoning perversely comforting, and it occurs to you that Romily's confidence and certainty, which have always seemed so desirable and effortless, may in fact be something she has been forced to cultivate as the elder sibling in order to protect you – that there is an inherent lightness to your position as the youngest that allows you the privilege of doubt and anxiety.

'This is on me,' you say when the bill comes, wanting to somehow repay her.

'Don't be idiotic,' she says, reaching for her purse. 'You can pay me back when you're on the red carpet.'

'I.e., never.'

'You better be joking. I'm banking on being your plus-one.'

The following morning, the two of you walk through one of the college gardens on your way to the train station. Thin drizzle scatters lightly over your face as though you are passing through a sprinkler.

'You can stop holding your cards to your chest now,' says Romily, not looking at you as she readjusts the hood of her jacket.

'How do you mean?'

'I mean you get off on analysing people but haven't debriefed on Sami since last night.'

'He's nice.' You keep your voice flat, not wanting to admit to his charm so soon after yesterday's discussion.

'Wow. Easy with the praise.'

'OK. Clever, attractive and nice. How's that?'

'Pretty generic as far as hat-tricks go, but fine.'

54

'I thought we were reviewing his personality, not my adjectives.'

She laughs, and the two of you pause while a guided group in identical navy anoraks poses for a photograph in front of a cultivated flowerbed. A gold stone turret looms in the background as the sun breaks through a cloud so that the effect looks like a computer-generated film set.

'That's the only drag about living here. It's rammed full of tourists.' The two of you continue walking in silence for a moment before she asks, 'You didn't see a long-term future with Nathanael, then?'

'At times I think I did, like I'd imagine what our kids would look like—'

'Fit.'

'Thanks. But then at other times I think I only wanted to, like I was engineering my image of the future to fit him into it rather than actually seeing him in it for real. Does that make sense?'

'Vague sense.'

'I mean, how do you work out the difference between what you want and what you're telling yourself to want?'

'This sounds like a Margot classic.'

'You think I'm overthinking things.'

'Well, yeah. But I also think it doesn't matter how you end up wanting something. What matters is just if you want it or not.'

'Maybe.'

'Listen, not to sound patronizing but you're still super-young to have worked out what you want anyway.'

'So are you.'

'I'm arguably young. You're irrefutably young.'

'Condescending but true.'

While you agree you have youth on your side, nevertheless

as you watch rain droplets inch across the carriage window on your way back to Paddington, you resolve that the next person you fall for you'll ensure you're more compatible with from the off. From now on, you can go on dates and sleep with men but won't permit yourself to get into a relationship with anyone who you don't clearly see potential for a sustained partnership with, setting your sights on finding a physical, intellectual and emotional match next time.

At this point you still consider Nathanael to be your first love but are about to meet Wren who will redefine your definition of love to the extent it will make you question what you felt for Nathanael. Wren will prove it's possible to have the love described in poetry, the kind that's desperate and absolute, that holds you underwater until you think your head will burst before shooting you up into air, into light.

5.   Wren

It's just a crush at first, instigated by a respect for his work which you think – or at least hope – might be reciprocated when he tells you that you're a bold performer, willing to take risks.

A professional actor and former student of the college, he's invited to attend a gala showcase to celebrate the opening of the school's newly built theatre. A mix of students from different year groups and courses have been selected to perform scenes from a range of popular plays, and your course tutor has asked you and Lillie to close the showcase with a duologue from *Twelfth Night* which you are currently rehearsing for your first public performance at the end of second year.

Before the performance begins, the school principal does a speech up on the stage, thanking various governors and investors and introducing each of the nine alumni in attendance – seated in the front row – of which Wren is one. You learn that he is currently in a West End production of *Twelfth Night*, cast as Sebastian in a modernized version by the RSC, which is shortly due to close after an extended run.

At the end of the performance, you find yourself standing beside him at the edge of the drinks table as you both select orange juice poured into wine glasses.

'Well done, that was great,' he says, as he turns and notices you. Petite and lithe, with olive skin and sable eyes, he moves with a boyish gait and energy but has a focus and a stillness when he talks that gives him a quiet gravitas.

You scrunch up your face as you reply, 'Thanks,' wanting to

acknowledge that you personally disagree, without sounding ungracious.

'No, you don't think so?' he says, with a laugh.

'I think it was probably fine, I just . . . I don't know. I always feel phoney doing Shakespeare, like I'm doing an impression of someone doing a Shakespeare play.'

He laughs again and then nods his head. 'I used to have the exact same feeling.'

'Really?'

'Yeah,' he says, rubbing the side of his neck.

'You said *used to*. What changed?'

'A director I worked with a few years back. She taught me a way "in" to the text.' He pauses and then says, 'Try something with me for a second.'

'OK,' you say, intrigued.

'Your ending soliloquy, have a go at speaking it again now but in your own words.'

'As in . . . ?'

'Just as an exercise, try improvising the lines. Let go of the language, but still make the intentions true to the scene.'

Feeling self-conscious about the people milling around, you do as instructed, and although you find it cringe-worthy to hear your off-the-cuff lines, this irreverence he has permitted you unlocks something so that, for the first time, you feel an emotional connection to what you are saying.

'Good. Now do it again,' he says, leaning forwards with a slight sway. 'This time with his words, but hold on to the feeling of what you just did. And if at any point you start to feel phoney, just go back into your own words.'

What follows is an odd mix of interwoven Shakespearean and modern-day dialogue, which makes you embarrassed at the start, awkwardly breaking into laughter at one point. But then comes a moment about a third of the way through where you feel yourself tuning into the text with a razor-sharp focus. After this, the rest of the soliloquy flows solely in verse, but feels natural in your mouth as though it's colloquial speech, so that by the time it gets to your ending line, you momentarily forget that you are 'doing Shakespeare' until your final word, 'Malvolio', reminds you of this fact.

You turn back to face Wren head-on and see he is now rooted to the spot, looking at you intensely. He nods again and then says, 'You're a bold performer, willing to take risks. Hold on to that.' You smile and thank him, trying to suppress your grin as your course tutor approaches, accompanied by the school's longest-standing member of staff – a voice tutor in his seventies – who looks delighted by Wren's presence.

Within moments, several members of your class have joined the circle, and you spend the next few minutes observing Wren, rather than partaking in the conversation. Your course tutor speaks about him with a distinct (and uncustomary) note of praise, listing his extensive credits and referring to him as one of the school's former 'star pupils'. Although this makes Wren look genuinely uncomfortable, he thanks her in a clear voice and with eye contact, indicating underlying humility.

He has a way of looking relaxed but alert as he listens and responds to comments from your classmates, joining his hands together with only the tips of his fingers touching, as though holding a small imaginary sphere. You watch him scrape the top half of his shoulder-length dishevelled hair into a knot with a frayed leather band he wears around his wrist, seemingly so absorbed in the discussion that you wonder whether he's even conscious of tying his hair up. As you stare at his silver wedding band, you try to visualize who he is married to. At one point he retrieves a bag of almonds from his satchel and offers them to the group before crunching on some himself. You don't take one even though you'd like to; you're not sure why but feel nervous of making physical contact with him in front of the others, as if they will immediately be able to detect your attraction to him.

Before leaving to catch his train, he offers the group discounted tickets to see his production in the final week before it closes, writing his email on a piece of paper which he tears out of a notebook from his satchel, and placing it on to the drinks table, saying to get in touch directly with him to arrange this. To your annoyance, your course director immediately proposes a class trip; you would have much preferred to have gone alone or just with Lillie but don't want to miss out on seeing the show and so you add your name to the list – jotting down Wren's email in your notebook as you do this.

You can tell from your classmates' response as they enthusiastically say goodbye that everyone has warmed to him, but you doubt if they feel this inexplicable connection to him that you do, as though you have known him before now, which is of course ridiculous because you have known him approximately seventeen minutes.

The following Thursday evening you go along with several members of your class to watch the show, aptly described in a review quote as *a high-octane romp of tangled love and mistaken identities contemporized to present-day Margate*. All the cast are strong, and Wren is no exception, making a lot of the role which is, on paper, relatively small and bland. Crucially, what you are attracted to is that he makes Sebastian feel real. In the climax of Act Five when he is reunited with Viola, you feel genuinely moved – something you've never felt watching Shakespeare until now.

In the bar afterwards, the more gregarious members of your class swarm around him which makes you hold back, frustrated at them for monopolizing him, but more frustrated at yourself for your silence and reluctance to get involved. Why can't you simply throw yourself in and become one of the group? Why is there this regrettable superiority to your character that has been part of you ever since you were a child, leading you to distance yourself from your peers, and which is currently costing you any form of exchange with Wren?

You notice how he divides his attention evenly so that while everyone is made to feel included, no one is marked out specifically. At one point he catches your eye and smiles at you, causing a spark to jolt through you like static. You smile back and give him a double thumbs-up, which you immediately regret, feeling juvenile and concerned you may have offended him with this facile response to his performance.

Just as you are working out a way to enter the conversation, Wren looks at his watch and says apologetically, 'I ought to get home, I'm in rehearsal all day tomorrow.' Several of your class simultaneously ask what he's rehearsing, and he says that he's doing a Clifford Odets play opening in a fortnight at the Young Vic, before redirecting the focus back on to the group by wishing you all the best of luck for your *Twelfth Night*. 'I think it clashes with my preview week but I'm hoping to make it along to your dress rehearsal.' Your class has been split in two, with roles jointly allocated so that you and another girl will be playing Olivia on alternating performances. You hope it will be your cast's dress rehearsal he watches, and wonder if there is a way you can contrive to make this happen, suspecting not.

'He's weirdly hot, you know,' says Lillie, as you watch him zip up his grey felt coat and put his satchel over his shoulder. 'Not in an obvious way, but in like an idiosyncratic way.'

'Yeah, I guess,' you reply, with a vagueness that makes you feel disingenuous. Yours and Lillie's closeness has been restored by not living together this last year, but you still feel a joint caution around the friendship – a guardedness on both your parts not to overstep the boundaries of this reframed relationship, for fear of tilting it off-balance once again.

Maybe it's because of Wren's youthful energy, or the way he seems to have positioned himself on a level with you and the other students, that means you are surprised when you google him later that night and discover that he is thirty-eight, making him a whole seventeen years older than you. His Wikipedia page states that he was born and raised in Hampshire to a Scottish mother who worked as a secondary-school teacher, and a father who was an engineer and is half Sri Lankan. You read the next line, feeling a stab of irrational envy. *He is married to a set designer, with whom he has two children.*

You draft him an email from your bed, which you send the following morning.

I don't think I properly thanked or complimented you last night. Shakespeare's not massively my thing but you and the show were great! Margot PS The caveat's meant to read as a compliment but I think I've failed on this (again).

That afternoon, throughout rehearsal, you check your phone whenever you are off-stage to see if he's replied, to the extent that your course director enquires as to whether you are waiting for an urgent health-related call or just displaying a general lack of unprofessionalism. Embarrassed, you apologize and turn your phone on to airplane mode.

'Do you want to run through lines at mine tonight?' you ask Lillie at the end of rehearsal as you change out of your practice skirt. 'Lukasz is back in Warsaw for the week so we can have free range of the kitchen.'

'Has he cut his thumbnail yet?'

'Do you know what I realized the other day? Presumably he's cutting it regularly cause it's not like record-breakingly long which means he must be deliberately trimming it to remain at that length.'

'Even weirder,' she says, unbuckling her doublet. 'I'm actually meant to be seeing that medic tonight.'

'On a school night? Rebellious.' You commend Lillie's determination to date beyond the realms of your drama school. Her taste for non-creative alpha-types is something you objectively admire, without viscerally sharing in.

'I keep having this fantasy about collapsing while I'm with him and him resuscitating me in front of a crowd of onlookers. I just think it would be such a turn-on.'

'I love how even your fantasies have an audience,' you say, turning your phone off airplane mode and feeling it vibrate seconds later with a notification.

'Obviously. Why, what do your fantasies involve?' she asks, as you look down and see a reply from Wren.

'That would be telling,' you say, trying to sound casual as you open up his email.

Thanks for your kind words (and the measured caveat). Shakespeare could totally be your thing if you wanted it to be. Break a leg for your opening night if I don't manage to make it along to the dress. Best, Wren

You reread the message several times that evening, trying to discern if there's any way it was intended to elicit a response from you, but cannot interpret his reply as anything other than friendly closure to the exchange.

The following week, you open your student production of *Twelfth Night*. Your course tutor reads out an email from Wren apologizing that he won't be able to attend as they're making lots of last-minute changes during preview week which means he's still tied up in rehearsal. There are rumblings of another group trip to see his show when it opens, but this time you are determined to carve out conversation time alone with him, and remain non-committal as dates are mooted by your classmates, later that day booking two tickets for you and Lillie for the week after next.

You google reviews of the production the morning after press night and see it's received a relatively lukewarm response from the critics – three stars across the board, largely due to criticism of the writing being dated and too much of a slow-burn plot-wise, but only positive things are said about the performances, Wren's in particular. *Perera is impressively convincing as Ben Stark, a lost and downtrodden dentist in a stifling marriage who is reawakened by the arrival of his new assistant, Cleo Singer (played with subtle yet explosive force by recent graduate Hannah Mead). Perera manages to capture both Stark's longing and fear of reigniting his muted dreams and ambition, as Cleo entices him to expect more, not just from his marriage, but from love itself.*

You wonder whether he drew on his own marriage for the role but suspect not when you see a photo of him and his wife at press night looking happy and attracted to each other. He has his arm low down around her waist so that it touches the side of her thigh which you find painfully arousing. You scrutinize the image, trying to find fault in her appearance, but can only find admiration for her tall stature and sleek auburn hair, tied in a high ponytail so that it accentuates her angular features.

You wait until a few nights before the show to email Wren to let him know you are coming.

Me again, hope you're well! Lillie and I have booked tickets to see Rocket to the Moon *next Friday. Looking forward to seeing it and you.*

You're disproportionately excited when he replies straight away. *Ah, thanks! It will be good to see you both. Sorry I missed your* Twelfth Night. *How did it go?*

Oh it was fine . . . Nothing to get excited about but fine.

I see your enthusiasm for the bard continues.

Ha. The old American dramatists are much more my thing. No pressure.

I'll try not to screw it up. And me too re the Americans but don't tell your course tutor I said that.

Your secret's safe with me (for the time being . . .).

I'll tread carefully.

You are pleased by the subtle flirtatiousness of this exchange.

The critics are right that the show is not without flaws, but you are engrossed, both by the writing and by Wren's performance, feeling staggering envy towards the actress playing Cleo, opposite him. There is a scene in which the two of them discuss Shakespeare, which gets a laugh from the audience, and you wonder whether Wren has ever thought about you during this dialogue. As you watch him wrestle against her advances before finally embracing each other just before the interval, rubbing his hands over her back and thighs, your desire to supplant her feels like a physical burn.

'Yeesh,' says Lillie, turning to face you as the house lights come up inside the auditorium. 'Intense.'

After the show ends, you and Lillie hang around in the bar, waiting for Wren, but after half an hour there is still no sign of him and you feel embarrassed that he has clearly forgotten you are coming, or perhaps he did remember and just didn't want to see you. Both options make you feel equally ashamed and undesirable.

Lillie is in conversation with an older actor in the show, their forty-odd-year age gap giving them the safety to flirt unashamedly without any expectation of following through on their suggestive remarks. Feeling superfluous, you leave the two of them talking and go to the toilet to take a minute alone to process your disappointment at not seeing Wren.

You are drying your hands when an email comes through from him. *Margot, I'm so sorry I had to dash. My wife's out of town and our babysitter messaged during the interval to say she's not feeling well. Did you enjoy the show?*

Buoyed, you reply, *That's OK! Enjoyed, no. Loved, yes.*

Re-entering the bar more energized now, you end up staying for another drink with Lillie and the older actor, following which Lillie leaves to meet up with a guy she's seeing in East London – to the older actor's visible disappointment, making you wonder whether he did in fact think he had a chance with her – and you catch the last train back to Sidcup alone.

On the train home you get a reply from Wren, surprised he's messaging so late, as it's now after midnight.

I'm really glad to hear that. The reviews have been pretty mediocre but I love it too. Odets is less popular than Miller and Williams and O'Neill but to my mind he's up there with the greats.

I completely agree! He really gets it. All life's yearnings and contradictions.

Has your phone been hijacked by a forty-year-old having a midlife crisis?

Ha. Nope. Just by my young and restless soul.

I had a hunch you had one of those. You'd make a great Cleo Singer in that case.

I'd kill to play her. You better warn your co-star to watch out . . .

I can contaminate her water bottle backstage if you like?

Yes please!!

Deal. (Just to clarify, we're joking in case our incriminating e-trail ends up in the wrong hands.)

I CAN CONFIRM THIS IS A JOKE.

Hm. There's something sinister about those caps letters.

i can confirm this is a joke. Less murderous?

Yes. But now it just looks like you don't know grammar.

Equally damaging to my reputation.

You carry on messaging in this bantering vein for the rest of the journey, so that when your train pulls into the station you see it is now approaching one a.m.

I've just got back to Sidcup so I'll sign off but thanks for the show and for the post-show chat. It was an unexpected bonus.

I feel that way about it too. Thanks again for coming.

You don't speak for the rest of the summer, although you think about him often and even get as far as drafting several emails to him which you fail to send because of their obvious transparency in revealing your crush on him, which feels schoolgirl and unreciprocated in its nature.

That August you go to the south of France and spend a whole month travelling alone along the coast. There is no particular point to the trip, other than the fact you desire it and are in a position of freedom to execute it. You're not sure whether it's thinking about Wren and the commitment he's made by getting married and having children, but you are acutely aware of your lack of ties to anyone at this point in your life which enables you to roam at leisure, at no cost or benefit to anyone else's happiness.

You had declined the offer of company from Amber and Rosie when they had volunteered to join you, as well as turning down their suggestion of a week's surfing school in Biarritz.

'But why would you actively choose to spend a month by yourself?' asked Romily, incredulous to learn of your plans.

'I've never done it before and it might be my only chance to experience it.' This line will seem laughable in the succeeding years in which you remain vastly independent and unresponsible for anyone or anything.

'You know you're not obliged to seek out every experience, right? Like even the bad ones, aka becoming a recluse.' But Romily has always derived her energy and purpose from other people, unlike you who – although extroverted when socializing – needs vast periods of solitude to recharge.

'It's not like I'll be completely alone. I can always hang out with people in my hostels.'

'Well, can you actually? Promise me you won't end up turning into a *total* hermit.'

Partly out of your promise to Romily, and partly because two weeks into your trip you are hit by a sudden craving for company, you infiltrate a group of Australian 'yachties' staying at the same crew house as you in Antibes who are bemused when you tell them that you are not here to work on the boats but that you are studying to be an actor in London (brushing over Sidcup's precise geographical location) and had found the crew house online, thinking it was an ordinary hostel.

The eldest in the group – a thirty-one-year-old Chief Officer called Aiden – takes on an older-brotherly air with you which, never having had a brother, you find novel. He introduces you to the Absinthe bar in town, full of Toulouse-Lautrec prints, piggy-backing you home after you consume too much of the aniseed green liquid, despite initially grimacing at its taste.

You share a room with a twenty-five-year-old blonde woman called Selina from Perth who wakes up at six every morning and puts on a crisp white shirt to go 'dock-walking' which she explains involves parading along the jetty and handing out printed copies of her CV as she looks for stewarding work. The woman in her fifties who runs the crew house tells you throughout the week, 'You'll end up staying another week, and then another one after that. Trust me. Once you've tasted yachtie life, there's no going back.' But as someone who has never been into ships or sailing, who has always preferred being in water to being on it, and whose calling to be on the stage has been resolutely unwavering since the age of eleven, you are not in any way surprised (despite everyone else's surprise) when after seven days in Antibes you happily pack your bag, settle your bill in twenty-euro notes, and say your goodbyes as you move on to the next leg of your journey.

As you weave the alleys of Nice's old town and hike the rocky coastal path, looking out over pine forest and aqua-patched sea, you feel filled with possibility – that so much is still ahead of you, and you are already living to such a full extent: exploring foreign towns, speaking in another language, pursuing your interests and staying no longer than you want or feel you ought when visiting a monument, gallery or museum. Inside the Musée des Beaux-Arts, one particular painting catches you off-guard and unexpectedly you start to cry. You can't work out why but it's something to do with the wildness of the sea and the sky. You lose track of how long you stand there, transfixed by this oil canvas of a shipwreck in a storm. When you turn away, you see a plaque on the wall next to it that says in cursive French text: *Art, because sometimes life is not enough.* You wonder if that's right or if actually it should read: *Art, because sometimes life is too much.* But perhaps the translation wouldn't work as well.

That evening you sit on the pebbled beach resting your back against the sloped stone wall of the Promenade des Anglais, your arms sticky with nectarine juice, and realize how content you are to be alone. It is not that you don't feel lonely at points, but there is a sharpness and a fullness to travelling without a friend or partner; both the highs and the lows are more pronounced, which you deduce is a balanced trade-off.

Almost a year has passed since you and Nathanael broke up and you have been single since. During this time you've had your first one-night stand (with a recruitment executive you met inside Sidcup's family-run Mexican restaurant), shared tapas with a *chef de partie* in London Bridge who had subsequently stopped replying to your messages, and been on several dates with a Bulgarian MA student who you'd wanted to be attracted to because of his refreshingly honest conversation but recoiled at the walking boots he wore and the way he asked you to gently tug his balls when you lay in bed together.

When you land in the UK nine days before the start of the new academic year, there's an email in your inbox from your course leader containing the cast lists for your third-year public productions. You scan the first attached document entitled *Spring Term* – simultaneously proud and disappointed to see Lillie's name listed next to the lead female role, without yours. However, this disappointment is immediately replaced by lurching excitement as you open the second attachment and spot the title of the autumn-term production and who you are playing. With legitimate reason to now message Wren, you email him that afternoon on the train back to Norwich.

Hi again! Hope you're having a good summer? Weird coincidence but I've just got the casting through for our third-year production and I'm doing Rocket to the Moon. *Am I destined to only ever do the same (slightly out of sync) shows as you from now on?!*

Four days pass back at your parents' house in which he doesn't reply, and you try to ignore the despondency that now permeates what would otherwise be enjoyable activities.

'You're quite morose for someone who's just come back from a month-long holiday,' says your mother, when you ask to abandon your game of table tennis halfway through.

'She's morose *because* she's just come back from a month-long holiday,' chips in Romily, from under the apple tree where she's lounging on a canvas deckchair.

'I'm not morose. I'm just bored of this game.'

'That's cause you're not even trying to win it,' says Romily, standing and gesturing for you to hand her your bat. 'Get ready to be thrashed, Mum.'

You are standing in the frozen-food aisle of Sainsbury's selecting ice lollies when Wren's reply comes through, three days before the start of your new term. You lean your lower back against the freezer as you open up his message, only registering that you are cold in your sleeveless dress after you look up from your phone and see the hairs on your arm are now vertical.

Apparently so! I'm happy and envious for you. I feel as though I'm still struggling to let that show go. I suppose all past productions stay with you to a certain extent, but I guess this one got under my skin in a big way. Do I assume you've been cast as Cleo?

Although tempted by the thought of conversing with him in real time, you force yourself to wait twenty-four hours before responding, enjoying picturing him thinking about you as he waits for your reply; you have no evidence of this occurring but in your hazy end-of-summer daydreaming can quite easily convince yourself it is.

Cleo yes! My wish came true (even without your offer of homicide). I know what you mean about past productions . . . When I finished my first panto age eleven they let me keep my elf hat and I slept in it for two whole weeks even though the bells pressed into my head. PS I'm sure you're busy being a father and successful actor but it would be great to maybe email you any questions about the show once rehearsals begin? I promise not to bombard you!

This time he replies immediately.

That sounds like an uncomfortable and jangly night's sleep. You and your director will have your own vision for the show and I don't want to impose but I'll welcome the creative stimulation. Bombard away.

And so, it begins. The emails feel fun and harmless at first, nothing inappropriate, mainly just questions and thoughts on the play – but invariably within these work emails, little facts about yourselves and questions to each other start seeping in so that you learn his wife is Welsh and called Cristyn and that they have a six-year-old daughter named Efa and a four-year-old son named Cai. In return you tell him about your family and reference your singledom in passing. Each time you see his name in your inbox you feel the area around your sternum thud, and sometimes you spend whole chunks of rehearsal, during scenes you're not in, mentally constructing your reply.

You feel completely immersed in the world of the play; your

71

waking hours are spent either in rehearsal or emailing Wren when you get home from rehearsal, so that it is hard to separate your feelings towards him and your feelings towards the show – both feel exciting and vital, in a way that belongs to being twenty-one, but is not necessarily simply because you are twenty-one. Or is it? It's difficult to distinguish causality from correlation.

There is always the premise of the play somewhere within the body of your emails to justify sending them, but lately they are getting to be six or seven paragraphs, sent nightly, often late in the evening or in the early hours of the morning. You have started to fantasize about him, so that you now regularly imagine a scenario in which his Young Vic production has merged with yours, with the two of you playing opposite each other, finding moments in the wings between scenes to fuck, no time to undress, wanting each other too much for that anyway, him just pulling up your white dental dress and pushing himself into you as he buries his face in your breasts. You allow yourself to indulge in these fantasies, because that's what they are: fantasies. You know he is married and that, save for two meetings, your entire three-month correspondence has been over email, but for the first time in your life you feel understood and cannot help pursuing this feeling, never believing that it will lead to an actual affair. The idea of this scenario materializing is so ludicrously far-fetched that your behaviour towards each other, although boundary-breaking, feels benign. But you have placed too much faith in the sanctity of marriage by convincing yourself that all your late-night correspondence is harmless, by thinking that you will be able to walk away from each other after what feels like having exposed your cores – an irreversible process like combustion or ageing.

It's the penultimate night of your show and he turns up unannounced so that you don't know he's been watching until you exit into the foyer and see him chatting to several of your classmates. You momentarily wonder whether he has been simultaneously emailing other students, and that perhaps you have misinterpreted your bond with him, but the look he gives you immediately discards this possibility.

You make your way towards him but are intercepted by Lillie who throws her arms around you.

'That was outrageously good. Also, seriously hot. I think even *I* wanted to bed you.'

Laughing, you reply, 'That was obviously my primary objective.'

'Really, though, I'll be amazed if you don't get signed from that. Did any agents show up, do you know?' You detect an edge of panic in her voice, along with genuine curiosity and goodwill. This underlying competition will continue to be present in your friendship over the decade that follows so that while you will share in each other's success, there will always be a slight tension surrounding it.

You shrug, less interested in the potential presence of any agents, in comparison to the concrete presence of Wren. 'I'm not sure. I'll call the box office tomorrow to see if their comps were collected.'

'You know who *is* here . . .' she says coyly.

'Who?' you ask, trying to sound relaxed.

'Your email buddy.' She delivers this archly, raising her eyebrows, before looking over at Wren and waving. He registers her wave with a smile. 'Let's go and say hi, then. Unless you're deliberately playing hard to get.'

'Why would I be doing that?'

'Because you clearly fancy him,' she says, grinning and turning to walk towards him without giving you a chance to contradict her.

You start to follow, but then some first-year students approach to tell you how much they loved the show, and you remember how in awe of the third-years you were when you were in first year, and so take time to chat to them and ask how their term is going.

When you look back over at Wren, you see he is in conversation with Lillie and your course director, while also now putting his coat on. Panicked he's about to leave, you detach yourself from the discussion, thanking the first-year students once again, and head towards him.

'Here she is,' says your course tutor. 'Watch out for your upper vocal range towards the end of the first act, but otherwise, no notes.'

'That's a first,' says Lillie. Your course director purses her lips, trying not to smile.

'I look forward to hopefully saying the same about your Nora next term,' she says, turning to strike up conversation with your movement tutor who is dressed in her usual black leggings and polo neck, with the touching addition of a navy velvet jacket for the occasion.

'Right. Let's ditch the theatre bar and head to the pub,' says Lillie. 'Coming?' she asks Wren. He winces as he says, 'I'd love to but I'm shooting an episode of *Casualty* in the morning. I technically should have been in bed two hours ago.'

'Wow. That's dedication,' says Lillie, not specifying what or whom this dedication is for, but looking back and forth between the two of you, knowingly. 'I'll wait for you by the door,' she says, turning to you, before walking off and leaving you, finally, alone with Wren.

'Thanks so much for coming. I thought you couldn't make it.'

'I wasn't sure I could. I didn't want to say I was coming and then not show up.'

'I'm really pleased you saw it.'

'So am I. You were superb.'

'Thanks. That's half due to you.'

'No, it isn't.'

'All right, a tenth due to you.'

'A lesser fraction than that but I'll take it.'

He opens his mouth and then closes it again as if he is on the cusp of saying something.

'Are you sure you can't stay for a drink?' you ask.

'It's a five a.m. call-time.'

'Ouch. In that case, even more thanks for coming.'

'I can't stick around tonight but I'm, um, I'm going to be in town rehearsing for the next couple of weeks if you're . . . about? This meeting feels kind of unsatisfactory. In terms of length, I mean.'

You laugh and say, 'Good to clarify you don't mean quality. And yes, I'd like that a lot.'

You hold eye contact until it becomes too intense and you have to look away or you're afraid you will do something inadvisable in a foyer full of people.

'What are you rehearsing?'

'It's a revival of *The History Boys*. The same production I was in five years ago.'

You smile, telling him you saw the original at the National when you were a teenager. 'I think it's the only time I've ever heard my dad give unreserved praise to anything.'

'He clearly hasn't seen you in this, then.'

'Oh no, he came last night and gave a full review of the show, including his criticisms.'

'He sounds like a tough man to please.'

You smile, rolling your eyes. 'I guess you must be playing the younger schoolteacher. I can't remember his name.'

'Irwin. To be honest, I'm probably too old for the role now but it's only a short run – a two-week tour and then two weeks playing in town, and I think it's probably time I got my head into something else.'

I wish you wouldn't, you think as Lillie shouts from the door, 'People coming to the pub, let's go!'

'Go, go and enjoy the rest of your night,' he says.

You hug and the physical contact feels like a sparkler has been lit inside you. As you breathe in his musty scent, you feel bereft at having to say goodbye to him, which seems unjustified, given you have only met in person three times in your life. But when he breaks away, you're quite sure he looks sad about leaving you too, which consoles you that at least you haven't fabricated the connection.

'You'll be getting an email from me imminently. I've got lots more to say about the show.'

'Throw in some caveats to balance my ego, won't you.'

'I'll do my best but it won't be easy.'

You walk outside together, where Lillie is waiting. 'Finally,' she says, dramatically shaking her hands in the air. Wren laughs and waves goodbye as he walks off towards the car park. 'He's definitely into you,' she says, as you turn to face her.

'He's definitely married.'

'My statement still stands.'

'Oh come on, we're just . . .'

'What, friends?' she says, eyebrows raised in the moonlight.

'Yeah. Or, I don't know, maybe more like mentor–mentee vibes. Anyway, why does it have to have a label?'

'It doesn't. Just so long as you both remember he's already got the one of Husband. Now let's step on it before they call last orders.' She links her arm in yours and breaks you into a run. You feel ecstatic and giddy, a wild horse charging down the street.

The following week, you arrange to meet Wren at a pub in London Bridge. It's the final week of term before the Christmas holidays and, although the production has been over for five days, your email exchanges have only intensified. Gone is the premise of work; you can no longer claim that this level of nightly correspondence is either professional or purely platonic. As such, you have persuaded yourself that the only logical and possible outcome of the situation is to release your feelings into the open, optimistic this might diffuse them. But do you really believe this? Or is it just persuasive reasoning that will permit you to divulge them in the hope they are returned?

He goes to the bar while you select a table in the corner and sit picking the edges of a beer mat, creating a pile of cardboard crumbs. You're embarrassed by the mess when he returns holding an ale for himself and a red wine for you, but he doesn't appear to notice, or at least doesn't comment.

'It's Malbec. Is that OK?' You nod because you like Malbec and because, even if you didn't, your feelings towards your drink seem trivial and irrelevant compared to your feelings towards him.

'How's rehearsal?'

'It's fun to be back in the room with the old cast but a revival hasn't got the same energy as an original production. It feels less about discovery and more about replication, which can be a bit . . .'

'Tiresome?'

'I was actually going to say something ruder.'

'But you didn't want to, in case it corrupts me?'

'Fuck no. I don't feel very old or responsible when I'm around you, you know.'

'I don't feel very young or responsible when I'm around you.'

'In a bad way? I don't mean bad as in naughty,' he says, catching himself. 'I mean in a way that makes you feel bad about yourself, because I really don't want that.'

'I'm not sure it's up to you.' And looking at him, you know it's time.

It's you who leads the conversation; in truth, you have convinced yourself that you have been the instigator of everything that's brought the two of you to this point. Yes, he proposed this evening's drink, but prior to this it was you who initiated each email correspondence, you who booked to see his show, you who repeatedly responded to his short replies with something longer, pulling at threads to reel him in, unable or just unwilling to ignore the connection you feel despite knowing he's a father and a husband.

'The thing is, I know technically I'm free and single but I'm also not. Because, well, I think I've fallen in love with someone who isn't available and now I don't know how to fall out of love with him.'

His eyes are so full of concern that for a hideous second you think your feelings won't be reciprocated, that he is humouring you for misunderstanding the situation, but then he takes hold of your hand and squeezes it under the table.

'I don't know either. I don't know how it happened, this thing between us, but it's real, isn't it? It exists.'

So he feels it too; happiness bursts through your valves, unblocking any doubt.

'It's just so rare and unexpected.' He looks lost and afraid, like a child inside an adult's body. 'I mean, it's not like anything I've ever experienced.'

You nod but are confused; does he mean, *since his wife*?

You will find this exchange melodramatic when you replay it in the years that follow – as though coming in cold to watch a fraught climactic scene without any prior build-up or context – but that evening you are so fully invested in the emotional stakes and drama of yours and Wren's story that his phrasing feels entirely fitting.

'I guess it will just disappear, though, right? If we don't do anything about it,' you say, half-hoping he'll refute your theory.

'I think so. If my circumstances were different I'd . . .'

'It's OK.' You don't want his condolences, can't bear to be pitied.

'No, but you should know that . . . What I'm trying to say is, it's just a sadness we only get one life. Because you see, the fact mine's already gone in a different direction to yours, well . . . that makes me quite painfully gutted.' He takes the leather band off his wrist and twists it in writhing motions.

Despite his angst, you cannot help smiling, a full beam at him across the table so that he smiles too. For you, at this point, this is enough.

Of course you would rather the two of you could be together in a parallel universe where he is not already married with two young children, but short of this happening you have succeeded in getting what you want: to be nothing but yourself and have every part of you accepted. You feel validated from this moment, believing in your ability to go forward and find somebody else you can feel this way about – someone who isn't already taken – and he assures you that you will. The two of you convince yourselves of it, agreeing to draw a line under everything that's passed between you and go your separate ways before anyone else gets hurt.

So it's a shock when, outside the pub as you say goodbye, he leans forward in the December night and kisses you. Prior to this moment there's been no physical contact aside from a singular hug, but now his tongue is inside your mouth, transferring the taste of ale and slight nuttiness of his breath, you feel a flicker of anger that he has crossed this line without asking. Nevertheless, you kiss him back, reasoning that it would be odd and offensive not to, surprised by how anticlimactic this exchange of cold saliva feels.

On the train home, you try to reassure yourself that the kiss was an end to what you've shared until now; you've said goodbye and have no reason to see each other ever again. But this thought, which is intended to comfort you, makes you mangled with longing.

That Christmas, you focus on trying to be a normal daughter, sister and granddaughter, even though it feels as though you're barely present, that you're a 2D cut-out in the room with these people, your family.

'Ah, of course, *creation*,' says your mother on Christmas Eve, holding up her pen with a flourish and scribbling on to her cryptic crossword.

'Here come the workings,' mutters Romily as your mother proceeds to recite the clue aloud to the room, congratulating herself in the process. 'Haydn's oratorio. Hostile reaction. Bit of a stretch for an anagram indicator. I'm sure that will leave a few people stumped.'

Romily rolls her eyes from where she's sprawled on the sofa, and you remember to roll them back in solidarity.

'Hands up for Aldi's finest,' says your father, entering the sitting room, dressed in a tailcoat and bow tie, holding a bottle of champagne by its neck.

'Hands up for actual champagne,' says Romily, raising her wrist limply above her head.

'This is actual champagne and you haven't even tried it yet. Anita, we've bred a snob.'

'Or I just have taste.'

'Taste and no money. A ruinous combination.'

'Have you come as Scrooge, Michael?' your grandmother asks from her upright position in the armchair by the open fire. She grits her teeth as she presses down on the nutcracker in her hand, batting away your offer of assistance. Her high-buttoned blouse, cashmere cardigan and subtle pink lipstick are a further reminder of the standards she upholds for herself.

80

'More profane than that, Mum. I'm paying homage to Charles Bradlaugh.'

'And I've bred a heathen,' says your grandmother, picking pieces of shelled walnut from her gnarled fist.

'Who's Charles Bradlaugh?' asks Romily, with a yawn.

'You must know Charles Bradlaugh,' says your mother, looking up from her crossword, aghast.

'Why *must* I know Charles Bradlaugh?'

'Political activist and founder of the Secular Society.'

'God, I can't imagine how I've survived in conversation until now.'

'Sarcasm works best when paired with knowledge, Romily,' says your father, popping the cork.

'I've got tons of knowledge. It just doesn't include your niche secular guy.'

'There's nothing esoteric about Charles Bradlaugh.'

'I bet Margot's never heard of him.'

'Unfortunately, that doesn't further your argument.'

You feel their collective eyes on you as you try to recall what's just been said.

'I know Charles Baudelaire?'

'Right century, wrong person,' says your mother, turning back to her crossword.

'See? If neither of us know about him, it's clearly an oversight on your part.'

'Girls, at some point, your education – or lack of it – ceases to be our responsibility.'

'Try telling that to Mum,' says Romily, reaching for a glass.

On Christmas morning, your grandmother asks to be accompanied to the family service at the cathedral – your agnosticism, held up against your parents' and Romily's atheism, making you the most susceptible to her request.

You watch as the youngest school-aged child in the

81

congregation is invited up to the altar to light the white candle inside the advent ring, disturbed that you have come so close to destroying a marriage and a family. How is it even possible you have this power? Aren't marriages meant to be strong enough to withstand the advances of a twenty-one-year-old? You want to atone for what you have done and at the same time rage that you have lost the first man to ever understand you.

At the end of the service, the two of you stay seated as the rest of the row files out.

'Grandma, you know the whole God forgiveness thing?' you ask, looking up at the stone vaulted ceiling.

'I do.'

'Do you ever feel it's just too convenient?'

'You're sounding dangerously like your father,' she says wryly.

'As in I sometimes think I'd like to believe, I just don't know how to.'

'In that case, I'll pray for you.' Her tone is matter-of-fact, as though she has agreed to pick up an extra grocery item on your behalf.

'Do you pray for Dad?' you ask, knocking the toe of your boot against the embroidered prayer cushion hanging in front of you.

'I don't pray he'll find God any more, no. But I do pray for him.'

'What about Grandpa?' As you turn, you see her face flash with fondness at his mention.

'Of course. He's top of my list.'

'You know, I don't think he'd mind if you fell in love again.'

Your grandmother looks at you with astonishment. 'What on earth makes you think I want to fall in love again?'

'Oh. I guess . . .' You tail off, feeling suddenly shy and mawk-ish. 'I guess I just figured who wouldn't want to be in it?'

'Margot, I loved your grandfather dearly but marriage and children take a great deal of energy and compromise. Especially if you don't have much money, and we weren't poor but we weren't well-off like your parents either.'

You sit up straighter against the hard wood of the pew and pull your shoulders back, trying to counter the collapsing of your insides as you think of Wren and Cristyn and their history of promises and compromises.

'We better get home to assist your father in the kitchen,' says your grandmother, reluctantly accepting the offer of your arm as she stands before firmly releasing it. 'We don't want another year of green stuffing.'

'Don't worry, Grandma, we've put a blanket ban on wasabi.'

You find points over the days that follow to extract yourself from family games and conversations to sit alone in your room where you go back through yours and Wren's emails, morbidly scrutinizing them like the collection of your milk teeth you kept in a small jar and as a teenager would tip on to your palm to examine their rusted roots. There is one exchange in particular you read repeatedly, even though it triggers a sharp stabbing in your chest.

I still can't work out what the audience is meant to think about Cleo. Odets presents her as this kind of naive and deluded temptress at the start, but by the end I feel as though she has a better handle on life than Stark or any of the characters. But maybe that's just because I'm young and still believe the kind of love she's striving for does and can exist. Mx

I think you're right to feel that, both about Cleo and about love. What I think Stark finds so attractive about her, beyond her physicality, is her refusal to settle for anything less than what she's looking for and I think he's both frightened and envious of that. Playing her with that hunger and aspiration is where her sexuality comes from, in my opinion. I wouldn't worry what the audience thinks about her. Even if they don't like her, the ones who really get the play will admire her. Wx

On Boxing Day, Romily comes into your room where you are lying in bed with your laptop rereading this conversation yet again. You minimize your browser as she sits on top of the duvet and inspects the tips of her hair.

'What's up with you? You're all mopey.'

'I'm just exhausted. They work us these ridiculous hours during term time and then constantly remind us how little we'll work when we graduate, and it's like, *then surely you could better prepare us for this scenario?*'

'Yeah, that makes literally no sense. They should be giving you loads of time to go out and meet wealthy old philanthropists who'll fund your careers.'

'I feel they'd struggle to get that on to the syllabus.'

'Extracurricular, obviously. So I take it there are currently no men in your life?'

'Not unless you count Middleton and Rowley.'

'Who?'

'Jacobean playwrights. Wrong audience.'

'I'm open to being educated.'

'OK, well they wrote this pretty famous play called *The Changeling*.'

'Go on.'

'So, the general consensus is that Middleton was probably responsible for the tragic plot, and Rowley for the comic sub-plot. More?'

'That was mildly interesting but no.'

As she lies back with her toes touching the headboard, you suppress your urge to confess everything; as much as you want her advice, you are afraid of her judgement, of her suggesting that the kiss was your fault for having led Wren on these last few months – something you already suspect and feel remorse about. Instead, you ask for more details of her recent trip to Sami's family riad in Tangier. Stretching out her arms, she basks in the memory, describing how light hit the centre of the courtyard every morning as they drank orange juice and ate baghrir dipped in honey and butter, and you bristle at how uncomplicated her relationship is.

Somehow you manage to get through the rest of the Christmas period and look forward to returning to school on the first day of the spring term, grateful for the distraction to occupy your thoughts. You throw yourself into your classes with vigour and feel the re-emergence of your old self, pre-Wren. You still pine for him, but have now punctured the belief that he is the only man you will ever love.

Lillie is straight into rehearsal for *A Doll's House* so you see less of her than you would like, but invite her over for dinner on Saturday evening, where she asks after your 'burgeoning email correspondence'.

'Did it burst into bloom over Christmas?' she says, picking pieces out of the bowl of cheese you are grating.

'The opposite. I'm pretty sure it's withered,' you say, feeling both remorse and relief to admit this aloud.

'Probably for the best. It's not like it was ultimately going to lead to any good.'

'Yeah, I guess not,' you say, turning towards the sink to hide your face, feeling yourself becoming hot as you recall the sensation of Wren's kiss.

'God, it feels good to have a day off from that practice corset. Trust me to go and get cast in the only period play.'

'Just be thankful it's only for one term and not the rest of your womanly life.'

'Hear hear,' she says, topping up her wine glass.

It is your father's fifty-fourth birthday the first Saturday in February and your mother has expressed a desire that you return to

Norwich for it, despite his insistence that he has 'no interest in celebrating this annual and unremarkable event'. You know from your research that Wren is currently on tour at the Theatre Royal – and the appeal of being in such close proximity to him persuades you to agree to your mother's request, but the moment you arrive back at your parents' house, you feel flat and tormented by Wren's nearness.

That Friday evening as you help clear the dinner table, you ask your mother what time she has booked the restaurant for the following evening, assuming you will be going to the family-run Bangladeshi three roads away from your house – your parents' staple venue for any form of occasion.

'We're actually branching out and seeing *The History Boys* instead. There's a touring production in town for a couple of nights.'

You can't work out if it's a dropping or rising sensation but something substantial happens inside your chest.

'What? Why didn't you tell me?'

She looks confused by your accusatory tone.

'I just assumed you'd be pleased. I'm sure I saw the website page up on your laptop at Christmas.' Yes, multiple times over the last month you have googled the production, not because you were ever planning on seeing it, just out of wanting to feel connected to Wren, but of course your mother doesn't know this. 'And you know how much your father enjoyed it the first time we saw it.'

'That doesn't mean he wants to see it again.'

'Margot, I don't know why you're getting all het up about this. Your father and I are going. You can join us if you like, and if not then you can call the box office and try and get a refund on the ticket, but I think it would be a shame given you've come home especially.'

You are torn. Your mother has technically given you an out,

but you agree that it would be pointless to have come back to celebrate and then to sit alone in the house all evening. You can't work out if this is a legitimate, or simply convenient, justification that convinces you to go along to the theatre the following evening, fuelled by both dread and excitement.

Although you are seated halfway back inside the darkened auditorium and know that Wren cannot possibly see you against the brightness of the stage lights, you are tense from the moment the curtain goes up. Your father laughs heartily throughout the first half and then begins listing an inventory of the show's flaws in the interval. As he analyses various cast members, you wait to see what he will say about Wren, but he gets distracted by the presence of an ice-cream seller and turns the discussion towards the pitfall of mint-flavoured ice cream – the inevitable disappointment of it not being pistachio. You tune out and think about Wren inside the green room backstage, only metres away from you; there is something deceitful about this occurring without his knowledge, and you wonder if he felt this way watching your performance at the end of last term.

When the show finishes, to your dismay you are forced to spend an entire seven minutes searching underneath the row of seats in front and behind for your mother's glasses case, which she insists must have fallen out of her bag and on to the floor, before remembering that she likely left it in the car when she got out her glasses to read the parking meter. Thanking and apologizing to the patient usher who had joined you on the floor on her hands and knees, the three of you exit the auditorium into the foyer, where you are on high alert, aware that Wren could come front-of-house at any moment.

As your parents begin heading through to the bar, you stop by the entrance of the theatre.

'I'm not feeling that well, actually; I think I'm just going to go home.'

'I hope it's nothing to do with that discounted quiche. Michael, did you check how many days it was past its sell-by date?'

'They're always overly cautious with those things. It's pumped full of preservatives anyway.'

'Nevertheless, we're not short of money. I don't know why we can't just eat in-date quiche.'

'What, and be the mug who pays full price for it? I don't think so.'

Your mother sighs and opens her mouth to object.

'It's not the quiche,' you say, keen to curtail the conversation. 'I'm just tired and a bit headachy.'

'Well, in that case take a taxi and get into bed when you get home, and we'll see you in the morning.'

'There's no need to take a taxi,' says your father, exasperated. 'The bus goes from right outside the theatre.'

'She's not feeling well, Michael. Margot, I'll pay for it.'

'It's not a question of who pays for it. It's all ultimately coming out of the same family pot which you lot seem to have no interest in preserving,' says your father, huffing as he takes a ten-pound note out of his wallet and hands it to you, gruffly kissing the side of your head.

'Thanks,' you say, hugging him and then your mother. 'I'll see you guys tomorrow.'

Exiting the theatre into the night, you feel gratitude mingled with regret to have made it through the evening without conversing with Wren, unsure which of these you feel in greater proportion.

You are crossing the street, heading towards the taxi rank, when you hear your name being called. You turn, holding your breath, and see him leaning against the outside wall of the building, smoking a cigarette.

As you cross back over the road and walk towards him, you

are so flooded with adrenaline that it is an effort not to break into a run.

'I didn't know you smoked,' you say, trying to sound casual but aware of the tremor in your voice and jaw.

'I don't normally,' he says, stubbing out his cigarette on the wall. 'I think it's being on tour. It makes me feel twenty-five again.'

You attempt to keep your face neutral as he speaks but have no idea if you are succeeding in this.

'How was your Christmas?' The question feels ridiculous the moment it leaves your mouth but you can't think of an alternative one that wouldn't be similarly drenched in subtext.

'I got through it. You?'

'Same.' There is a pause, following which you say, 'I'm not here intentionally, by the way. I mean, my mum booked the tickets for my dad's birthday. I didn't know we were going until last night.'

He nods with understanding. 'I did think of you. Being here in Norwich. It's good to see you.'

'You too.' Although 'good' feels unsuitable to convey the wealth of conflicting emotions you are experiencing.

'Well, maybe not good,' he says, voicing your thought. 'More like a cross between wonderful and horrific.'

You laugh, feeling a stab of pain. 'Yeah, that's exactly it.'

He looks down at the ground and then back up at you.

'Sorry. I'm still processing you being here. You seem to be dealing with this a bit better than me.'

'To be fair, I've had longer to adjust. I've just been watching you onstage for two and a half hours. You were great, by the way, but there's nothing new in that.'

'It's a fun show but I'll be glad to get home. It's the small things you miss when you're on tour.'

The implication of him missing his family knocks the air out of you as though you've been winded. 'I'd better go. I told my parents I'm not feeling well to avoid staying for a drink.'

'So they're in there right now?' You nod. 'You know I'm going to go straight to the bar in that case and desperately try to work out who they are, don't you.'

'It won't take you long. Just look out for a woman in an anorak next to a bearded man forensically studying his drinks receipt.'

Wren laughs and then looks sorrowful. 'I think I won't hug you, for obvious reasons.'

'That makes sense.'

You smile at each other, and you watch his Adam's apple go up and then down as he swallows, feeling a thick ball in your own throat.

'Bye,' you say, turning and walking away, feeling intensely proud that you have resisted any form of physical contact. But this brief restraint offers a dangerous form of confidence which then allows you to turn once again, now you are at a safe distance, and say, 'Maybe we could get a coffee in daylight tomorrow morning.'

He pauses, giving you both long enough to assess the wisdom of your suggestion (or lack of it), before replying, 'My train leaves at ten, but the tour ends next week. How about we meet in London when I'm back? Do you think we could handle that?'

'We've handled it tonight.'

'It's a date, then. No. I mean, it's categorically not a date.'

You both laugh, and just like that, the two of you convince yourselves that you are in a safe position to share an innocuous drink, as a reward for your abstinence, when in actual fact this meeting will undo the last six weeks of work and be the striking of the match that scorches all stable ground as you currently know it.

★

Despite the pact you make with yourself on your way into town – that you will not do anything that breaches the contract of his marriage – there is a feeling of charged inevitability from the moment you arrive to meet each other outside Greenwich station the following Thursday evening.

Your initial suggestion of a daylight coffee has seamlessly transitioned into an evening drink, without either of you drawing attention to this alteration. Is this how affairs progress? you wonder. With each person expecting the other person to behave more responsibly?

He greets you with a kiss on the cheek, asking if you like jazz, saying he knows a small venue around the corner. On the way there he discloses that he used to play the euphonium in a college band called The Honkers. This piece of information is delicious and compulsive, like the residue of toffee stuck in a molar which you keep returning to, gleefully mocking him with it for the remainder of the walk.

'Why do you think there's no status imbalance between us?' you ask.

'Oh there is. You just don't notice because it's tilted in your favour.'

You dare to touch his shoulder as you reply, 'I'll go easy on you tonight.' The felt of his coat feels coarse against your fingers.

The bar is subterranean with soft lighting, giving the impression of privacy despite being a public place and only a forty-seven-minute train ride from campus. Still, you remind yourself that there is no need to be covert; you are permitted to share a drink with a married man.

It's early, the small circular tables dotted around the room are still empty, their candles presently unlit. On the platform stage a saxophonist is doing a sound-check, his fluctuating fingers on the distressed brass keys producing notes that are thick and full of bass.

'Red wine?' asks Wren.

'I'll get these.' You feel assertive, as though you are riding a wave you have caught at the exact right moment.

'If you're sure?' You nod. 'I'll have a bitter, please, whatever they've got on tap.'

When you return to the table, Wren is typing on his phone. You wonder whether he's messaging Cristyn, and what their childcare arrangements are.

'This is for you, by the way,' he says, taking a worn exercise book out of his satchel and sliding it across the table. 'Well, on loan.'

You open it and see his signature scrawled in the top corner of the inside cover. *Wren Perera, London, 1995.*

'It's my diary from the year I graduated. I was reading through it at Christmas, trying to keep myself occupied, and realized I was the same age as you are now when I wrote it.'

As you begin turning and scouring the pages, his voice takes on a hesitancy. 'Just tell me if you're not interested, I don't want to inflict my twenty-one-year-old musings on you, I just thought, since you didn't know me then, it would be a way of . . .'

He tails off, and as you look up at his flushed cheeks, at his small dark eyes flitting between your face and the book, you feel an urge to protect him with sincerity.

'This is great. Honestly, it's really cool.'

'I warn you now, I wasn't as mature as you are.'

'Obviously. You're still barely a match for me.'

'Rudely accurate.'

You look back down at the diary and begin reading aloud: '*Andy and I saw* The Young Gods *at Kentish Town Forum last night. Andy doesn't think* Only Heaven *is as strong as the first four albums but I like what they're trying to do with the more ambient sound. "Loin-taine" is probably my favourite track.*'

'Yeah, so this is going to be painful if you're going to read it aloud,' says Wren, reaching for the diary.

You smile, snatching it away. 'Who's Andy and who are The Young Gods?' you ask, enjoying his discomfort.

'Forget about Andy but you ought to know The Young Gods.'

'What's their vibe?'

'Swiss industrial rock. I'll play you some.'

'Please don't.' Wren laughs and you turn the page, selecting another extract at random. '*Yesterday I got my ear pierced at one of the stands in Camden Lock market. It's gone a bit red but the man said it would be sore for the first couple of days. I hope it looks OK once the swelling goes down.*'

You look at Wren's ear and notice a tiny mark on his left lobe. 'How long did you wear it for?' you ask, grinning.

'It kept getting infected but I persevered for a good few months.'

'So, what were you – a punk?'

'Trying to be.'

'I can't decide if there's anything sadder than trying and failing at counter-culture.'

'Are you planning to barb me the entire evening?' he asks, shaking his head and smiling.

You lean in towards him as you reply, 'That depends if you keep providing this level of bait.'

In the dimly lit bar after a glass of wine, your pact to maintain self-control seems of increasingly less relevance than giving in to your desire, which argues your right to be reckless and make mistakes at twenty-one, that it is not your responsibility to look out for his wife; it is his. As you get older, you will grow in allegiance to your own sex and feel deeply ashamed to have ever held this view, so that in your thirties you will feel compelled to stress the importance of female solidarity to younger women, but as much as possible will resist this urge: partly because it feels hypocritical to preach about loyalty when you consider your own betrayal to Wren's wife, and partly because you suspect most twenty-something-year-olds already hold higher moral standards than you did at this age – and as for the ones who don't, surely they should be allowed to learn through living, as you did?

It's sometime after the second glass that you let your hand brush against his knee and that he reaches out to take hold of it and keep it there. It's sometime after the third that he moves his chair closer to yours and you start to kiss, allowing your hands to rove under the table, and sometime after this that you say, 'I'm pretty sure I saw a Travelodge near the station,' and Wren looks surprised before slowly nodding his head.

'I think I can make that work, I just need to make a quick call home. Shall I meet you outside in a few minutes?'

You nod, wishing you had a partner to phone and lie to as he gets up from the table and exits the bar. Your singledom makes you feel flimsy and disposable, as though you are constructed of plastic while he is made of oak.

You're both quiet as you walk the eight minutes along Greenwich High Road. All the intimacy you'd had in the bar seems to have dissipated so that the notion of holding his hand now feels out of the question.

He pauses outside the lit-up entrance, the crassness of the chain logo somehow equally shameful as cheating on his wife.

'You know, I could book us somewhere nice, if we waited and planned this properly.'

You shake your head. 'If we're going to do it, it might as well be tonight.'

Although repulsed by the idea of committing adultery, you want him so much, enough to convince yourself that even if you were to walk away and once again attempt to bitterly get over him, you would only later relent further down the line, and find yourselves – a few weeks or months from now – at this same impasse. The futility of going through all of this only to end up at the same point makes you want to scratch your skin until it bleeds.

'Yes, hi, good evening, we'd like a room, please,' he says to the receptionist inside the foyer. Her slicked-back hair and blazer look uncomfortably tight. You wonder if she knows, just from glancing at you, that you are about to sleep with another woman's husband.

He puts the room on his card. There's no question of you paying for it; you're a student. While it is about so much more than the physical act of having sex, you recognize that there is an additional urge in him from having slept solely with the same person for the last twelve years which means he needs this more than you. Is that true? It feels true.

The light inside the room is harsh and grey. You turn it off and let the glow from the skyscrapers in Canary Wharf permeate the thin net curtains, the walls becoming blue and shadowy. When you kneel down and take his penis in your mouth, he groans so deeply it startles you; his hairs feel wiry against your cheeks and smell sweet and yeasty. As he enters you, you too groan loudly, want even more of him as you press your palms into his back and push him deeper inside you, wishing he could penetrate every part of you; there is nowhere you don't want him.

Afterwards, sprawled in each other's arms, you breathe deep and slow, your head rising up and down on his chest like horses on a carousel.

'It's not normally like this. Is it?' You detect a vulnerability in his voice, a fear that you have felt this present feeling with some-body prior to him.

'No. At least not that I know of,' you say, keeping your face turned away, not wanting him to see the tear inching down your cheek both from what you have done and the idea of not being able to do it again.

Later, when you wake, it feels so obvious to find yourself there next to him, like the sun rising because it can't not. You feel both heavy and light – the heaviness from the guilt and impossibility of the situation, and the lightness because here you are, naked and held by the person who most understands you.

After this, you lose count of how many times you try to end it, each time falling back into each other's arms after weeks of abstinence. You – who are known to be disciplined and measured, who can resist an open box of chocolates, and wakes early to do articulation exercises every morning before class – are utterly failing to resist temptation, and it frightens you.

As the affair continues, because that's what it is now, you become increasingly reckless: jumping off trains to greet each other, kissing in broad daylight on the platform, boldly holding hands as you walk along the South Bank. Does a part of you want to get caught? Or are you both too full of the confidence that comes with love, to care?

By Easter you feel like a husk having to keep this secret away from the people you are closest to, yet are simultaneously the fullest version of yourself you've ever been. There are no triggers for your waves of despair or, similarly, for the sudden bursts of joy that arrive without warning. During these bursts you send him poems, playlists, photos, wanting to share everything with him that seems to personally reflect your love, as if all art has been created with the two of you as its muse.

When your parents go on a cycling holiday to Romania, he comes to stay with you in your family home for a night while Cristyn and the children are in Wales visiting his in-laws. He cooks spiced pumpkin curry as you read on the sofa, filled with such contentment that you can't fathom ever being unhappy again. After you have sex that night, you lie facing each other in bed, talking for hours as if there will never be enough time – because there isn't.

The next morning, he takes a scenic route back to London. At one point a car speeds past on a narrow country lane, clipping the wing mirror of the passenger seat, making you consider what would happen if you crashed and your injured bodies were found together, what justifiable explanation you'd give. But these sombre thoughts subside when Wren parks the car next to a nearby field and suggests stretching your legs. You walk hand in hand, stopping to drink from a carton of apple juice while he picks wild flowers, yellow, white and purple, and puts them in your hair as though you are his bride.

During your despair, the guilt consumes you, causes insomnia, curbs your appetite, cuts you off further from your friends and family who you can't confide in.

Romily messages you at the end of April. *Can you call Mum to confirm you're alive so she can stop calling me to check you're alive? PS You are alive, right?*

Alive, yes! Sorry . . . Meant to reply to your missed calls . . . Deep in rehearsal for our showcase next month and have a panel of directors assessing our monologues tomorrow . . .

Just so long as you're eating/breathing/sleeping? Break a leg for the panel!

Thanks! And yes x 3

I'm fine btw . . .

Sorry! How are you?

See above

Seriously though?

Not getting any data off my flies and had another fight with Sami but other than that fiiiiine

I'll call you next week

I live in hope . . .

Promise xxx

Good job we're blood related or I'd have culled you by now x

During sleepless nights you write lists of why you and Wren cannot be together, memorizing the bullet points by heart before setting fire to them with the scented candle in your room in case your housemates were to accidentally discover them; for years after, the smell of vanilla makes you want to retch. You text him saying you need to speak, asking him to call as soon as he wakes and can get away, and when he does, you cry down the phone to him, delirious from lack of sleep and loneliness that you cannot do this: you cannot keep seeing each other. He always agrees, never pressurizes or tries to persuade you otherwise. And it's always you that breaks and comes back to him. In this respect, you have the power in the relationship in which it otherwise belongs to him – as the one who is largely unavailable and whose schedule you orchestrate your meetings around. After all, you cannot call him whenever you have the impulse but he can always pick up the phone to speak to you, and you'll almost always answer. You have lost track of the number of times you've lied to Lillie about who you're talking to or why you sometimes suddenly make excuses to leave the room when your phone rings.

'Another call from your mum?' says Lillie one evening, twiddling a strand of hair as she alters her position on the sofa in your living room.

'I don't know why she's suddenly got all clingy. She never used to be.'

'Ageing, I reckon.'

'I hope not or else it's only going to get worse.' You press your phone to the side of your thigh, hiding the screen from her as you stand. 'I'll just be a couple of minutes.'

'Want me to pause it?'

'No, it's fine, I've seen it like a dozen times.'

'Meta.'

'Huh?'

'*Groundhog Day*? A dozen times?'

'Oh right, yeah. I'm losing my edge.'

'I won't affirm or deny that but yeah . . . something's different about you.' It's remarks like this that make you wonder whether she knows about the affair – or at least suspects it – but is protecting your friendship by not asking you outright in case your response is to lie to her face.

You're not sure why Wren seems less affected by guilt than you when it is his wife the two of you are cheating on. You ask him about this one evening inside your hotel room as you come back from the bathroom and lie your ear on his axilla. He pauses as if wanting to make sure he gets his answer right, and says, 'I suppose it's because she seems happy.'

This makes sense to you, at least in part. While all you can do is visualize Cristyn's pain and anger if she were to find out about the affair, unlike you, Wren can go home and attempt to offset his betrayal with small acts of goodness; you picture him bringing her coffee in bed or taking Efa and Cai swimming on Saturday morning so she can read the paper, and feel gladdened by these superficial thoughts.

'She had an affair once.'

'What?' You wonder if you've misheard as you draw your head up to look at him.

'At the start of our marriage. She only told me about it a few years ago.'

'Weren't you angry?'

'I was but I forgave her. We got through it. Maybe that's partly why I feel justified doing what we're doing.'

You are stunned; there is so much you don't understand about his marriage or, for that matter, any marriage.

And so, it carries on. Another two months pass in which you turn twenty-two, but all the while, the idea of simply accepting the affair as your new modus operandi feels deplorable. The whole thing becomes tarnished, not only with shame but with sadness – that you will never enjoy the ordinary everyday acts of meeting each other's parents, making mutual friends, sharing a home and building a life together.

Sometimes Wren shows you videos and photos of Efa and Cai on his phone and you glance at his face while watching them, see the genuine delight and interest he has in these two miniature people, and ache that they are not your children too. Even when you fantasize about having his child, it is marred by the fact that you cannot compute him loving it as much as Efa and Cai, or rather your specific concern is that even if he loved it the same, he would not like it as much.

When Cristyn is in the videos or photos, Wren scrolls quickly past them; you are too embarrassed to mention that he might as well not bother, that you have returned to that press-night photo of the two of them countless times, staring into her yellowish-green eyes from the safety of the screen, each time muttering the same feeble apology, *You don't deserve this*, to the static image in front of you. But your contrition is conflicted with jealousy – that she met him before you did, that Efa and Cai come from her body and not yours, that she has the prize label of *wife* and *mother* while you are just *the other woman*. The absurdity is not lost on you that she is part of a competition she is not even aware she's entered.

Finally, when the strain gets too much, when you once again arrive in distress to meet him, cupping water over your face from the basin of your hotel bathroom, you turn to him and say, 'I don't know how long I can keep claiming "I can't keep doing this" without actually doing something about it.'

'Then I think there's only one solution, isn't there?' You're not sure if you're more terrified or ecstatic about what he'll say next. 'Neither of us can go on like this. It's not right or fair on anyone, Cristyn too.' You flinch at the sound of her name; he so rarely mentions her unless prompted by you.

'We've tried ending it and each time that's failed,' he continues, as if ticking off a checklist for the benefit of you both, so that when he says it, when he says out loud the sentence that will change everything, that will transform this five-month affair into the rest of your lives, it will feel like the logical and unavoidable solution made by two rational people – not by a thirty-eight-year-old who feels as though he's been reawakened by the passion and adoration of this young woman who he doesn't have to discuss curtain fabrics and school pick-up times with – and not by a twenty-two-year-old who doesn't want to wait to discover if she can find someone else she might be able to feel this way about, despite knowing that given how many people exist on the planet, the odds of you finding someone else to spend your life with are high enough to risk letting him go.

'The way I see it is we're going to have to be together.'

The line turns your legs to a mercury consistency. Sitting on the side of the bed, you don't answer him for several seconds, cannot fully process that he is offering you the thing you most desire and equally fear.

'Are you sure that's what you want?' you ask.

'It will be tough, at least for a while. And we'll probably have no money for – well, basically, forever. But I don't think we'll mind that too much, so long as we're together, will we?'

You shake your head. 'What about . . . I mean, there are things you've already done that I haven't had a chance to do yet.'

'Children?'

You pause before answering, trying to convince yourself that you could be OK without them – being a stepmother to his and never having your own – but the lie bounces off your gut and refuses to settle. You nod, adjusting your focus to the bark on a plane tree through the window, its pale and dark patches like the marbling paintings you and Romily produced in abundance one August. Your mother had stuck them on the fridge and then across the kitchen walls when she ran out of space so that by September she gleefully announced, 'Who needs the Royal Academy, girls? We've got our own summer exhibition!' It strikes you as unnecessary that your life has become sad and hard, given the head start you had at happiness.

'Margot, I'll do it all again tomorrow if it's with you. If you want them, that is.'

You turn back to face him, annoyed at yourself that you've started to cry. 'Really? Because I do. I mean, not yet, but I definitely do want them.'

'Then we'll have them. No more discussion needed.'

Laughter splutters out of you in a succession of gasps; your throat tastes salty and granular.

'Oh my love, come here,' he says, pulling you in so that you're sitting on his lap, rocking you as though you are a child.

'I'm squashing you.'

'No, you're not. Well, you are but I like being squashed by you.'

'I'm not sad, you know. I'm crying because I'm so happy I get to be with you.'

He kisses you all over, with each kiss pushing away your doubts – of depriving two innocent children of their father, of being despised by his wife, of what your friends and family and the staff and students at your drama school will say. You let yourself be soothed by his reassurance; he will take care of everything, you trust him so implicitly that it is unfathomable he could ever let you down.

Now the plan exists to be together, in one sense you feel you have regained some integrity, as you can no longer accuse yourself of sleeping with another woman's husband without committing to a life with him. But on the other hand, surely the decision to come clean and pull apart Wren's family in the process is arguably more selfish than continuing the affair in secret? You start to wish that you yourself came from a broken home, determining you'd have more right to cause the rupture of his family if your own had been severed by a third party.

'So, do you reckon you were ultimately better off with your parents separating?' you ask Lillie as you lie next to each other on the grassy school grounds, studying the clouds as they morph above your head. It is the end of June and your course has just finished; you are impatient to move further into London and begin your new life with Wren and as a working actor, but also feel incubated by this vacuum of time as though it is necessary preparation for everything to come.

'I don't know. It was pretty shit with them arguing all the time but it was also pretty shit when Mum left.'

'It all turned out OK in the end, though, didn't it?' You want empirical evidence that Efa and Cai will not be irreparably damaged by your actions.

'Well, I mean, sure, everyone's happy now but it took years to get to the point where Dad would even be in the same room as her again. Why? Are you thinking of divorcing someone?'

'Oh right, yeah, this is me telling you I'm secretly married.'

'I wouldn't be surprised if you were, or at least I wouldn't be surprised if you were having an affair.'

You are grateful to be looking up at the sky so you can avoid eye contact as you deliver the requisite response: 'Ooh, go on. Who would I be having an affair with?'

'My money's on Wren.'

'Interesting. What makes you say that?'

'The fact you're always disappearing into town to date

various guys I never get to meet. Plus the fact you go red and smile anytime I mention his name.'

'Good sleuthing. You've got me,' you say casually, pulling at tufts of brown grass like moulting hairs and scattering them over your top.

'Good double-bluffing,' says Lillie, rolling on to her side to face you, unconvinced by your so-called admission.

'Who says I'm bluffing?' you ask, risking this next line. 'We're madly in love and he's leaving his wife for me.'

'And let me guess, the sex is dire.'

'Oh no, the sex is great,' you say, exhaling with relief that your candidness appears to be acting as your cover. 'But all the lies and secrecy, ugh. That bit's definitely overrated.'

'Yeah, sure, I bet sneaking around is a real turn-off,' she says, lying back down again, seemingly accepting of these truthful statements disguised as lies.

Your deceit gives you a prickling feeling across your neck, but you reason that confiding in her properly would not only be a betrayal to Wren but would make her complicit in the affair, which would surely burden her in a way that would be equally undesirable.

'How's it going with Luke, by the way? I feel like you haven't seen him for ages.'

'That's cause I haven't. Do you know what's less attractive about dating medics? Never actually getting to go on any dates cause they're always working.'

'My cousin's married to a consultant anaesthetist and he spends most of his time kite-surfing. You just need to somehow bypass the medical-school bit.'

'What, go for them when they're forty? Ew.'

'Forty's not that old.'

'All right, Humbert Humbert.'

'You're twenty-one, not twelve.'

'Exactly. The prime of my life. This is our time to be young and free.'

She fans her arms above her head as you try to suppress your panic at having essentially committed to spending the rest of your life with Wren. The following evening, you stand at the window of your hotel room, pull back the curtain and see the city shrinking in front of you. The rooftops seem traversable by foot, too many telegraph poles obstruct the horizon, suddenly you swear the sky has walls. You want to ask Wren if he feels it too, the tightening sensation of things closing in, but are ashamed of your fear; he is leaving his family to be with you and you are worried about not having 'lived' enough. Surely this is already an imbalanced trade? And so you push down your doubt, remembering Wren's words – that love like this is rare. What choice do you have but to accept it?

That July, you leave Sidcup and join a house-share in Turnpike Lane, tenuously sourced by a friend of your mother's whose godson is looking for someone to fill his room. It is a crumbling detached Victorian build with a bath inside the living room (a prop from a theatre show left by a previous tenant) and an overgrown fig tree in the garden. The tiled floor in the hallway is subsiding and the kitchen has a hole in the roof which leaks water when it rains, but its occupants – an assortment of actors, comedians, writers, artists – are prepared to overlook its derelict condition on account of its charm and ludicrously low rent charged by the landlord who had requested your height when you'd come to view the low-ceilinged attic room. Besides, you conclude that it is only a temporary living set-up anyway, as you and Wren will soon be moving in together. You feel guilty about the short-term nature of your tenancy as your father spends his Saturday morning loading packed boxes from your room in Sidcup into the car and driving you to North London where he spends a further several hours unloading them and reassembling your furniture.

'Thanks, Dad,' you say, watching him wince as he man-oeuvres his way across the floorboards on his knees to tighten the screws of your bedframe. 'I really appreciate this.'

'I'm just doing my parental duty,' he replies, cursing as he stands upright and hits his head on the eaves. 'Although it would be nice to know if there's an end-date to my services anytime soon. In my day you hit twenty-one and were out on your own. Either you fended for yourself or found a partner to take on the role.'

'I'm sure you'll soon be supplanted,' you say, wishing that he could share in the irony of your remark, and wondering how he will react to yours and Wren's announcement when it comes. How long exactly until this happens you're not sure; whenever you discuss details Wren is vague but suggests that sometime in the summer holidays would probably be optimum to give things a chance to settle down before the start of the new school year for Efa and Cai.

You wonder if there are other factors you and Wren ought to discuss, such as him no longer waking in the same house as his children so that he won't be there to hear Efa announce at break-fast that cornflakes aren't really proper flakes like snowflakes and that the next time it snows she's going to build a snow-woman instead of a snowman. Or that he'll no longer poke his head into her and Cai's bedroom when he gets home at night and listen to their shallow breathing as he tucks their small hot limbs back inside their duvets. But you are anxious of bringing this up in case it makes him change his mind, and so convince yourself that he has already thought of all this and is simply not confid-ing in you in order to protect you.

You have few, if any, regrets at this point in your life but this will become one of them – that neither of you force yourselves to have this discussion about what it will take for him to leave his children, to lead both your minds to this dark harsh place in which you truly envisage the cost of what he stands to lose.

By doing this you believe you might have avoided the harrowing ending that happens instead.

The night he tells Cristyn he's leaving he doesn't tell you he's going to do it. You have no concrete cause to suspect that tonight is different to any other night as you sit in the garden of your new house-share, dressed in an oversized cardigan reading Wren's copy of Rilke's *Letters to a Young Poet*. But intuition tells you something is wrong. Later, you'll try and justify this feeling by rationalizing it, deciding that perhaps he'd messaged less that day or there was something in the tone of his last text sent to you that afternoon to suggest a hint of what was to unfold that evening. But right now, at ten to nine at night, there is no reason to think he has just launched a grenade inside his house, no reason other than something inexplicable connecting the two of you from opposite ends of the city.

You send him a message. *Is everything OK? I suddenly feel weird.* He doesn't reply but this in itself is not that unusual. He isn't always able to message in the evenings, sometimes it isn't possible. You can always message him, though, he assures you of this, has changed his passcode on his phone to your date of birth and made sure his notifications don't show on his locked screen so there is no chance of Cristyn discovering them.

You don't sleep much that night and when you do it's only in intervals, checking your phone each time you wake. It's the start of August and you haven't seen him for over a fortnight; the summer holidays make childcare more difficult and mean it's harder for him to get away. The four of them are going on a family holiday to Inverness two days from now, but he's due to fly back early to do research and development for a new play at Chichester. The plan is for you to meet him at Heathrow and travel there together to stay with him inside his rented apartment for the week; the thought of getting to live with him for seven whole days makes your pelvis smoulder like kindling.

In the morning, when you see he still hasn't messaged, you start to feel nauseous, convinced that something is wrong. You have a casting beginning in two hours' time inside a converted church on the Isle of Dogs, are thankful for the provided distraction and journey across town.

The casting has come through your newly acquired agent, an ex-soap actor and cruise-line entertainer looking for a career change, who runs the agency from his flat in High Barnet but strategically pays for a postcode in Soho where work-related mail is directed. He is assiduous and enthusiastic about you and his small list of clients, but doesn't have the calibre of contacts to get you the sort of castings you long for – classical roles with the RSC, the Globe, the National, which are accessible only to graduates of the top four and most exclusive drama schools.

The casting is a workshop format, run by a newly formed theatre company whose young founders are putting on a movement-based adaptation of *Antigone*, allocating themselves the principal roles while on the search for a Greek chorus made up of keen graduates who are willing to work for free simply to be able to say they are 'in work', despite not being paid for the privilege. Although this seems contradictory to your definition of a job, you try to quash your niggling sense of injustice, aware that there are a multitude of other actors willing to take your place, that you are currently expendable in an overcrowded industry that has no need of you.

And so you take your place on the dusty floor along with thirty other hopefuls, all dressed in black leggings and tank tops with subtle outfit variations in an attempt to stand out, which take the limited form of red lipstick and colourful knotted headbands. You are required to writhe around and make guttural noises at the young director's command. Ordinarily you would undertake this with commitment, but are cautious in your current condition – concerned that if you engage with any primal emotion you may not be able to regain composure – and so focus on a hair ball that is rolling across the floor. You clearly don't make a striking enough impression as you are not asked to stay behind for the afternoon's recall.

Checking your phone again as you leave the hall, you see there is still no message from Wren. Outside, the bright sunlight feels tacky and inappropriate for your mood. Your inability to eat anything since last night has left you lightheaded, and so you buy a pineapple juice with a straw from a corner shop and take small sugary sips from it as you walk. You don't know where you are going, only know you don't want to go home to wait inside your bedroom where, alongside his diary, Wren has left his Nikon camera and favourite linen shirt as tokens of proof he's coming back to you.

For two hours you follow the river until you arrive at the South Bank. Everywhere you look is a reminder of him but surely your body must want this, need this, or else why would it have led you here? The sky starts to leak hot summer rain and you stand under it while people run for cover before it breaks, watch as a group of children chase each other in circles outside the Royal Festival Hall, squealing at how soaked they're getting.

It is seven minutes past three when he calls. You will remember this exact time as though it is etched into you from this moment on, so that in the future when you happen to look at a clock and see the small hand on the three and the big hand somewhere between the one and the two you will always think of him, not necessarily with an intensity of feeling, just as a reflex that's pointless to resist.

When he says your name, his voice is as you've never heard it before, high-pitched and breathy like a whimper.

'What is it? What's happened?'

'She knows, I told her, I told her everything. It's . . . it's a

mess, it's a complete mess, I don't know what to do . . . She . . .
she knows. It's . . .'

You try to get clarity, to calm him; it's an utter reversal of
your roles so far, where until now he's always been the stabiliz-
ing one.

'What did she say? How did she react?'

'It's just such a mess. I can't . . . I can't speak right now, she
doesn't know I'm calling you. I have to go, I can hear her coming up the stairs.'

'It's OK. It will be OK.' You have no idea if you believe this
as Wren ends the call, but say it anyway.

Instinctively, you go to dial Romily's number before stopping yourself; just days ago she'd sent a distraught message to
you and your parents explaining the temperature control inside
her lab had malfunctioned and as a result her flies had died, losing her two years' worth of data. She'd once admitted to you
that as the older sister she felt your pain in the way a parent
would, that it wasn't the normal empathy you have for a friend
when they're sad or distressed, but that it went into her own
body as though via osmosis. To add to her weight right now
would be nothing but selfish – something you are already too
identified with being, having robbed a wife of her husband and
two children of their father. And so, too ashamed to call your
parents and unsure what else to do, you walk into Foyles and
pick up random books, flick through the pages but the words
don't mean anything, are just black outlines of shapes like
hieroglyphics. At some point you realize you're freezing in
your damp clothes and go home. Your tongue feels furry and
redundant.

It's not until later that evening you hear from him again. The
tone of his text is hurtfully formal but you suppose Cristyn is
now overseeing all of his messages, hovering over him as he
types, not allowing him to sign off with a *x*. *We're still going to*

Scotland tomorrow for the children. You can meet me at Heathrow one week from now but please don't contact me before then.

You don't know how you're going to get through the next seven days without speaking to him, other than the fact you have to. You take him at his word, trust he knows what he's doing, how best to handle the situation, so that it doesn't even occur to you to go against his request and try making contact. You have no doubt at this stage that he is doing anything other than what he said he'd do, which is to leave his family to be with you – the bravest and hardest step of which he's surely already taken by telling Cristyn. You assume, as he said, that they are going ahead with the holiday for the sake of Efa and Cai and that they will use the time to work through the logistics of their separation.

To your memory, you have never been called naive, but your faith in Wren at this point is so unwavering that it's hard when you think about it now, with the distance of more than a decade, to label it as anything other than naive. You believe in him with every fibre of your body, the way a child looks to a parent to tell them whether it's safe to cross a road or if they'll be hit by oncoming traffic.

The next six days and nights are amorphous. As much as you can, you fill them by rereading Wren's diary as you lie in bed dressed in his linen shirt, trying to inhale his scent and muffle your moans while you conjure him hard and fast until your hand aches. Thankfully your new housemates keep irregular sleeping and working hours which means you have little contact with them, aside from periodically crossing paths on your way to the kitchen or bathroom. The only other woman in the house – a petite stand-up comedian called Ishani with small pimples below her hairline – corners you by the fridge on one of the afternoons and offers you the use of her blender. She swiftly follows this by an invitation to be her required plus-one at a gig later that night.

'Thanks, but I'm not really into live comedy.'

'What, you're not into laughing?'

'No, I am, just . . . not massively right now.'

'No offence but you look like you could do with some.'

'Maybe another night.'

'Your loss,' she says, swinging her ponytail of purple braids over her shoulder as you scurry out of the kitchen holding a piece of unbuttered toast. What you'd like to say is, 'Listen, you've met me at the oddest time in my life and this isn't really my personality,' but that would just elicit questions you don't want to answer.

You get a text from Wren the evening before he's due to land back in London. All the message says is his arrival time and which terminal to meet him at. Again you notice the absence of a *x* and this time feel a stab of rage that he has done nothing to reassure you these last six days. But what could he have done? Perhaps he tried to sneak away and call you, but Cristyn is still monitoring him.

The following afternoon, you get on the Piccadilly Line and ride all the way along it, right to the end, watching as the carriage empties. One woman has matching Burberry suitcases, all in different sizes like Russian dolls. You don't understand how she's going to get them off the train; perhaps you'll be required to help. But a man in a trench coat with a hook-handle umbrella offers his assistance and you are left empty-handed.

As you stand by the steel barriers waiting for Wren, you suddenly regret your outfit. It's too youthful: a frayed denim skirt and strappy top with bare shoulders, sandals that show your girly painted toenails. You should have dressed more demurely. No, not demurely but severely. Something that would have conveyed the trauma of the last week and acknowledged the hardship for everyone involved, an outfit which reads, *I understand the grown-up seriousness of this situation.* But you don't think you have any outfits which say that.

You're not sure whether to smile at him when he enters the arrivals hall. Will it seem too frivolous? But not to smile at all would feel unthinkably cold. He needs you to comfort him, to look after him; it's your turn to be the strong one and you're ready to be it. But the moment you catch sight of him you feel your stomach becoming acid. He looks robotic, walking towards you as though you're a stranger he hasn't been programmed to recognize, as if you've been lasered from his system.

You open your arms tentatively and he drops his rucksack and grips you tightly, hugs you so forcefully that you believe you have imagined his detachment, that it will all be OK. If you knew this would be the last time you'd hold each other, would you cling on longer? Or break away sooner? When you part he looks at you, his eyes steeled against warmth.

'We have to end this.'

You assume you've misunderstood, notice his clenched fists and the way he's biting down on his bottom lip as he says it again, two more times.

'What are you talking about?' You're shaking your head now, fast and repeatedly.

'The pain. The pain I – we – have caused everyone is unimaginable.'

'But we knew that. That's what we knew it would be like.' You feel your entire body becoming gas as though loose particles of you are floating off.

'Not like this, this is . . . no.' He's gritting his teeth, almost snarling.

'But how? How is this different to how you thought it would be?' To you, the entire world has just fallen apart to the extent that you are confounded to see out of the corner of your eye a woman nibbling the corner of a giant Toblerone. How can life be going on as normal around you?

'I've been punched by my wife, OK? I've watched her throw

up in front of me, multiple times.' He's spitting the words out, bobbles of saliva landing around his mouth; you've never even seen him angry before, let alone seething.

'But I can't . . . I can't understand what that changes.' You know you ought to acknowledge Cristyn's suffering but are too shocked by what he's saying to think of anything other than you and him, the two of you as one unit just as he'd planned and promised.

'I've barely even seen my children this year.' You cannot believe he is only realizing this now; has he been deluded the entire time you've been together? You'd thought that your minds were fused but now you wonder who this man is standing in front of you saying aloud this obvious statement, and in a tone that makes it clear he blames you for this fact.

'I can't leave them. I can't leave my children.' He says this on a loop; whatever justifications you throw at him, whatever you remind him of – how happy the two of you will be together in time – he will keep coming back to this. His tone gets more venomous, his face scowling and full of accusation, until you can see that you are not only no longer his love, but his enemy – someone who has committed an atrocity which he and his precious family are now paying for.

You're crying, not lightly or reluctantly, but heavily and with conviction, don't care about the fact you're in a public place, only care about changing his mind as you frantically plead with him. But he is utterly unmoved.

When he picks up his rucksack, you are stunned to realize the conversation is over. He hoists it on to his back and just walks away, pausing momentarily as a girl in a Mickey Mouse T-shirt runs in front of him.

As you watch him go, you hear yourself calling out, 'Don't leave me. Please don't leave me. Please.' But he doesn't look back, only walks out under the glowing green and white light, exiting your life.

Bleating, you make it over to the rows of stuck-together chairs by the window, slumping forwards and clutching your side where the pain is stabbing. You know you need to pull yourself together – that this is not sane or acceptable behaviour for a grown woman inside an airport – but you are unravelling from the inside, don't know how to reel yourself back in again.

'Excuse me, can I do anything to help?' Feeling a hand on your shoulder, you look up to see the concerned face of a stranger, her features full and expressive. She wears a navy jumper without a logo, the sleeves rolled up to her elbows.

You shake your head, repeat the same line over and over as if she holds the answer. 'How could he leave me? How could he just leave me?'

The stranger's name is Leanne. You know this now because after a few more minutes your crying weakens and your breathing settles and you become aware that, unlike Wren, this woman has not left you, but is kneeling down next to you, softly rubbing your back. You tell her that the man you love – who had told you he'd walk through a burning building to save you, that he loved you with the same ferocity he loved his children and couldn't wait to grow old with you – has just effectively killed you.

If she judges you, she doesn't permit you to see it; all she does is listen and nod until eventually you stop crying.

'Sorry. I don't want you to miss your flight.' You're not thinking properly, have forgotten this is the arrivals hall.

She says for you to take your time, that her daughter has already come through the gates. You look to where she's pointing and see a teenage girl with a fishtail plait on the cusp of womanhood, spinning two young children on a luggage trolley holding a *Welcome Home* sign.

'Where's she come back from?' You're not sure if you're asking because you're genuinely interested or whether it's simply crucial in this moment that you prove you can go on function-ing without Wren, which means making polite conversation with compassionate strangers.

'Her gap year. She's been teaching at a school in Uganda.'

'You should go and be with her. Thank you for stopping, though. I mean, really, thank you.'

'I'm going to give you my number and then maybe you can text me at some point to let me know you're OK?'

Two hours later, as you sit on a National Express coach back to your parents' house, you text Leanne at her request, thanking her again. She replies, *You take care, it's hard to see it now but good things lie ahead. They always do. x* You don't believe this, not even as a con-cept, but find her faith comforting even if you can't share in it.

That evening, as you sit at the kitchen table in front of an untouched plate of teriyaki salmon and wild rice, you tell your parents a condensed version of the story. Although visibly shocked to learn of Wren's plan to leave his wife and children, they listen with a calmness and radical acceptance of the situ-ation that gives you a stability you have otherwise just lost.

'I think you've dodged a bullet here. I really do,' says your mother, scrunching her knuckles down on to the place mat, attempting to take control of the situation while clearly still trying to process it. 'You know, I did think something was up,' she says, cocking her head sharply. 'Nothing sappy like mother's instinct but you were very evasive when I asked about men. Not that I expected anything like this. I mean, this is . . .' She tails off, looking lost for a second, which is so unlike her that it makes you want to cry again.

'I had no idea,' says your father, a flake of pink flesh falling out of his mouth and landing on his beard. You wonder what this admission will be followed with but he stays silent, looking at you with an expression of curiosity, as though you have just become someone he might be able to respect.

'It does sound as though it was his children that made him change his mind, don't you think?' says your mother, sawing into her overcooked salmon before dropping her knife and fork on to her plate and crossing her arms. 'I mean, they're so young. They're still in their key developmental years. The damage would have been . . . No. He definitely did the right thing, staying. I mean, it took him long enough, and he's behaved appallingly. But even you can see that in the end he did the right thing, can't you, darling?'

This is precisely why you couldn't confide in her during the affair, because Wren's decision to leave his marital home would have gone against everything your mother stands for – the value of a stable nuclear family. Even your father, despite presenting as nonconformist, as far as you know has never been unfaithful. His lifestyle choices are in fact far more traditional than those he purports to advocate.

You run your fingers along the edge of your fork, embarrassed to be sitting opposite them, as though you embody a threat to the monogamy they represent.

'It's his wife I really feel sorry for,' says your father, staring up at the canvas painting above your mother's head. His tone is reflective, as if he has already carved out a distance between you and the event.

'Michael, I don't think now's the right time—'

'You see, Margot, you get to move on,' he says, turning to face you, his voice gentle but firm.

'But I don't want to move on.'

'Not right now, no. But you will.' He delivers this with such conviction that for a moment it almost convinces you.

'He's right, sweetheart.'

'At least have some yoghurt,' says your father, pronging your salmon fillet on to his own plate.

Later that night on your way to the bathroom, you hear your

mother on the phone, cannot hear what she is saying, only her hushed low voice, but infer minutes later from Romily's text that she has filled her in.

Marg, I'm devastated for you. Don't ever think you can't call. Flies are flies, you're my sister. Get some sleep and we'll speak tomorrow. Love you always x Rom

The following morning, when you wake to discover the situation has not been changed by the arrival of a new day, you howl on the bay windowsill of your childhood bedroom, wondering if you will have to endure this concentration of pain every day for the rest of your life and how your body will withstand it. You hear your father calling urgently for your mother, detect the panic in his voice on discovering she isn't in and that he'll have to deal with this bereft creature himself. Although never physically absent, he's always left anything emotional to his wife to deal with, but now here he is, entering your room and striding over to the window, hugging you to his chest with fierce determination – not so much seized by an impulse but an understanding of what's required of him – and you discover that he is surprisingly good at it, more than capable.

'Oh Gotty,' he says, using your childhood nickname as he strokes your hair, 'oh my darling Gotty.' You wait for him to undercut his sincerity with another remark but he just keeps holding you, soothing you.

'I don't know how to live without him.'

'Not yet. But you did before and so you will again.'

He's never been a protective father; perhaps it's his lack of protectiveness that meant you sought it in Wren but that also feels too simplistic. Your father understands the nuances and contradictions within people, that things are so rarely black and white. In the past you've found his abstrusity frustrating but now you value his ability to see the grey, how Wren is neither right nor wrong, good nor bad.

It is your father who will persuade you to send Wren's diary and camera back to him – the camera he'd used to take the first photos of Efa with when she was born – and to keep the cards and books he'd given you and ticket stubs of the shows you'd been to together, pointing out you might want to look at them later. And so, returning to London the following week, you box up Wren's camera and diary, wrapping them inside his linen shirt, and post them to him, without any form of a note in case Cristyn opens it instead. And besides, what would you even write? *You have shattered my heart.*

As you bag up the other items to store inside your parents' attic – if not out of mind, then at least out of sight – you have the sudden thought that Wren will not be able to keep any of the things you've given him. Now that Cristyn knows about you there will be no corner of his personal space left unturned. Of course Cristyn has every right to destroy every note and poem you ever gave him but in doing so she is wiping out evidence of the affair's existence and you are not ready to be erased.

On your way back to Norwich you meet up with Lillie inside Liverpool Street station and tell her everything, apologizing for your deceit, even though lying to her no longer feels like a significant part of the story. But to Lillie your betrayal of her friendship is the primary strand of the narrative and a point of hurt, shock and injured pride.

'So you basically lied to me for a year.'

'OK, but that really wasn't my intention.'

'But as a by-product that is what happened.'

'Lils, I'm sorry. I didn't want to get you involved.' You watch as a group of pigeons congregate around a discarded piece of baguette on the floor.

'But why? I'm your best friend. Why didn't you involve me?'

'Because I knew you'd tell me to stop seeing him and I couldn't do that, I'd tried already.'

'Yeah, well I probably would have done. But I also would have been there for you if you'd even given me a chance.'

You don't know what to say, know Lillie has a right to feel aggrieved but are too tired and hurt to comfort her in your wounded state. And so the two of you sit on a metal bench inside the concourse with distance between you, each too coiled to put your arms around the other one, until one of you moves in closer, or both of you do; you can't remember now.

Inside your parents' house, you transfer Wren's things into your grandfather's old leather suitcase. It's tan-coloured with stitching around the sides and a rusty metal clasp. As you click it shut, you wonder how many years it will be until you open it again. Will it even next be opened by you or by someone else, one of your children perhaps? You like the idea that you now officially have history. Perhaps this is what it costs – this level of hurt – to have a life that future generations will look back on and consider fully lived.

On the upstairs landing your father is pulling down the steps to the attic from the door in the ceiling, coughing from the dust. As you hand the case to him and watch him climb, his generosity and decency towards people strike you as limitless. Where did he learn this? Can you learn it too?

Your mother is also generous and decent, but your suffering pulls on her as if it's her own, maybe because the two of you were once joined by a literal cord.

'I'm angry, you know,' she says, turning on the light inside the sitting room to find you hugging your knees in the dark.

'I am trying, I'm trying to stop crying, I don't know why it's not working.'

'I'm not angry at you, I'm angry at him. He was older and married and he took advantage of the situation—'

'No, don't do that, don't try and turn me into a victim. I'm not one.'

She sighs and you can see that she agrees, that as much as she would like to absolve you, you are a twenty-two-year-old consenting adult who – wrongly or rightly – has experienced something beyond your years and been badly stung.

'I just don't want you to become one. Promise me you won't do anything stupid like wait for him to change his mind.' The phone rings and she shouts for your father to answer it who yells back that he's in the bath.

But your mother needn't worry; even in your grief you never contemplate Wren coming back to you. It's so definitively over after that day at Heathrow because he's dismantled the only thing that would have been strong enough to hold the two of you together: the belief that your relationship could survive everything to come, so long as you had each other. In leaving you so decisively and abruptly he does what each of you had tried and failed to do earlier – implodes your love.

There's an alternative scenario you sometimes consider, in which he leaves his family that day and comes to live with you but then weeks or months later leaves you to go back to be with them – how much more intolerable that would have been. There's another scenario in which he stays with you, determined to make it work, to stick with his decision, even though he misses his children terribly but is too appalled by the trauma he's already caused them to admit he's made the wrong choice and beg forgiveness from Cristyn, who may or may not be willing to give him another chance. And then of course there's the scenario in which he meets you at Heathrow, as planned, to start a new life together and, after the initial drama and difficulties which overshadow the first few years, you do in fact share the most phenomenal love for the rest of your lives. This scenario you try not to think about; the potential happiness of it is so sharp that it cuts you like glass until at some point the feeling becomes comparable to that of sandpaper, and then finally just sand.

Years from now, you'll move in with Noah and discover the local corner shop sells bags of almonds on the swinging rack beside the till, surprised you've never realized how much they look like hard wooden tears. You'll think of Wren, as you often still do – not with pain but something akin to awareness – with the knowledge that he can't not be part of you, like touching your wrist and registering you're made of bone.

6. Oliver

In the months that follow, your body feels tender as though it's a bruise that emits pain when pressed but is no longer dark purple and sore to the faintest touch. You have no frame of reference to rate the speed or quality of your recovery, whether you are healing at an adequate rate. Your behaviour at points feels tentative – you are wary of getting hurt again – and at other points reckless, as if you're equally afraid of not capitalizing on your newly returned freedom.

Depending on your mood, the weight of experience you now carry can make you feel chosen and unique, as though powered by an invisible source of light, and at other times like a home-wrecker and a whore. You feel the latter most acutely in the presence of children, which you discover when you sign up to work as a promotional assistant at a festival in East Sussex at the end of August. You are surrounded by young families, by wives who address their husbands as 'Daddy' while you stand at a trestle table and spoon samples of fruit puree into small plastic pots, smiling as you shrivel inside.

You are expected to wear a pale yellow T-shirt (a colour your mother has advised you never to wear on account of your complexion) and to be knowledgeable and passionate about the brand you are representing. You would prefer your acting skills were being put to use on a stage, but are accepting at this early phase of your career that you will have to do menial jobs to earn an income, that this is a requisite first rung on a ladder which you assume you will continue to climb in linear fashion so that by the time you reach your late twenties, you envisage you will be successfully making a living doing the thing you love. And so, you memorize the product's unique selling points and say emphatically, when asked, 'Yes, that's right. Made of one hundred per cent pure fruit, great for the little ones.' You pretend you are in an advert.

Lillie's mother and stepfather throw a party at their farmhouse in Devon to mark the end of the summer which the two of you travel down from London for. You get drunk on flat cider and at one point find yourself on the lap of one of Lillie's schoolfriends inside the bathroom. He wears a white cricket jumper and salmon shorts which you unzip and intermittently stroke his penis while the two of you personify the floral porcelain jars around the basin. He doesn't come that you remember; it's more playful than sexual, and most importantly feels void of any threat – sharing this experience with a friend of a friend rather than a stranger. Afterwards you rejoin the others outside and a group of you skinny-dip in the river that backs on to the garden; you duck your head under the water, its cold darkness like a baptism as you come up to the surface, spluttering.

'I dreamt I gave birth last night,' you say to Lillie the next morning as you walk through a series of fields belonging to a neighbouring farm.

'Watch out for that ram,' she says, pointing to a fawn-coloured sheep, its placid face framed with curled horns. 'He'll try and hump anything that moves.'

'Noted. It was weirdly empowering. Just me alone inside this cow barn pushing it out.'

'Gross.'

'You can't gross childbirth. That's like grossing nature.'

'Grossness and nature aren't mutually exclusive,' she says, plucking a buttercup from the grass and peeling off its petals.

'I just felt completely bereft when I woke up and realized it wasn't real.'

'I think that might just be your hangover.'

'You've never had that before? Not specifically the cow-barn bit but the giving-birth dream.'

'I've dreamt I'm pregnant and it's been the total opposite for me when I woke up. Sheer relief.'

You kneel down to pick up a handful of grass and sprinkle it back over the ground.

'I don't actually want a child right now. I mean, that would be insane. I just . . . fell so in love with it, in like a physical way. I still feel it now, like I'm missing something.'

'God, I hope I start to get some maternal instincts at some point. Currently I'm dead in that zone.'

'I think that's normal. I feel weird and old for knowing I want one already.'

'Was it Wren's?'

'If it was, he wasn't there.'

Lillie shudders. 'This is way too grown up. We need to do something young like cartwheel.'

'OK, but I might throw up a bit.'

'It's fine, the sheep will eat it.'

'Ew.'

'Natural and gross, see.'

'Touché.'

You raise your leg off the ground and outstretch your arms. As your hands press into the grass, you look up at the grey blotch of sky between your legs and try to feel young and fey but it's more an aspiration towards the feeling rather than the actual feeling.

Back in London, you browse the rails of vintage jackets and retro shirts inside the charity shop around the corner from Lillie's flat in Holloway, trying to cultivate a look of effortless androgyny. You go on nights out in Hoxton and Shoreditch where everyone smokes and wears black skinny jeans, and so you buy some too even though they don't flatter your figure and restrict the range of motion around your calves.

Your overriding feeling is one of intimidation and awe as you immerse yourself in the city, always wondering if this is the London of your twenties you're meant to be living, checking you're experiencing it all so you can have no regrets later. But even in your moments of wildness you still feel cautious, as if other people are freer than you. You're not sure if this is because of what happened with Wren which has made you more discerning or just because of who you are as a person, how difficult you find it to be wholly uninhibited.

One lilac evening at the start of October, you cry on to the floorboards of your bedroom, pressing your knuckles into the slots between the wood as you rock back and forth on your knees. Afterwards, you wash your face, exchange panda eyes for smoky ones, and catch the two buses to the bar in Highgate where Lillie works and has instructed you, under no mitigating circumstances, to join her. Lillie will not allow you to wallow in your grief – partly because you mean too much to her and partly because she needs you to be fun and twenty-two with.

She slips you a double rum and Coke on the house before going to serve another customer while you watch a man in a sailor shirt with a handlebar moustache run his hands through his shoulder-length hair. Later that night you find him on the dance floor and slide your shoulders up against his for the duration of Rihanna's 'We Found Love' before catching the two buses home again where you allow yourself another cry, proud for accomplishing this small goal.

Autumn arrives and that November you go with Lillie to a bonfire party on Walthamstow Marshes, wake fully clothed on a canal boat the next morning to find a man sleeping next to you on the thin single mattress below the brass porthole window.

He stirs as you stretch and, on discovering you there, begins to kiss you which you reciprocate because even though you're not particularly attracted to him, sometimes just the feel of another body assuages loneliness. But then a small grey cat climbs on to the bed and you lose all interest in the man who, after a few further attempts to start kissing again, gives up and rolls over to face the wall, leaving you to delight in the softness of the cat's fur and its steady vibrating engine. You feel warm and calm inside this stranger's bed, bobbing on the water, with the presence of the small grey cat who has removed any expectation or pressure for you to sexually offer yourself to this sleeping man beside you. You've slept with no one since Wren and won't do until you meet Oliver six months from now. You're not sure what you're waiting for exactly but think maybe you're holding out for love again or at least the feeling that comes before it, the one that says, *This has the potential to turn into love.* You're also disturbed by the idea of Wren dominating your thoughts while it happens, and so decide it's essential you choose someone kind who'll be sensitive and understanding, should you need to stop and possibly even explain your history, and Oliver will be exactly this person, as well as so much more to you.

It's in a bar in Spitalfields on the night of your twenty-third birthday that he approaches the table where you're sitting with Lillie and Ishani — as well as Amber, Holly and Rosie who are visiting for the occasion — and is introduced by Ishani as '*another comedian*'.

Ishani has welcomed your character change since Wren's departure — accepting your generic explanation, 'I was involved with this guy but it's over now,' without prying — and subsequently the two of you have become friends as well as housemates. You now regularly spend at least one night a week in the backroom of a pub watching her try out new material at an open-mic night, laughing loudly in support, even when you don't always find the material particularly funny, but at least she isn't bitter like so many comedians. Ishani finds a way of making her lack of cynicism – her resilient belief in finding 'true love' – the butt of the joke, rather than succumbing to actual cynicism in order to get a laugh.

Oliver's limbs are what you notice first, not just how tall and gangly they make him but the way his arms and legs appear to move with their own conviction. He's wearing a royal-blue cardigan and thick-rimmed glasses as if these statement pieces might detract from his loose-jointedness, but which conversely draw more attention to it. When he smiles he looks surprised, as though he's been caught off-guard by his own reflexes.

'You're welcome to join us, Oliver, but it's Margot's birthday,' says Ishani, pointing at you. 'So I warn you now, we're intending to get very drunk.'

Oliver laughs awkwardly and replies, 'Happy birthday. I certainly don't want to get in the way of that happening.'

'Well then, why don't you start by getting us all a drink,' says Ishani, drumming her hands on the table.

'I'll do that. Shall I?' He directs the question at you, looking unsure whether to stay.

'We could definitely use your height getting served at the bar.'

He smiles, bolstered by your response. 'I'm told functionality is my biggest social asset. What would you like?'

When he returns carrying a bottle of Prosecco and a handful of glasses, he takes a seat at the opposite end of the table so it isn't until the next bar that you get to properly speak to him. In contrast to the boldness of his physical appearance, his speech is soft and precise. A lot of people, yourself included, use filler words like 'ah' and 'um' but he doesn't. He takes time to select each word, as if he has a duty both to language and himself to most accurately convey his meaning. These small beats of silence create tension each time he opens his mouth.

'Sorry about gate-crashing your birthday. I've ruined your symmetrical numbers.'

Smiling, you say, 'We were meant to be seven anyway. My sister had to stay in Oxford at the last minute to work on her thesis.'

As he pauses, you study the small wrinkles around his eyes, trying to work out his age, concluding he is decidedly older than you but younger than Wren.

'Do you think lazy and unproductive people exist in Oxford and we just don't hear about them?' he asks. 'Or do they syphon them all off into Reading and Swindon?'

'I reckon the syphoning option,' you say with a laugh.

He smiles and then adds, 'I probably should have checked where you studied before I asked that.'

'You're safe. I went to drama school in Kent.'

'How was that?'

'Mixed. I mean, I haven't worked since I graduated nine months ago. But it was good training for life, I guess.'

'That's not a bad takeaway. I could have done with more of that myself.'

'Where did you study?'

'I did Classics at Reading. Hence why I'm still gigging in the backroom of pubs.' You let out another laugh and you expect him to follow this with another joke but he looks reflective and says, 'I thought I wanted to be an actor but I dried doing *Hamlet* at college and developed awful stage fright. Someone's father in the audience ended up shouting out the line to me. It was mortifying.'

'But now you do stand-up. Isn't that worse?'

'No, because if I forget a bit I can just improvise. Thankfully, my material's less well known than Shakespeare's.'

You laugh again and feel your core firing up; it's the first flicker of outright connection you've felt since Wren.

You add Oliver on Facebook the following day. He accepts your friend request and, when he doesn't message within the following twenty-four hours, you message him. In his reply he references having got on several wrong buses home that night, giving him the sensation of being trapped inside an Escher drawing, but concludes, *It was worth it for the very nice evening.* You have to google Escher before replying, unperturbed by the fact Oliver possesses knowledge you don't. In fact, you like this about him, for the same reason you prefer to ask questions rather than answer them, finding it more exciting to be told new information than to tell someone information you already know.

The two of you exchange Facebook messages for several days before arranging to meet at a speakeasy in Holborn. As with Wren at the start, you are aware that you are the one primarily doing the pursuing, moving the conversation forwards, but feel protected this way, as though you are overseeing the operation from above while simultaneously partaking in it at ground level.

Arriving fifteen minutes late, Oliver bounds over to the table where you're sitting beside a tassel lampshade against a backdrop of chintz wallpaper. A row of empty Verve Clicquot bottles line the mantelpiece above your head.

'I'm very sorry about this, I got lost. Again.'

'That's OK, it's given me a chance to acclimatize to the wartime vibe.' You gesture to the dusty Union Jack on the wall.

He looks awkward as he says, 'I hoped you'd be into borrowed nostalgia and alternative drinking vessels, but we can go somewhere else if it's a bit much?'

'Oh no, I'm a sucker for this stuff.'

'Phew.'

Still apologetic, he insists on buying the first two rounds of drinks – gin cocktails that arrive in china teacups with dried orange peel on the saucer, followed by a sweet rum concoction served in tin mugs.

'It's odd, though, isn't it?' you say, watching Oliver fiddle with the rim of his collar. 'We've glamorized drinking out of jam jars and this whole period of history that was presumably pretty horrendous to live through.'

'True.'

'Like, I wonder what bad things from this era our ancestors will end up thinking are cool and retro.'

'A recession-themed bar? IKEA tumblers served with selfie sticks?'

You watch him try not to smile as you laugh and say, 'Was that lifted from your stand-up set?'

'No, but it might make it into a future one.'

Listening to him speak, it's not so much a physical urge you feel but an attraction to his thoughts and observations. This admiration you have in place of desire doesn't worry or concern you. On the contrary, when you kiss for the first time outside Chancery Lane station, it feels all the more unique that it's gentle, light and measured. Twice on the lips: one, two, no tongues. And much like his distilled sentences which leave you wanting more, so do these kisses.

The following evening you go to watch Ishani perform at a gig, knowing full well that Oliver will be there. He's listed to open the show with the first five-minute slot, and when he catches sight of you by the bar, you can tell he's nervous at having to perform in front of you from the way he shifts his weight from one foot to the next, as though unsure where to settle. Watching him mount the small platform stage, you're nervous too because what if he suddenly isn't funny and you don't feel attracted to him any more? Once love is there as a foundation you'll be able to watch him 'bomb' (a rare occurrence) and only love him more, but at this early stage of knowing him his skill is in direct proportion to your attraction to him. But you needn't have worried; his dry understated wit wins over the room within seconds, and you find you can relax and just enjoy listening to his set and the orchestrated laughter he conducts around him.

'That was very funny,' you tell him in the break between sets.

'That's kind of you to say. And kind of you to come.'

'To be fair, I'm here to see Ishani. You just happened to be the opening act.'

He laughs and says, 'I find it's a solid spot for inflicting myself on unwitting audience members.'

You smile at him as you reply, 'OK, I lied. I was very much witting.'

He goes slightly red and looks uncomfortable but is clearly pleased by your overt flirtation.

It's not until the seventh date that you sleep together. You feel no pressure from him and are enjoying the slow pace of things, the process of falling for him further with every apposite message he sends and each evening you spend in his company.

The night it happens you are both wearing green, a coincidental but satisfying detail: Oliver's sage shirt, your jade dress, his huge shadow on the wall cast by the lamp on your bedside table. Curiously, the apprehension you've felt leading up to this moment – in case the two of you have spent the last month dating only to discover you're sexually incompatible, or that the memory of Wren will pervade with force, making you unable to go through with it – leaves you now. You feel steady and sure and entirely present as you kiss and unbutton each other with a tenderness and respect which will always be present in the sex that you have, so that while it is never not good, there will often be a leftover urge in you when it is finished, an irrational need to have been taken and briefly owned – but not tonight. Tonight you only want sex to be kind and mutual and Oliver epitomizes these qualities.

But while he is kind, he is also frightened of commitment and reluctant to get into a relationship. Rather than telling you this outright, in the ensuing months he'll go hot and cold towards you, pushing you away before pulling you in again until finally, after half a year of knowing him, you will confront him while walking over Waterloo Bridge shortly before your ushering shift is due to start, and tell him what he has been avoiding telling you himself.

'Here's what I think's happening. I think you enjoy my company and are attracted to me but that you want to indefinitely just continue dating. And, well, that's not an option for me cause my feelings have moved beyond that. I can't hold them back now even if I wanted to and anyway I don't want to. So, yeah, that's what I think. What do you think?'

'I think you're right,' he says, his forehead creased with concern. 'All of what you said.'

You wait to see if he'll add anything before concluding, 'Well, then I guess that's it, in terms of us seeing each other.'

'I really don't want it to be,' he says, inhaling deeply and standing upright at his full height as he gazes across the river, his pale grey eyes flickering when he looks back down at you. 'But I understand why it has to be.'

You want to say, *But it doesn't have to be. You can choose for it not to be,* but the statement feels too close to pleading, and you refuse to ever plead again to make someone stay.

Wrapping your arms around his protruding ribcage, you blink rapidly as you step back to look up at him, resolving not to cry; his lasting image of you as a predominantly happy person feels important and worth preserving. 'Bye, then.'

'Goodbye.'

As you walk along Waterloo Road and turn on to The Cut, you try to work out how you've once again fallen for someone who's ultimately unattainable, only this time without even realizing; you want to glean meaning from your loss of Oliver, to give purpose to your pain, but in truth it just feels pointless.

Entering the chandelier-lit foyer of the Old Vic, you make your way downstairs to the pit-bar toilets. As you pass your duty manager on the spiral carpeted staircase, you force a smile, catching sight of its falsity in the gilded mirror, your face a tightly pulled band vibrating with resistance. Inside a rose-pink cubicle, you change into your uniform and walk up two flights of stairs to the dress circle where your team briefing is already underway.

On autopilot, you stand by the door of the auditorium checking people's tickets and directing them to their seats. You point with a straight arm in the style of an air stewardess as you repeat the reminder, 'It's a ninety-minute running-time with no interval.' The wealth and married status of the diamond-ringed women who waft through the door, reeking of floral perfume and white wine from plastic cups with lipstick-smeared rims, makes you feel lowly, as though the life you want – one of success and of being held on to rather than let go of – is out of your grasp.

Because, unlike you, Oliver is someone who tends to let life happen to him rather than make decisions, it is all the more surprising that when you finish your shift later that night and exit the theatre, you find him waiting by the door.

'Oliver.'

'Hello.'

'What . . . what are you doing here?'

'I ran after you, a few minutes after you left, but never caught up. You're very adept at weaving through crowds. I assumed you'd have started your shift by the time I got here so I've been waiting outside.'

'But that was three hours ago.'

'I did get a decaffeinated tea at one point.'

'OK . . .'

'Because, well, watching you walk away made me realize how much I want you to stay. In my life. And so if that means being your boyfriend then I'd like to be it, please. If that's still on offer.'

It's almost disappointing that you can't experience what this moment would feel like without the canon of Richard Curtis films lighting up inside your head. Would this line land with the same charm if you weren't comparing him in this moment to a taller, more ungainly, Hugh Grant? Either way, in a film this would be the end scene, when in actual fact – although you share a tingled kiss, believing this to be the beginning of your future happiness – it will go on being a battle at every stage over the next three and a half years you're together to get him to commit: to introduce you to his friends and parents, to call you his girlfriend in public, to use the pronoun 'we' when discussing plans for the weekend, let alone the future like one day moving in together.

But the future is relatively easy to push to the background when Oliver's companionship offers so much in the present foreground. You delight in his lightness – his wit and bumbling lack of practicality often leave your chest heaving and short of breath, not through crying as with Wren, but through laughter.

Although talented at stand-up, it's films and books he really wants to write, and as far as you can see, he's brilliant and you can't understand what he's waiting for. You'll learn over the years through endlessly interrogating him that his caution derives not only from fear and self-doubt, but that he (much like you in this respect, although your fear of stasis won't allow for indecision) is in love with possibility. And that, for him, the pleasure of imagining his ideas as a screenplay or novel in their perfect form is more appealing than the act of having to commit these ideas to the page and invariably lose part of them in the process.

You love watching films and TV shows with him, how he always seems to be able to condense a story into one piercingly simple and pertinent line. He is never clever for the sake of being clever; his interest is in refining the truth to as few words as possible, something you feel is a lost art, despite living in an age of Twitter.

And so, you are mostly able to suppress your doubts when they surface, but it concerns you when a year and a half into the relationship you arrive late one afternoon at his house-share in Tufnell Park and follow his elongated strides up the stairs to his room.

'I've got something to show you,' he says, standing with his back to the wardrobe, his arms pulled behind him as he fiddles with the knobs on the double doors.

As he turns and opens it, he steps back and you are confused; there is nothing inside except for his clothes and a top shelf half full of old journals.

'It's for you. The other half of the shelf, for your essentials. I cleared it this morning so you won't have to keep bringing all your things every time you come over.'

He looks so pleased and relieved to have reached this milestone at the age of thirty-four that you feel it would be cruel to point out that most of your friends, if they are not already living with their boyfriends, have half their possessions scattered inside each other's rooms.

'Thank you. That's really sweet,' and you realize with a pang that Oliver may only ever be willing to offer you the corner of a shelf.

There is also the issue of children; he is openly unsure about wanting them, giving you further cause for concern. But his ambiguity and the fact that you are in no immediate rush to become a parent keeps you holding on – especially when the idea of not being together feels largely inconceivable, given your perpetual interest in what the other one has to say, how repeatedly you understand each other when those around you miss your meaning, how invested in each other's careers and intertwined your lives are.

Together you go to New York the spring you turn twenty-five. You take the glass elevator to the top of the Rockefeller where, on the observation deck, your hair blows upright in the wind so that in photographs it looks like a vertical crown above your head, and you and Oliver will make the comparison to Marge Simpson at the exact same moment. He buys a salt-beef bagel from a deli on the Lower East Side and counts fifteen slices of beef with comic revulsion before offering it to a homeless woman holding a sign saying *Hungry*. 'No meat,' she says, shaking her head. He hands her an apple from his rucksack instead.

The two of you spend most weekdays stationed at opposite ends of Oliver's bedroom while he writes copy for various household appliances and you email the theatre directors of recent productions you've seen, trying to craft flattering sentences about their work without sounding desperate or obsequious, in an attempt to foster your own contacts to make up for your agent's lack of them. Despite the frequency with which you do this – determined to be productive and not stagnate – you can't help feeling it is a thankless task when most of your emails go unanswered and, on the rare occasions they convert into an audition, you only ever receive the generic feedback via your agent, 'Unfortunately it went another way this time but they really liked you. Next time!' You'll masochistically end up googling the cast list to find out who got the role and will invariably see it's someone with an impressive stream of credits and more of a profile than you which is, of course, a vicious cycle.

'How am I meant to build up my CV if no one's willing to take a punt on me?' you exclaim to Oliver one overcast morning in February as you close the lid of your laptop and throw yourself on to his bed where you punch a pillow in jest and then do it again in genuine frustration.

'Hang on three seconds,' he says, midway through typing, his eyes flitting between the screen of his monitor and the vacuum-cleaner manual open on the desk. 'Right. Sorry. You were saying?' he says, swivelling in his chair to face you.

'I just hate how exclusive it is, the industry. Why is no one letting me in?'

'I know it's difficult and annoying and you probably don't want to hear this, but, well, these directors don't owe you anything. Nobody does.'

'Well, you say that but . . .' But as much as you would love to dispute his point, you are forced to accept its validity. 'All right, fine. Then I hate how hard it is.'

'It is hard but you're good and you're persistent. Those are two things in your favour.'

'There's no guarantee, though, is there. I mean, not like with other jobs which you train for and then actually get to work in.'

'True. You are choosing to do this, though.'

'I didn't choose to *want* to do it, though.'

'That's a solid loophole.' He pauses before adding, 'Can you think of a synonym for dust?'

It's Oliver who encourages you to begin writing your own material which initially you try out in the form of stand-up comedy, signing up to a one-day taster course in Camden, following which you get drunk and force yourself to book half a dozen gigs. Although you get a positive response, shown by clustered laughs from the small crowd, you feel restricted by having to elicit laughter as the primary response to your writing rather than a multitude of reactions, of which laughter might be one. It's at this point you switch to writing your own one-woman show, *I Hate You at Least Nine Times a Day*, which follows the lives of three characters over twenty-four hours as they intersect across the city – discovering you get as much pleasure from writing it as you do performing it.

You showcase sections of it at various scratch nights before hiring an upstairs theatre in Islington to deliver it in its entirety. Stepping out on to the stage and into the hot white of the lights, the probability of vomiting seems as high as delivering your first lines. But as your eyes acclimatize, the sight of Oliver's long legs crossed in the aisle at the end of the third row stabilizes your nerves, and you start to speak, stunned when fifty minutes later – sweating, exhausted and creatively fulfilled for the first time since you graduated – you realize you're approaching the climactic finish.

'Mate, that was way better than I thought it would be,' says Ishani with customary bluntness as she hugs you in the foyer afterwards. 'When you said you were doing a one-woman the-atre show I was like, ew, cringe, but that was actually good.'

'Exactly what she said,' says Lillie, laughing and joining the hug.

Despite the show's acerbic title, it's described as a 'comically poignant ode to strangers' by an enthusiastic reviewer in the *Scots-man* when you take it up to the Edinburgh Fringe that summer. Thanks to this favourable review and a string of others that fol-low, the show garners the attention of several producers who want to talk about the possibility of adapting it for television, and consequently you're able to upgrade agents – to a formidable woman in her fifties with an established list of comedy acting and writing clients. She speaks with a disarming combination of charm and curtness that makes you feel on edge during your brief and nerve-wracking phone calls in which you are keen to prove yourself to her. You are still working as an usher to support yourself, but finally it feels as though you are on your way, and – although impatient to get to where you want to be – you take from Oliver that you are still young and have time; he never seems to be in a rush like you are, despite being almost a decade older.

The two of you break up and get back together multiple times, to the extent you lose track of the various dates and locations where these fraught conversations happen; that is until the final time. This day you remember clearly because, unlike the other instances which had always involved an element of fight and therefore the belief you might reconcile, there's a resignation to your conversation, as you walk the quiet Sunday streets of Clerkenwell, that reeks of finality. In voicing aloud your doubts and concerns about the very essence of each other's characters, you maul any belief you have left that the two of you are ultimately suited enough to stay together. While you reason you could easily spend another couple of years in the relationship feeling equally fulfilled and frustrated, if you can already see that you and Oliver lack compatible levels of drive and desire – the kind required to sustain a lifelong partnership – then surely it is only cowardice that would make you delay its inevitable ending?

As you pause outside a boutique shopfront, trying to process the realization that you are breaking up for good this time, you note the window display with tangy laughter: a trio of headless mannequins in ivory bridal gowns, their embroidered bodices glinting through the glass.

'At least we've saved ourselves the cost of a wedding,' he says with a comedic grimace, his long arms rocking backwards; his determination for lightness even in sadness makes you suddenly panic about letting him go.

'But wait, what if we're wrong, though, and we don't end up happier with other people?'

Two women with heavy fake tan approach the bridal shop. As you step aside to let them enter, their apple-scented perfume lingers in the air. Oliver bites the inside of his mouth before replying.

'I don't think fear should be a reason to stay together, should it? Something tells me that's not the right way to live.' And this line hurts acutely because of its laconic truthfulness – qualities of Oliver's that had made you fall in love with him in the first place.

Together you walk to King's Cross where you hug outside the entrance to the Tube until you can no longer justify holding on to each other any longer. Eleven minutes later, as you surface at Finsbury Park and walk up the station rampway, you message Romily.

Are you in? Can I come round?

I'm on a comedown and housemates are on a rollover . . . Tomorrow night?

It's over with Oliver, as in actually over

Fuck. Are you OK?

You reject her call and type back.

Can I come anyway? I'm five mins away

Putting the kettle on as we speak! We can hang in the kitchen/my bedroom xxxxx

Approaching the stoop of Romily's house-share, you see her housemates inside the front room, dancing in an assortment of colourful spandex and sequinned jackets. Cans of beer clutter the table alongside sprawling plants in mosaic pots. Noticing you through the window, they break out into a cheer. You summon your best acting skills and wave vigorously.

'Oh Marg,' says Romily, opening the door to you and hugging you on the step. 'What happened?'

You follow her through the hallway to the kitchen, holding your hand against your neck to stabilize yourself as though you are in danger of breaking.

'Nothing happened. We were just walking along together and then we were suddenly walking along not together. I just . . . It honestly feels like I've just lost my best friend.'

Your voice cracks and Romily slides in her socks across the linoleum floor and hugs you again. 'It's so hard, I know, but this is the shit bit. It's only up from here.'

'Only if it was the right decision.'

'But you think it is, right?'

You nod. 'I actually wish I had more doubt so I could still be with him. I think that means it must be.'

'When did you get so wise?'

'Somewhere around the time you became a doctor?'

She rolls her eyes and flicks the kettle switch. 'What a waste of money that was. I barely even need an undergraduate degree for this job.'

'It's still science.'

'Pharma marketing, but thanks. Also, not to continue to make your break-up about me, but it's good timing with my London move. We can go out and have tons of fun together.'

'We would have done that anyway.'

'It's not the same, though. We've never been single at the same time in the same city.'

'That's cause you've basically never been single.' You can't help hearing a resentment in your voice, fuelled by an inkling that Romily will once again soon find herself in another long-term relationship. Whether or not this is her intention, it is a pattern nonetheless.

'True. But I intend to make up for lost time.'

'Have you spoken to him?' you ask tentatively.

'Only about the deposit. There's not really anything to say.'

'I can't imagine not having anything to say to Oliver.'

'You say that now but give it a few months and I bet you'll feel differently.'

'I won't,' you say resolutely. 'We've already agreed we're going to stay friends.'

'Sure,' says Romily, with a note of scepticism.

'I mean it.'

'OK, then.' But she says it with an irritating smile that is equivalent to having the last word.

The next time you see Oliver will be three months on from that afternoon, at a Christmas party you and Ishani are hosting. You will chat on the sofa into the early hours of the morning when everyone else has either left or gone to bed, and as you hug goodbye on the doorstep, it will be a physical wrench to watch him go.

'Why are you bothering, Marg? With the friends thing,' asks Romily later that morning when she finds you, back turned, shoulders convulsing, as you transfer empty bottles from the kitchen counter into a bin liner, peeling your feet off the sticky floor. 'I mean, why are you putting yourself through this?'

The acrid scent of spilt beer pervades the room; through the window a sparrow is eating crisp remnants off the garden table. Everything feels too much and, at the same time, not enough.

'Because this is the hard part, it won't always be this way, will it.' You don't remember whether you add a rising inflection to the end of your sentence, if you are asking her for confirmation or telling both yourself and her that it won't. You know it is in Romily's nature to want to protect you but feel she is concurrently defending her own position in relation to Sami.

As far as you're concerned, there is everything to be gained by keeping Oliver in your life, but it is a slow, intricate process which both you and he handle with care, as though joint guardians of a valuable item that requires sensitive exchanges back and forth. It's with tact and consideration that you invite each other to events, giving the other one the option to decline but also ensuring their presence is made to feel welcome. It takes months but the two of you successfully persist, so that almost a year on from the break-up you are able to conclude that your perseverance to carve out a friendship with Oliver has been painful but unequivocally worth it.

Five years later, on his fortieth birthday, he invites you and Noah to a pub in Marylebone to celebrate with him and your mutual friends. As you stand chatting to Oliver next to a framed Smiths vinyl, you observe Noah in his dark grey flannel shirt navigating his way back from the bar, a tripod of drinks in his broad palms. He stops to let an elderly couple cross in front of him, says something to them and they laugh; Noah's courtesy and ease with strangers always makes you unduly proud, given you're in no way responsible for it. As you take your drink from his hold, he hands Oliver a glass of white wine.

'Thank you. Margot must have told you I don't drink beer.'

'I didn't, actually.'

'OK, stalker-confession. I found an old stand-up routine of yours on YouTube. You do that bit about nine Stellas and a Sauvignon on your friend's stag? It's really funny.'

'That friend's since divorced and remarried and I still haven't written twenty minutes of new material.'

The three of you share a laugh; its collective noise feels full and delicate like a bed of camomile.

'Cheers,' says Oliver, holding up his glass at an angle, liquid spilling over the side. 'Nice to finally meet you.'

'Likewise,' says Noah, raising his pint, his rolled-up sleeves showing his perennially tanned arms. 'And happy birthday.'

As you turn to each of them and clink their glasses, you consider it significant that you have got here to this point, standing

144

beside these two men — one who you are in love with and the other who you still have love for.

'It's really great what you guys have,' says Noah as the two of you exit on to the street later that night and stand under the amber glow of the pub's Victorian wall lanterns.

'It is, isn't it.'

'I hope we'd stay friends if we weren't together.'

'I'm not sure I'd want to.' Your Uber pulls into the kerb and Noah holds open the door for you. 'I mean, I think it's different what I have with you, in a good way.'

The car smells sweet and has a purple strip of light above the floor. The driver offers you water, tissues and mints which you decline with thanks while Noah gets in beside you and kisses your knuckles. As Carly Simon comes on the radio, you feel almost unbearably loved.

7. Malik

As someone you meet only three times in your life, Malik's influence is owing to what he represents. You first encounter him on the one-day stand-up comedy course you sign up to during the time you and Oliver are still together. The tutor asks you all to form a circle on arrival and each briefly introduce yourselves with a line about why you're here. Most of the group are frustrated actors or writers, on the hunt for another creative outlet, but Malik's a policy and public affairs advisor – keen to experiment with injecting humour into his lobbying to make him more persuasive – which, to your mind, immediately gives him the most interesting motive for being on the course.

At lunchtime, a subset of you walk down Oval Road to Camden Lock. Passing a piercing shop, you momentarily think of Wren, and consider the vastness of your life since he left it, wondering what it might currently look like with him still in it. You will continue to speculate on this at random points over the years as if this hypothetical imagined life that didn't happen with him is running in parallel to your actual one, with your overwhelming feeling being that of relief at the life you got, by his choosing.

Inside the food market, Malik pauses by a stand serving crispy sweet and sour chicken which is thick and gelatinous and luminous orange.

'How about it?' he says, addressing you directly. 'Shall we risk some iridescent poultry?' You like the way he's almost made the decision for you; the fact you're still with Oliver at this point means you find any kind of male assertiveness novel.

You nod and say, 'Let's do it,' and so you fill up two Tupperware boxes and sit on the hot stone bank overlooking the canal, your legs dangling above the water.

'I'm intrigued by your reason for doing the course,' you tell him.

'Yeah? What about it intrigues you?'

'It's just very original and, well, kind of manipulative.'

'Oh, do I detect some disapproval?'

'That depends who you lobby on behalf of,' you say, smiling.

He shrugs and replies, 'A fracking firm.'

'Then, yes, definite disapproval.'

'I still get points for originality, right?'

You pause before replying, 'I'm still working that out.'

'I await your judgement,' he says, grinning and putting a whole piece of chicken into his mouth. 'I'm joking, by the way. I work for an NGO.'

'Do you actually?'

'Yes,' he says, holding up his business card in front of you.

'In that case, full points for smugness.'

You expect him to smile or laugh but instead he looks at you quizzically and asks, 'Have you done this stand-up stuff before, then?'

This would be the opportune moment to mention Oliver but because you're enjoying Malik's attention and want it to continue, you say, 'First time. But my housemate's a comedian, so I'm only one degree removed.'

Of course by not mentioning Oliver you're then obliged to come out with the line, 'I should probably say I've got a boyfriend,' when Malik asks for your number at the end of the afternoon.

He just smiles, holds eye contact and says, 'That's allowed. I'm still going to take your number, though.' You give it to him and he dials it in front of you so that now you have his number too.

Neither one of you does anything with this exchange of digits. That is until a fortnight after you've broken up with Oliver for the final time and are scrolling through your contacts trying to work out who to offer the spare ticket to that you now have for an Ionesco play at the Barbican next week, and land upon his name.

Not sure if you remember me . . . we met on that stand-up course in Camden last year? x Margot

How could I forget that chicken. What can I do for you?

I'm looking to sway my MP on a fracking ban and could do with some advice

Are you serious?

No. Wondering if you're free next Thursday and into absurdist theatre?

I'm not not into it

Barbican at half 7 if you can make it?

Let's do dinner at 6

Sounds good

I'll be coming from a parliamentary committee meeting so you'll have to excuse the suit

I bet it suits you

I take it your stand-up career never took off

Haha. See you Thursday

See you then

The play's in French btw

Is this another joke?

Non. Il y a des sous-titres

Impressive

Generous. I would've gone with pretentious

Let's go with both

As it is, he's held up at his committee meeting and so you

leave his ticket at the box office and he slides into the seat next to you during the latecomers' entrance, whispering, 'What have I missed?' You notice he doesn't apologize for being late.

'Not much. It's not exactly plot-heavy,' you whisper back.

The play's over within two hours so you're able to get dinner afterwards. He says he knows a place around the corner which turns out to be full of men in suits like the one he's wearing, and women in silk blouses and court shoes, making you feel out of place in your frayed jeans and leather jacket.

He asks if you drink red wine before selecting a bottle from the middle of the wine list, rather than the house wine you ordinarily drink. You both order the chicken and share a knowing smile at the nod to your lunch in Camden; it's oddly comforting how the two of you already have history with each other in the form of an in-joke from those six hours you'd spent together over a year ago.

'So, what's an attractive woman doing with a spare ticket to the theatre?' he asks as soon as the wine arrives.

You want to correct his assumption that only unattractive women have spare tickets to the theatre, but also don't want to be pedantic and know the question he's really asking is: *Where's your boyfriend or have you broken up?*

'Well, when I booked it, I was still with Oliver—'

'Your boyfriend.'

'And now we're not together,' you add for clarity.

'I'm sorry to hear that.'

'Are you?'

'No, I'm pleased.'

You smile at each other and simultaneously take a sip of wine.

'So did you win over MPs today with your tight-five?' When he looks confused you offer up, 'It's a stand-up term for a well-crafted set. A five-minute one.'

'I did get them onside actually, yeah.'

'And what is it exactly you want from them?'

'Well, it's not just me, but a group of us have been trying for a while to get the government to increase their overseas aid to 0.7 per cent of GNI and—'

'GNI?'

'Gross National Income. And yeah, today it finally looked like there was movement in the right direction.'

'Congratulations.'

'I thought you'd approve.'

'Not to rain on your parade but 0.7 per cent doesn't sound like much.'

'It's just over eleven billion pounds.'

'OK, that sounds like more.' He laughs and takes another sip of wine.

'And was their change of heart thanks to your persuasive wit?' you ask. 'Or just to the sudden discovery of their moral compass?'

'They tend not to score high on the latter so I'm going to take it as a personal win.'

'Funny. A minute ago I could have sworn you said it was a team effort.'

He doesn't laugh this time – not now the joke is on him – just frowns and changes the subject, does this repeatedly throughout dinner whenever the topic of conversation ceases to suit him. He has strong views on the wine and the food which he presents as facts rather than opinions – a trait you find offensive but also regrettably a turn-on. There's a definite thrill to being in his company in terms of not knowing what's going to come next, as well as a relaxation on account of his dominance; his strong preferences mean you can allow yourself to be led after years spent leading Oliver.

'My treat,' he says when the bill comes. You're not going to argue; his salary is presumably multiple times more than the

London Living Wage you earn as an usher, and besides, you paid for the theatre tickets. But it does now feel as though you partially owe him something. And so when he says, 'Fancy going to a health spa? I know a place that stays open late,' it's partly your curiosity and partly the fact you feel indebted that makes you say yes.

You assume he'll flag down a taxi, but he leads you to a nearby bus stop, making you recalibrate your impression of him as flash and well-off. 'I didn't picture you and your suit on public transport.'

'Policy advisors don't get paid much, you know. At least not the ones who work for NGOs. The private-sector guys do it for the money, we do it for the love and for the greater good.'

'Ah, like actors. Minus the social justice.'

You get off by Kentish Town station and walk for about a minute until he stops outside a shopfront that looks like a cheap travel agency; generic images of palm trees, turquoise sea and white sand cover the opaque windows. Above the door *Jacuzzi. Sauna. Steam. Plunge pool* is written in coloured block font.

'I don't have my swim stuff,' you say, oddly only just realizing this.

'That's OK, you won't need it.' He pauses before adding, 'It's a nudist spa.' You study his face, trying to work out if he's joking. 'They don't mind if you keep your underwear on, though.'

As you weigh up your options, you move your foot across the pavement, tracing the imaginary outline of a circle. Yes, you could simply cross over the road to the nearest bus stop and head back home, but the thought of doing this makes you feel neglectful towards the part of you that craves new experiences. And so rather than object, you say, 'How do I not know about this place?' as though you are someone who ordinarily frequents late-night naturist venues and have inadvertently missed this one off your list.

It seems legitimate enough on entering, looks similar to the reception area of a regular swimming pool. Inside the changing room, you toy with whether to take off your bra and knickers; your drama-school training has made you at ease in your body but the combination of being naked both in front of a group of strangers and someone you've now shared two meals with demands a level of confidence you regrettably don't have.

Malik is already inside one of the Jacuzzis when you enter the pool area and beckons you over to join him. You try to look relaxed as you approach, feeling intimidated by the backdrop of nudes as you sink down into the hot bubbles. An overweight man with oiled hair and a gold chain stares at you and you turn away, keen to avoid eye contact, but several minutes later you accidentally meet his gaze and he asks, 'Do you play?' Not understanding the question, you shake your head, trying to seem uninterested rather than ignorant, thankful when Malik suggests getting out to use the sauna.

It isn't until he stands that you have confirmation he's been naked all this time. There's an almost deliberate slowness to his walk as he steps up out of the water as if wanting to prove he isn't fazed. You're struck by his poise, his round stacked buttocks, his boldness compared to Oliver's.

As you pass by another Jacuzzi on your way to the sauna, you spot a visibly aroused couple, touching each other under the bubbles. They catch you looking at them, which you assume will make them stop, but your acknowledgement appears to have the reverse effect as they up the intensity of their underwater movements, grinning at you as the woman lets out an audible moan. You turn to Malik in shock, but he has already walked on ahead of you and is now opening the door to the sauna, and so you follow.

Inside, you feel your body being assessed as you cross to take a seat next to Malik who is sitting with his shoulders pulled back and eyes closed on the wooden bench furthest from the door. A naked couple to the other side of you are massaging each other. You stare straight ahead, trying to make yourself as inconspicuous as possible, but are distracted by the sight of the man's partially erect penis in your peripheral vision, juddering as it attempts to stand upright. 'You can hold it if you like,' says the woman, smiling as she rubs it so that it becomes fully hard in her hands.

'Oh. No, thank you,' you say, trying to suppress your mild panic as you glance at Malik who still has his eyes closed. 'Hey, I think I'm done,' you whisper. 'Shall I meet you out the front?'

He opens one eye and nods. 'Sure thing. I'll be out in ten.'

Relieved by the cooler air that hits you as you leave the sauna, you head back towards the changing rooms, passing a row of men with towels around their waists, lying on sunloungers eating curry from takeaway containers. Still puzzled by the place, you retrieve your things from the yellow locker inside the changing room and begin getting dressed, realizing that you now have no dry underwear.

You end up wearing your wet knickers on the bus back to Malik's flat so that they're warm and damp by the time you arrive, feel like the sticky air inside the tropical nursery at Kew Gardens you once visited with Oliver. Malik lends you a T-shirt and pair of boxer shorts which he removes as soon as you get into bed and begin kissing, but the heavy food and wine and fact that it is now early morning have left you with more desire to sleep than have sex. Although clearly not what he was expecting, he accepts your weighty limbs and drooping eyelids as a signal to roll over and turn out the light.

Leaving his flat the next morning, you message Lillie.

I ended up in this weird spa last night and everyone was naked

Is this inside your dream?

Actual life! Kentish Town

Loooool you went to Rios?!

You know it??

It's an institution

Have you been?!

I'm too prudish and scared of catching an STD. Was it wild?

I still don't fully understand what it is?!

YOU WENT TO A SEX SAUNA

WTF?! I DID NOT KNOW THIS

So worldly yet so green . . .

How come I'm such an ingenue?!

Tbf I don't think ingenues hang out at sex spas

They do inadvertently

That's what they all say . . .

Are you around? Want to trawl through casting breakdowns together? After I've showered!

Could do . . . I've kind of committed to making pancakes

I thought this George guy had a job?

He's taken the morning off

Pancakes and late mornings and you're still claiming it's not a relationship?

They're non-exclusive pancakes

You're both ridiculous. Enjoy x

You arrange to see Malik again a few nights later, but on this third encounter find the way he steers and shuts down conversation, and at several points corrects you, not only patronizing but verging on controlling. And so, leaving the restaurant you claim you have a casting early the following morning which prevents you from staying at his. You deliberately don't do your best to sound too convincing; you don't intend to see him again, therefore see little point in implying you do.

As you catch the bus home, leaning your head against the window – unsure whether you're mimicking being a character in a film or if your head naturally finds the angle agreeable – two conflicting feelings occur. The first is regret: the ache you feel that Malik isn't Oliver who you miss profoundly. The second is hope: that men like Malik, who are unabashed to walk out of water stark naked, do exist.

If Malik and Oliver are a Venn diagram of opposites, you deduce there must be a middle, overlapping circle representing a group of men who share both Malik and Oliver's traits: men who are confident but modest, self-assured while respectful, interested as well as interesting. To look at it another way, Malik has helpfully provided you with a cut-off point to your scale so now you have him at one end and Oliver at the other. Between them, they've marked out two posts at either end of your playing field, and in doing so have refined your criteria in terms of what you are looking for in a partner.

You wonder if your expectations might be unrealistic, but reason you aren't abstractly chasing perfection, rather methodically working on honing your search – and why should you be anything less than scrupulous in your quest to find someone to share your life and have children with? You can think of a commitment with no higher stakes.

'Yeah, except you can't use logic to find a partner,' says Ishani, as you recount your findings the next morning while helping her pack. After four years of living together, she is moving back to her parents' place in Croydon to use as a rent-free base while she spends the next three months touring the UK as the support act for a high-profile female comedian – a hard-earned gig following years of grafting on the circuit. 'Love, attraction, connection, it's all random, isn't it.'

'Why, though? I mean, who says it has to be?'

'How do you use the Marie Kondo spark-joy approach for electrical appliances?' she asks, rummaging in a bag of cables and wires.

'I think if it has utility you're just allowed to keep it,' you say, treading on the sporadic patches of grey carpet between the boxes on her floor. 'I mean, if you think about it, it's probably the biggest decision you'll ever make.'

'Whether I keep a spare laptop charger?'

'Tying yourself to another person.'

'Oh, we're back on that.'

'Especially if you end up having children together. Surely it actually makes sense to arrive at the decision through a series of adjustments based on previous results?'

'You and your clinical theories,' she says, shaking her head and laughing. 'Why not accept it's all basically down to chance? Take the pressure off yourself.'

'Thanks but I'd rather take a bit of pressure than forfeit control over something as big as this. What? Why are you looking at me like that?'

'It's just even the way you say "forfeit", like you actually think you have control over it in the first place. When love decides to hit, it'll hit. All you can do is be open and ready for it.' She tilts her head and looks full of longing for a second before gesturing for the roll of parcel tape next to your foot. As you roll it towards her, you picture her heart as a cartoon image, floating in the air, absurdly red and bursting.

8.   Zach

You weave through Romily's crowded hallway wearing high-waist jeans, a long-sleeve black crop top, silver brogues and your grandmother's gold chain necklace. Moments ago you left the basement where someone has just taken over on the decks, turning the funky house into drum and bass which you find problematic to dance to. Inside the kitchen you fill a pint glass with water and note the arrival of pizza without interest.

As you climb the stairs of this four-storey townhouse, passing more bodies on the landing, you feel bright and charged. Eighteen months from now you'll watch a cocaine documentary outlining the human bloodline required to produce a single line, and will vow never again to take it, but right now have only recently discovered it and have decided it's your drug.

A tall woman comes out of the bathroom in a top hat holding a man on a lead; both wear thick eyeliner and have small noses. She smiles in recognition that you are someone she knows by association and you smile back, proud when she says to the man, 'That's Romy's little sister.'

You hear the word 'limbo' shouted with elongation from the neighbouring bedroom, watch as Romily's housemate Ciaran bends his knees and arches his back, inching forwards under a held-out umbrella. His skinny legs look zebra-like in his black-and-white-striped leggings. As he stands upright, he notices you and winks.

'All right, Marg?'

You love this house and its occupants; the fact that Romily and her housemates treat you like one of them, while simultaneously looking out for you, gives you a security that allows you to behave with abandon. You smile and nod, and begin ascending another flight of stairs, while contemplating the present whereabouts of your sister, out of curiosity rather than concern.

As you enter the attic, Romily's friend Silas leaves the conversation he's in and comes over to chat to you, a regular occurrence of late. Romily has expressly advised you to stay away from him, warning it will disrupt the group dynamic if anything happens between the two of you. Her assumption that you will not be able to resist his advances is both amusing and mildly offensive. Firstly, he has a mohawk, and secondly he always talks at length about his job as a sales manager for a craft brewery in East London. You have little interest in beer (only drinking it when you're abroad) and so always find talking to him a lot of effort; even with your acting skills, there is a cut-off point to your feigned interest in fermentation.

As you swivel on a velvet office chair, trying to look attentive enough so as not to be rude but not so attentive as to lead him on, you become aware of another man's eyes on you. You've never seen him before but there are plenty of people you don't know at the party among the many others you do. It's the ideal blend of strangers to give the night possibility, and of friends and connections to make you feel part of an inner circle.

This new man wears a black T-shirt and red baseball cap, appears short leaning back at an angle against the wall, one Nike trainer flat against the skirting board. His face and arms are hairless, giving off an almost-teenage vibe, yet he has a surprising level of assertiveness as he unashamedly watches Silas attempt to flirt with you.

You let a closed-lip smile out of the corner of your mouth before swivelling back to face Silas and coolly asking, 'Shall we see what's happening downstairs?' He nods eagerly, as though this casual proposal is confirmation of your interest, and heads towards the door. You stand and begin following him out of the room but, just before exiting, turn back to the man in the baseball cap and say, 'Maybe see you later.'

'Let's make that happen,' he says with a nod. It's a needless dialogue, given you could continue the conversation then and there, but the exchange feels fun and provocative and more appealing than conceding to your immediate availability.

Inside the kitchen, you spot Romily by the sink, her arms wrapped around the neck of her colleague Aaron, their lips millimetres from touching. 'Catch you in a bit,' you say to Silas who looks briefly perturbed before turning his attention to the remaining slices of pizza, congealing in their boxes.

'Hey, can I borrow you?' you say, swooping in and pulling Romily away.

'What are you doing?' she asks with lacklustre irritation, as though she is manufacturing annoyance in order to cover up her sheepishness.

'What are *you* doing? You told me he said he really likes you and that you don't feel the same way.'

'Well, maybe I've changed my mind.'

'Have you?'

'I was in the process of trying to work that out.'

'Really? Or are you just tired of being single and wanting an easy out?' You'd intended your tone to sound light-hearted, but it had subconsciously tilted towards sincerity.

She frowns and then scoffs. 'Margot, it's a party. Lose the psychoanalysis and loosen up.'

Her comment irks you, firstly for the fact that anytime you are told to loosen or lighten up it has the opposite effect on you, and secondly because she is refusing to acknowledge the truth in your remark.

'That doesn't give you free rein to mess around with his feelings.'

'Why do you even care? You barely know the guy.' But having shared in each other's dwindling enthusiasm for dating these last couple of months, you resent that Romily has a back-up option in the form of Aaron at her disposal, which she is now considering taking.

'I just don't think it's OK to dick him around because you're lonely.'

'But it's OK to sleep with another woman's husband?'

Her comment lands like a slap across your skin, stunned by the shock of it as much as the hurt. You haven't spoken about Wren for several years now, and, anytime you have, it's never been met with anything other than condolence, or her criticism of him. That she is using the experience to now attack you feels preposterously unjustified and out of the blue.

'I was in love with him. And it tore me up.'

'And I didn't judge you, so I'm just saying don't judge me.'

'I wasn't judging you until just now.'

You turn and walk with defiance out of the kitchen, a steely determination overriding your anger – your mood's refusal to be defeated by this altercation. You feel surprisingly liberated by the absence of any guilt; Romily, having wildly overstepped the mark, can be the one to stew.

Descending the steps to the basement, you pass the man in the baseball cap at the foot of the stairs, adjacent to the make-shift DJ booth. He leans in towards you, putting his mouth close to yours, and says over the music, 'You again. You better tell me your name.'

'Mm. You can have the first letter,' you reply into his ear.

'Go on, then.'

'I just gave it to you.' You walk off before he can reply but not without looking back over your shoulder to see his eyes narrowing in appreciation as he nods his head and shifts his tongue around inside the roof of his mouth, slightly altering his face shape.

This silently acknowledged game, in which the two of you pursue and subsequently deny yourselves to each other, carries on throughout the night. When you meet on the dance floor, you grind your thighs against his without turning to face him. Brushing each other's arms by the drinks table, you exchange no more than glances. At one point you cross paths on the landing and he says, 'Mary?'

'Less biblical.'

'Molly.'

'Less cute.'

'One more strike and I'm out,' he says, grinning at this raising of the stakes. You hold eye contact, smiling as he looks you up and down. 'Martina.'

Taking a step towards him, you tilt your head and say, 'Game over.'

He moves in closer so that you're almost touching. You assume he'll kiss you but instead he removes his baseball cap and places it on to your head.

'Is this my prize for you not winning?' you ask, trying not to sound disappointed.

'You wish,' he says, removing it from your head and putting it back on his own before walking off, leaving you feeling somehow cheated by his exit.

When once more you encounter him, this time in the living room in the early hours of the morning, finally the meeting feels earned and worthy of giving part of yourself away.

'M for Margot,' you say, holding out your hand in surrender.

'Z for Zach,' he says, shaking it brusquely from his seat on the arm of the sofa. 'And what do you do, Margot?'

'In terms of a job or just generally?'

'I meant for a living but generally's also fine.'

'I'm an actor.'

'Nah, my aunt and uncle are both actors. You're too smart to be one.'

'Do you normally insult your extended family in your pick-up lines?'

'It's not a pick-up line and my family are cool, they're just not clever.'

'What makes you think you've got a gauge on my intellect? We've barely spoken.'

'Enough to get a read on you. So, go on, what else do you do?'

Flattered, you acquiesce. 'All right, technically I also write.'

'And what do you write?'

'Well, I wrote a theatre show which got some TV interest so now I'm dabbling in the world of *showbiz*.' You emphasize the word, wanting to mock it. You don't tell him that the formal option on your play-turned-TV script expired several months ago without being picked up by any channels. You are still pitching new ideas to various production companies but, with this year's set of Edinburgh previews now in full swing, producers are already looking ahead to fresh talent, and you are finding your emails less frequently replied to. You also don't mention the notable decline in castings coming through your agent now that the initial buzz of being her newest client has worn off and you have not landed any of the parts she's put you up for.

'That makes more sense,' he says.

'And what about you? What do you do for a living and/or generally?' you ask.

'I'm the founder of a food-delivery app. We've just closed a five-million-pound seed round.' You're not sure what a seed round is but understand the line is intended to impress you.

'And all before you turned twenty-one. Congratulations.' He smirks at this, stroking his hairless chin. 'Seriously, though, how old are you?' you ask.

'Twenty-nine. You?'

'Twenty-seven.'

'So now we've established we're above the age of consent . . .' He takes hold of the chain around your neck, pulling you towards him. His kiss is unexpectedly rough and he pushes you away after a couple of seconds before pulling you in again, toeing the line between thrill and annoyance.

The timings of the night are hazy, but you know that when dawn arrives a group of you are out in the garden. It's the spring bank-holiday weekend; the coral sky is misty, the lawn wet with dew so that strands of grass stick to your trainers like shreds of green paper. A guy you vaguely recognize takes hold of your neck to re-enact part of an anecdote he's telling and, although it's done in jest, Zach immediately intervenes, pulling the guy off you and announcing, 'Oi, that's my neck.' To hear him take ownership of your neck, while against your feminist values, is electrifying. So when he turns and says, 'Come on, let's get out of here,' you follow him obediently down the garden path and back into the house without question, as if connected by an invisible current.

You haven't seen Romily since the argument several hours ago, presuming she's snuck off with Aaron somewhere. But as you retrieve your coat from the pile draped over the banister, you hear her distinct laugh coming from the kitchen, and catch sight of her profile in the mirror in the hallway, animatedly gesticulating to her friend Phoebe. You stand for a moment watching her.

'That's your sister, isn't it?' says Zach. You nod. 'You gonna say bye then, or what?'

Feeling a surge of entitlement to behave without acknowledging her, you turn to him and say, 'Let's just go.'

It's approaching five a.m. when you leave the house and walk down the road where you climb the iron gates of Clissold Park. As you jump down on to the other side, you feel emboldened by the latest residues of cocaine in your bloodstream and by the company of this stranger who will allow you, by not knowing you better, to be the most daring version of yourself.

You cut through the park on to Church Street and from there into Abney Park Cemetery, this time have even bigger gates to climb and dismount as you exit on to Stoke Newington High Street. Cold, muddy and on a comedown, you buy takeaway tea in polystyrene cups from a cafe that looks like a kebab shop and take the bus back to yours. He doesn't say much on the journey, leaving you to do most of the work conversationally. The sex is also surprisingly bad, rough like his kissing, his fingering harsh and jabbing, making you suspect he's only ever had a series of one-night stands before – that no woman has taken the time to help him locate the clitoris.

When you wake, you're at ease getting showered and dressed in front of him, removing last night's make-up and not bothering to put on any more; you don't assume you'll see him again following this weekend, making un-mascaraed eyes inconsequential.

Later that afternoon, you ignore the string of calls you receive from Romily as you and Zach consume Bloody Marys and pick at lamb roasts inside a Georgian pub garden in Angel. He is oddly couply, hooking his arm around your shoulders as you sit side by side under the wisteria-covered pergola, even kissing the top of your head. You enjoy his tactility in your hungover state, but nonetheless feel relaxed and uninvested in him, so that it only bemuses you when at the end of the afternoon he stops abruptly outside the entrance to the Tube and says, 'Just so you know, I don't do relationships, they don't work for me. But you're cool so we should hang out again as, you know, friends with other stuff. That kind of thing.'

'You flatter me.'

'Yeah, well whatever, I'm just warning you now, don't get attached.'

'In that case, I'm not sure if I should admit this, but I'm already, well . . . deeply unattached.'

He grins and hooks his arm around you again, pulling you in tightly; your dismissiveness only enticing him.

As you leave Zach by the ticket barriers, deciding to walk part-way home, you get a message from Lillie.

How was the party? Gutted I missed it!

Quite wild! How come you weren't there?

Quite as in not much or as in very?

Leaning towards very. Where were you??

George's friend Joel was DJing at a warehouse in Hackney Wick. You need to meet him so we can double date!

You do a disgruntled exhale, despite Lillie not being there to witness it, deciding not to reply. She has repeatedly bailed on you of late; you are unimpressed by her prioritizing of George's friends over her own, and had predicted her absence last night would be attributed to him.

When you get back to your house, you find Romily inside your living room perched with crossed legs on the edge of the sofa.

She looks up from her phone as you enter and immediately stops typing.

'Your new housemate let me in.'

'Does this mean you've lost my spare key?'

'It means I forgot you gave me a spare key.'

You glance at the bunch of rainbow tulips on the table.

'They're for you,' she says. 'Obviously.'

Trying not to smile at their vibrancy, you walk past her into the kitchen. 'I think this is only about the fifth time you've ever been here.'

'To be fair, I worry about its structural integrity,' she says, looking up at the ceiling as you re-enter holding scissors and a vase of water.

'Weird. I assumed you'd come to apologize, not insult my house.'

'OK, look, you know I'm shit at saying sorry which is why I've worked hard to make an acceptable level of offensiveness part of my personality, but last night I was way off. Even by my own standards.'

'At least we can applaud your self-awareness,' you say, not looking at her as you trim the base of the tulip stems.

'Marg, what I said about you and Wren was . . .'

'Pretty outrageous.'

'It was heavily outrageous, as well as outrageously naff.'

'It did sound quite soap opera.'

'Eugh. Don't. I'm ashamed enough already.'

'Of the melodramatic line?' you ask, glancing up to look at her.

'I mean, yes. But no. More cause of how it made you feel. It's honestly the worst, hurting your younger sister. Like it goes against the natural order of things.'

'I feel that term ought to be reserved for children dying before their parents, but sure.'

She smiles gratefully and strokes the spine of a cookbook on the shelf. 'Nothing happened with Aaron, by the way.'

You shrug and hold the silence.

'You were right about what you said, though. I'm done with dating.'

'You always claimed you like being single.'

'I did like it, past tense. Now I'm not liking it, present continuous.'

'You can't actually use stative verbs in the present continuous.'

'Oh my god, I think Mum just died and went to heaven.'

You laugh and begin arranging the tulips inside the vase. 'If you want my opinion, I think you're going for the wrong kinds of men.'

'Go on,' she says, shaking her head. 'Annihilate my big-sister pride.'

'All right then, I think you should ditch these flaky musicians and try dating some guys with more solid jobs and less solid egos.'

'So basically Aaron-types but not Aaron.'

'Guys you can imagine being good dads. I mean, you want kids, right?'

She looks at the bookshelf before looking back at you with an expression caught somewhere between realization and acceptance. 'Yeah. Yeah I do.'

'Well, there we go,' you say, placing the vase in the centre of the table.

'You know, it's a bit/a lot disarming having your younger sister point out something that now feels very obvious.'

'I *think* there was a compliment in there somewhere.'

'I deny all knowledge of one,' she says, holding out her arms, beckoning you in.

You hug, and for the second time that day, you feel the top of your head being kissed.

'By the way, technically you haven't said sorry yet.'

She squeezes you tighter and mumbles something into your ear.

'What was that?' you ask, smiling as you pull back to look at her.

She laughs and sniffs your neck. 'I said you smell of boy.'

'I may have gone home with someone,' you say archly, raising your eyebrows.

'Who?' she asks, her eyes glinting.

'Zach somebody. He's a friend of a friend of Ciaran's.'

'Not that Forbes Under 30 guy?'

'Probably.'

'You sound wildly apathetic.'

'That's cause we're wildly different. I'm pretty sure it was just a fun bank-holiday thing.'

'You're not going to see him again, then?'

'I might but I'm not going to push for it. I don't care enough either way,' you say, and you genuinely mean it.

But in the succeeding months you go from being in control of your feelings to feeling as though you'd do almost anything Zach asks, including letting him have sex with you without a condom, pulling out just before he comes, despite his open admission that he is sleeping with other women. He ignores most of your messages, refusing to make plans in advance to see you, and instead calling only when he feels like it so that you drop whatever you're doing to go out and meet him, pretending you were already in town even though you can see from his smirk that he knows you're lying. For the first time in your life you feel you have become a *pathetic woman*, although hope that in acknowledging this it gives you a degree of separation from actually being one.

At points you wonder if you're now attracted to 'bad' men but it isn't because of the fact he doesn't respect you that keeps you coming back for more; it's in spite of it. You can't deny that by holding you on a tether he fuels your desire, but it's what he does and says to you when you're together that sustains your limerence: the way he both mocks and validates you, making you feel continually challenged and stimulated by him so that in the end you can't discern if it's him you crave or the version of yourself you are around him.

Your attempts to sever contact fail repeatedly, as you try blocking him on WhatsApp – writing his number on a scrap of paper and tucking it inside the sleeve of your phone case before deleting him from your contacts – but, after several days or weeks, always end up relenting. Each time you message he seems entertained that you've felt the need to both reject and elicit his company when he appears to be largely indifferent to yours. You fear this pattern will simply go on indefinitely, that nothing will be able to break the cycle of your self-sabotage, as though you are watching from the sidelines while Zach derails your pursuit of a compatible partner, powerless to stop it.

'He sounds like a total dick,' says Romily, as the two of you sit on a bench inside Lincoln's Inn Fields around the corner from her office on her lunch break.

'I know that bit already. The bit I don't get is why I still want to see him.'

'Cause you're bored? Cause you grew up chasing approval and validation from Dad and now you're playing it out in your relationships by dating unavailable men?'

'Er, OK, very Freudian and very out of nowhere.'

'Hardly. Wren, Oliver, now this Zach guy,' she says, pushing the end of her falafel wrap into her mouth.

'Yeah but if that was true then you'd be doing the same thing.'

'Not necessarily. The Dad thing always bothered you more than it bothered me.'

'Why is that?'

She shrugs as she swallows. 'I dunno. I guess I'm just less into unrequited interest.'

You turn your head and look across at the bandstand, feeling lost and forlorn. 'Do you think I need therapy?'

'No, Marg. I think therapy is for people who have had actual shit happen to them. Not people like us with mildly emotionally unavailable fathers.'

'But how do I cure it?'

'I haven't just given you a cancer diagnosis.'

'All right, fine, how do I change it, then?'

'You'll change it when you care enough to change.' Her phone pings and she looks at her screen, smiling ineluctably.

'Who's the guy?'

'Who says it's a guy?'

'Your face?'

She grins and presses her phone to her sternum. 'His name's Alec. And it's only been one date.'

'I'm inferring it was a good one.'

Still smiling, she puts her phone into her bag and stands. 'I should get back to work.'

'Hang on, why are you being so coy?'

'He's just so not my type.'

'Sounds promising already. What's he like?'

'Scottish and old and wears a suit.'

'Hot. How old?'

'Forty-three.'

'Acceptably old.'

'He's asked me out again on Saturday.'

'Saturday night. He's keen.'

'I think I am too,' she says, scrunching the wrapper of her falafel into a ball.

'If you end up marrying him, it'll be all thanks to me.'

'We won't be getting married, and I repeat – it's been one date.'

'How do you think marriages begin?' you ask gleefully.

'I'm more interested in why his ended,' she says, throwing the wrapper at you.

'Huh?' you ask as it lands in your lap.

'Oh, right, yeah. He's also divorced.'

'Anything else I should know about him?'

'Did I mention he works in oil?' she says, grimacing.

'Un-ideal, but whatever. I've got a good feeling about him.'

'Me too. Plus, I figure if it goes anywhere I can just lie and tell Mum he's in renewables.'

You don't hear from her much over the next fortnight and then the following week she messages out of the blue.

Dinner next Thursday? Me, you, Alec?

Wow that's soon no?! I take it things are going well?

Pretty sure it's meant to be the other way around?!

Explain??

You beg to meet him, I say no it's too soon, you say plssssss etc . . .

I forgot to say the yes bit! Yes plsss! etc etc

Great, I'll book somewhere

Not too nice, I've got no money

Standard. I'll pay x

Standard. Thank you! x

Despite your happiness for Romily, you feel uneasy at the prospect of Alec disrupting your sisterly dynamic, knowing that she will have increasingly less time for you. Your concern is not an irrational one, having further lost Lillie to George who she is finally official with after a year of dating, and is now taking on the role of girlfriend with a fervour and commitment that precludes any form of activity not involving him.

'So do you two exclusively come as a pair now?' Ishani had asked the two of them last Sunday as they sat wedged next to each other inside the pub, holding hands under the table while eating off the same plate. 'Like, I'm just curious what happens when one of you needs to go to the loo or take a shower and you're forced to separate.'

George grins and looks sheepish as Lillie replies unabashed, 'There are creative ways around that.'

George and Lillie's closeness is a two-fold grievance; there is the loss of Lillie's undivided company, as well as the stark and constant reminder that she has the thing you want and lack.

The following Thursday, you enter the waterfront restaurant in Granary Square where Romily beckons you over to a table by the window. As Alec stands to greet you, you're immediately struck by the obvious age gap between them – his grey hair and soft paunch, the capillaries of wrinkles framing his eyes.

'Upfront disclaimer,' he says as you sit down. 'If I come across as remotely twattish or dweeby tonight, it's because I'm nervous to impress you.' The quietness of his voice and Aberdonian accent force you to lean in when he speaks.

'Ha. Thanks. I think.'

'He's got it into his head that you're my favourite person and so now he feels the need to win you over. You're not, by the way; you're like my third favourite.'

Alec holds his index finger up and mouths, 'Number one,' at you across the table, making you involuntarily laugh.

When he gets up to chase down the bill at the end of the night, Romily waits until he's left the table, and then says with a speed that divulges her nerves, 'So, obviously I care what you think to a certain extent, but I'm also into him enough to not care.'

Infusing your voice with as much earnestness as you know she will allow, you reply, 'Rom, he's great. Like truly great.'

'He is, isn't he.' She runs her finger around the rim of her glass, looking pleased.

'Do you think he wants children?'

'I know he does. His ex-wife never did and he said that was a sticking point in their marriage.'

'Convenient.'

'Right?' Your phone pings, prompting her to ask, 'You're not still seeing that awful guy, are you?'

'I love how you claim not to know his name. And no, I'm not.'

As soon as you say it, you realize it's not a lie, or at least it doesn't have to be; Alec's enthusiasm and maturity have inadvertently made Zach's aloofness less appealing, shifting something subtle but definite in you over the course of the evening which you are determined to act on.

Following your goodbye to Romily and Alec outside King's Cross, you delete Zach's number before removing the scrap of paper from the sleeve of your phone case and dropping it into the bin with an odd-sounding exhale that resembles more of an impression of relief rather than genuine relief. As you walk away, you expect to feel panic at the thought of not being able to contact him but instead feel as though you are gliding underwater, pushing through a weightless wall, your ears cool and billowy.

Of course, he still has your number, and in the weeks that follow you regard your phone with underlying anxiety, as you confine yourself to your attic bedroom and try to focus your energy on creating another show. Having spent the last year churning out TV treatments, chasing the zeitgeist, you perceive you are in danger of falling out of love with the industry that you have spent the last half a decade trying to infiltrate, unless you return to producing work that viscerally excites you. As you write, trying to blot out the appealing sound of laughter from your housemates through the floorboards, you try to remove any expectation that this second show will catapult your career in any way (while obviously still hoping it will) and to be led by your instincts in terms of what you find amusing or interesting, with the aim of evoking these responses in your audience.

'I'm writing in the dark and just hoping it will connect with people,' you admit to Oliver when he lures you out of your hermit's cave to meet him in a coffee shop near Old Street station. 'But I wish there was some way of knowing in advance if it will resonate.'

'Can you not road-test sections of it like you did with the last one?' he asks, blowing on to his peppermint tea.

'Maybe, but this one makes less narrative sense out of context. I'm thinking I'm just going to have to commit to it and then find out in one big whack whether or not I've landed on anything good.'

'That's why theatre is for brave people and stand-up is for cowards,' he says, attempting to take a sip of hot tea with a wince.

'Ah, but you have to hear the sound of instant failure if they don't laugh. I can just tell myself they're quietly moved.'

'Let's call it a truce and declare we're equally insane to be doing this with our lives,' he says, smiling.

You nod and smile back. 'Insane. And insanely lucky.' You leave a beat and then ask, 'How's Sophie?'

He fiddles with the string of the teabag, pausing for a long time even by his standards, before replying, 'Good. I think I've finally found my compatible demographic when it comes to dating.'

'Older women?'

'Older women who aren't interested in children or marriage or cohabiting.'

'So, basically, zero commitment.'

'I'm actually meeting her family next weekend,' he says, looking at you tentatively as though this news may affect you.

'Oliver, that's great. I'm really happy for you.' And you genuinely are.

'And you? Is there . . . anyone in your life at the moment?' He always has a slightly awkward, almost fatherly, air when asking after your relationship status, or at least more of a protective and embarrassed air than your actual father.

'Nope. Just someone I'm trying to get out of it.'

'Good luck with that. I hear pepper spray can be very effective.' You laugh, and consider how your friendship with Oliver is perhaps your greatest achievement of the last couple of years, leading you to conclude that your professional accomplishments of late have been somewhat lacking.

When you eventually hear from Zach the following month, you are relieved to find that you are not stirred into a frenzy. His *Oi, where are you?* leaves you more bewildered than flustered at the fact you were ever enamoured by someone so lacking in basic courtesy. Then again, you consider you might still be having your affections mauled by him were it not for Alec's embodiment of decency. You like to imagine you'd have found the self-restraint and integrity to move on regardless, but recall the flinching pleasure of dipping your fingers in hot candle wax as a child, the cooling liquid setting on your skin, the satisfaction you got from those hard little caps forming on your fingertips like tiny trophies of pain.

9. Frank

It's the sex you think of most when you think back now on Frank; the frequency and quality of it, as well as the openness you shared in bed, to this day remains unrivalled by any other man. But the two of you had the advantage of never falling in love and so were able to maintain a level of distance that generates that kind of hungry erotic desire.

You meet him in August at the Edinburgh Fringe where you've taken your new show that year. He's an assistant editor for an online comedy guide, up there for the month to review a dozen shows a day. Born and bred in Sunderland, he's voluble and ebullient; his self-professed hobbies comprise 'comedy, clubbing and shagging'. Although the same age as you, he's an old soul – doesn't do social media, prefers having a pint in person rather than messaging, favours traditional stand-up over experimental character-acts or meta-plays like yours that break the fourth wall. Your show is listed in the official Fringe guide under theatre rather than comedy which excludes him from reviewing it anyway, and besides, neither of you are out to use the other to climb further in your careers; if you use each other for anything it's as a source of buoyant sex and company.

He's pale and skinny, in contrast to the colour and fullness of his personality. When you have sex, you feel his hip bones sliding against you but there are no sharp edges to his character; he's indisputably kind. You're comfortable being naked together, telling each other what feels good and what doesn't, although the latter is barely relevant as most of it feels insanely good. He apologizes when he takes ages to come, saying he wants to hold on, doesn't want it to end – isn't affronted when you roll your eyes and say, 'I do also need to sleep tonight, I've got to be flyering at nine unless you want to do it for me? Unpaid of course,' just throws back his head as he concedes, showering you with adoration as he climaxes.

Although your show does well – is repeatedly sold out thanks to word of mouth and your dogged approach to market it every morning even when it rains (which, being Edinburgh, it does most days) – it doesn't land with the same force as your first one, largely because it isn't your debut and therefore doesn't attract the same swarm of producers in search of the next 'big thing'. Still, you enjoy the month you spend up there getting to work in your chosen profession without having to do paid work on the side. Yes, you will have to pick up extra shifts at the Old Vic on your return to compensate for your loss of earnings, but for this month alone are able to live solely as a creative.

When the Fringe ends you find cheap flights to Mallorca and a hostel for twenty euros a night where you spend four days decompressing on a beach outside Palma, welcoming the dry heat after a month of being predominantly damp. You feel calm and present – are able to blot out concerns about the future, such as how you will ever make a living from your career – as you lie topless on the hot sand reading Raymond Carver short stories and drinking beer which you buy from the guy who walks up and down the shore calling out in a high-pitched voice, '*Agua, cerveza, patatas fritas.*' You swim intermittently throughout the day whenever you need to cool off and then reapply sun cream, dotting each mole like piping icing on a cake. When a line in one of the stories is so good you have to share it with someone, you photograph the page and WhatsApp it to Oliver or Lillie – alternating this with sending Frank photos of your naked breasts which look starkly white in the sun, convinced there must be a man out there who'd be equally happy to receive both the Carver quotes and your pasty chest. But where is he?

You wonder if you've misjudged Frank, send him a line from the next story you read, saying, *Agree or disagree? I think it makes me feel both (younger and older).* But he replies, *You're a strange cookie. More tit pics please!!* followed by a photo of his throbbing cock.

You're open with him that you see the arrangement as casual. Back in London over the coming weeks, he continually jokes he's going to marry you, and rather than coyly smile and say, 'We'll see about that,' you feel a duty to be honest, and so tell him bluntly and sincerely, 'Listen, this genuinely isn't going to turn into a relationship.' You ardently know and mean this, but it's hard to tell whether he believes you, especially when such lines are commonly used to make the other party fall further and therefore might be construed as tactical.

Your agent calls a fortnight into October, late on Thursday afternoon as you are packing to join Lillie and George in Devon for a long weekend to celebrate Lillie's birthday.

'Listen, it's mad in the office today, but just a quick one to check you got the sides I sent across?' She sounds calm and unhurried – a confusing dissonance between her vocabulary and tone, leaving you unsure about the level of detail and urgency you are required to respond with.

'Oh, right, no, I haven't seen them yet. I'm experimenting with turning off my notifications, not like permanently, just for small windows of—'

'So, it's a biggie,' she says, interrupting with a purr-like quality to her voice. 'A pilot for HBO. Not the lead but a nice meaty role. Fifties Manhattan, set inside a media company, so think glamorous, but it's also a satire so they're looking for strong comedy chops. Sort of *Mad Men* meets *The Thick of It.* The sides are chunky but I think it would be really good to get you off-book for this.'

You put her on speaker and open up your inbox, scanning the attached fifteen pages of script she is expecting you to memorize.

'The casting director's in LA. She wants you to self-tape and send it across to her by the end of the weekend but with the time difference that'll give you until late Sunday evening or even first thing Monday morning.'

'That's, um, soon,' you mumble, unsure whether she's heard you when she continues, 'Do at least a couple of takes of each scene and maybe try and use a prop; you know, something to really stand out.'

'Sure,' you say, casting your eye around your bedroom for any 1950s-looking objects.

'Listen, I've got to go, but look, we've not had a great streak lately and I think we really need to turn that around with this tape, so really go for it, OK. Really make it your own.'

She hangs up and you throw your half-packed bag from your bed on to the floor, scrunching your fingernails into your palm so that they leave small indentations in your skin.

'It's a total waste of time,' you say down the phone to Lillie. 'It'll go to a name or at least someone with a profile. I don't even know why they've asked me to tape for it.'

'You might get it.'

'I won't get it.'

'If you really think that then come to Devon.'

'My agent will drop me if I don't do the tape, though. She basically said as much on the phone.'

'OK, so do the tape, then.'

'It's just so ridiculous that we're expected to cancel our plans at the whim of some casting director who's probably not even going to watch it anyway. We're like the plants of the food chain, right at the bottom even though the system would collapse without us.'

'You say "we're" but I'd kill for the castings you get.'

'You'd probably actually get the parts too.'

'Maybe I would but I don't know because I don't get the chance to go up for them.'

You pause, feeling both guilty and relieved about this.

'Look, do the tape or don't do the tape but don't complain to me about being asked to do the tape.'

'Sorry.'

'It's fine. Just let me know if you're coming and we'll pick you up from the station.'

She puts down the phone and you grab hold of your pillow, enjoying the salty texture of the worn fabric as you bite into it. Attempting to muster gratitude, you open up the attached document and scan the pages again, trying to ascertain how quickly you might be able to memorize them, wondering if you can somehow go to Devon and simultaneously learn and record the tape; but you've never been adept at multitasking, and if you go and spend the whole time worked up about the casting, you risk ruining Lillie's birthday with more than just your absence. Resigned, you send her a message: *I'm going to stay here and do it. Really sorry to miss the weekend. 'Lils extended bday celebrations' going into my diary for next week. Let me know which afternoons you're free and I'll take you out for a fancy tea xxx*

You stay holed up inside your room for the duration of the weekend, declining Frank's offer of assistance to help with your lines, partly as self-inflicted punishment for your poor-friend behaviour, and partly in the knowledge that preparing you for your casting will be his secondary focus.

'This is so civilized,' says Lillie the following Friday, glancing up at the chandelier as she rests her forearms on the white table-cloth. 'You know I was joking when I said the Ritz, right?'

'You were half-joking. Plus, to be honest, it's basically the same price as a return train fare to Plymouth.'

'You could have totally lied and told me you were squandering your savings to take us here,' she says, flicking a loose strand of hair behind her shoulder as she scans the room.

'Ah, see that's the difference between us. I'm all about the truth, you're all about the charm.'

'I'll drink to that.' She picks up her cup, overtly sticking out her little finger, and winks.

'Here's to your birthday,' you say, raising your cup to hers in a toast. 'And sorry again about missing it.'

'Hey, I'd have done the same thing.' She leaves a tentative pause before casually asking, 'You haven't heard anything yet?'

'About the tape?' She nods and you shake your head. 'I won't either. It's just out there in the ether not to be acknowledged. And then eighteen months from now I'll turn on the TV and see some C-list celebrity doing the part I went up for.' You note the flicker of frustration across her face and catch yourself. 'Sorry, I'm doing it again. Just hit me next time, go full on Pavlovian.'

She softens and sits back in her chair. 'You know, it was actually quite useful having that conversation, in like a moderately painful way. I thought about it when I got off the phone to you and I realized I've spent the last six years calling myself an actor but I don't even do any acting.' Her fervent attempt to sound light-hearted reveals the depth to which she cares.

'Neither do I really,' you say, determined to boost her self-esteem. 'Not unless you count auditioning.'

'You're making your own work, though.'

'True. But you could do that too.'

'Exactly,' she says, shrugging. 'I've figured I'm going to have to.'

You feel a familiar surge of panic, immediately imagining that whatever Lillie creates will be funnier and cleverer and more meaningful than anything you could come up with. The only way you have ever been able to keep up with her is by working twice as hard, thinking back to your drama-school assessments where you had matched each other mark for mark, but whereas your A grades were gained through hours of slog, hers arrived as a result of innate talent.

'So, what kind of thing are you going to do?' You wonder if she can detect your feigned breeziness in an effort to mask your insecurity. How absurd and humbling that just moments ago the scales of your balancing egos were weighted in the opposite direction.

'I dunno yet. Maybe film-making, having a go at making my own short. Writing, directing and acting in it. The full caboodle.'

You feel placated that she is choosing a different medium where your success and hers can less easily be compared.

'Hey, you might end up being the voice of our generation.'

'Well, no, cause Greta Gerwig's already that.' You laugh and take a bite of cucumber sandwich.

'I think you'd be really good at film-making. I mean, you're way more visual than I am.'

'Speaking of which, I don't not like that dress, I just don't think it's actively doing anything for you.'

'Seriously? I literally just called you charming.'

'I'm doing honesty – your favourite!'

You shake your head and throw a piece of cucumber at her, making her squeal.

'Are we actually having a food fight?' she asks, grinning.

'No,' you say, firing a crust at her.

'So louche, I love it,' she says, hitting you with a macaroon.

'OK but that's it now cause it's approximately five pounds a throw. Plus, it's kind of off-kilter with the vibe.'

'Kicked out of the Ritz would be a good anecdote, though.'

★

Returning to Frank's house-share later that afternoon – your dress urgently discarded on to the floor – he looks up from planting kisses across your stomach, and says, 'Fuck it, we should just have a baby.'

'Sure,' you say, nonchalantly reaching across to the box of condoms by the bed.

'Nah, obviously I'm joking, but also kind of not.'

You freeze as you imagine him impregnating you – flashing forward in your mind to a year from now, his infatuation worn off, and no other foundation on which to raise a child. You have not come this far in your quest for a compatible life partner and co-parent to discard your game plan on Frank, wonderful as he is.

You have no objection to two consenting adults having sex without commitment, but the notion of maintaining a mutual level of detachment proves once again to be an unrealistic ideal; just as you'd been the one to fall harder in the case of you and Zach, it's undeniably clear to you in this moment that Frank wants more from the arrangement than you do.

It's partly out of care for him that you end things, but also out of care for yourself. While your present-self at this stage would happily go on spending the majority of your free evenings off work with him, so long as you are doing this you are not making yourself available to other men who might offer you a future as well as a present, and this has always been – and still is – your ultimate goal.

With your mind made up, you message him the next day. *Are you around for an early drink this eve?*

I'm at a mixed-bill night until 10ish. Can come to yours after though? ;-)

Ah that's OK. I'm going to have an early night

No hanky panky, can just do cuddles?

You start typing and then stop, do this repeatedly without sending a reply.

Everything OK? I know I can come on strongly, I'm just a bit smitten

I'd kind of wanted to do this in person or at least on the phone . . .
Do what?

You don't know how to respond and so go into the kitchen and make an omelette. By the time you come back to your room he's sent four more messages, all in quick succession.

You still there?
I can't speak right now, the next act's about to come on
Can you message?
I may be a big softie but I've got tough skin x

And so with his permission, feeling guilty you've got away without meeting, you type: *I've really loved hanging out with you these last couple of months – you're unquestionably great. I just need to be elsewhere right now in terms of dating. I hope you understand? xx*

Your fondness for him is only amplified by his reply that he sends later that evening.

Not to worry, pet. I don't go in for schmaltz but knowing you has been one of the happiest times of my life. You take care and let me know if you ever fancy a meet-up for old times sake x

But despite his open invitation, and the urge you feel on nights of acute loneliness for the press of his bony frame on top of yours, you don't message him again; you don't feel it would be fair.

Four months later, you pass him outside a pub on Old Compton Street, customary fag and pint in hand. He locks you in a hug, tells you he's got himself 'a gorgeous girlfriend', and that they're moving in together next month, winking as he adds, 'Touch wood she doesn't suddenly realize she's way out of my league.'

Smiling, you reply, 'She'd be a fool to let you go.'

He smiles back at you and says, 'She wouldn't be the first.'

Walking away, you want to thank him – for belting Prince's 'Let's Pretend We're Married' to you on the night bus home, for the time you got a cold and he tucked you up in bed, for the tissue he folded and snuck under your pillow when he thought you were asleep – want him to stay exactly as he is but you no longer have the privilege of knowing him; it had to be that way, or rather, you chose it that way. People talk about forks in the road determining major life choices, but what about all the smaller tracks leading off those bigger ones? Aren't they equally part of the story?

10.   Patrick

Suddenly, at twenty-nine, you are palpably aware of your body clock; whereas before you understood it to exist in an abstract sense, it now manifests inside you as underlying noise like the persistent buzzing of a wasp or tinnitus. You know you're not old but friends around you have started getting engaged, causing spikes of doubt about the path you've chosen in which you've experienced being with a number of men, rather than staying with the same partner since your late teens or early twenties.

It isn't superiority you feel towards these friends; on the contrary, you've both envied and admired them at points over the years. But you do believe that the route you've taken is the more desirable one, as given you intend to live until ninety and not have children until you're in your thirties, you'd rather meet the person you're going to spend the rest of your life with after a decade spent with other people, because well, who wouldn't choose a period of variation before embarking on a fifty-odd-year commitment?

However, here's the crux: your approach has always been predicated on the condition that it will ultimately lead you to the same endpoint as your friends – the opportunity of having children and growing old with someone you love. But for the first time, it now also feels like a risky course, one that may have diverted you so far off-track that you are in danger of not getting the future you want.

It's at this point after Frank that you date relentlessly – signing up to four different apps, so that any evening not ushering is spent scouting for potential partners. But on multiple occasions you meet with someone whose messages you've found promising, only to discover an absence of any chemistry.

'It's just such a let-down when I get there and I'm immediately not attracted to them,' you bemoan to Lillie inside the kitchen of George's parents' house in Muswell Hill where the two of them are temporarily living. 'Like, we've wasted hours having this protracted dialogue on WhatsApp which could have been short-circuited if we'd just met for one second in real life.'

'So then just meet them without messaging so much,' she replies, taking a wonky kiwi out of an assorted box of misshapen fruit and absent-mindedly picking at its skin.

'Well, no, cause I've tried that too and it's an even bigger fail. At least this way, even if the attraction's not there, we've got our conversation history as back-up.'

'Yeah, I get the predicament. Do you want some ham, by the way?' she asks, pointing to a leg of Iberico on the side of the counter.

'Why do you have that?'

'George's parents got given it as a pearl anniversary present.'

'Wouldn't oysters have been more appropriate?'

'That's what I said. Anyhow, we're all hammed out, so I've been instructed to ply anyone and everyone with it.'

'Grim.' You are alarmed by the ease with which Lillie has assimilated into this grown-up environment, feel as though you are losing her to bougie hams and ethical fruit subscriptions. When did your lives become so subtly yet vastly different?

'Do you think these men ever feel let down by you when you meet?' she asks.

'I'm sure they do. Also, just to be clear, it's not about looks, it's about chemistry.'

'Sure.'

'Why are you smiling?'

'I'm just not convinced the disappointment's reciprocal.'

'Sweet, I appreciate the ego boost but I actually think my ego is part of the problem, like it makes me feel entitled to all the things.'

'What are the things?'

'Physical attraction, emotional connection, a shared sense of humour and values, minimum my level of intelligence but preferably higher, ideally financially stable . . . shall I go on? Actually that's it.'

'That's just standard stuff. I don't think you're being picky, I just think you need to be more savvy, like FaceTime them before you arrange to meet.'

'A bit weird but I'd actually be up for that if they'd go for it. Not a bad idea.'

'Great, now I can go on your Tinder as my reward.'

'No you can't.'

'Oh, come on, why would you deny me the most fun game?'

'Because it's my actual life?' You try to sound amused as though you are willingly making a joke at your own expense, but feel frustrated by Lillie's insinuation that your single status holds any genuine allure.

'Too funny,' she says, but in a more sober tone than before. 'Go on, I'll find you someone good, I promise.'

'You've got as long as it takes me to wee,' you say, conceding and sliding your phone across the table. 'And don't swipe right just cause they've got a puppy. It messes with the algorithm.'

You resolve to put Lillie's FaceTime suggestion into action following a final date you have scheduled for that evening. Therefore, naturally this date happens to be with someone who you not only find attractive and intelligent but who also lives locally and shares like-minded views.

It seems that every man you go out with is a direct reaction to the man who preceded him. While Frank is unfashionable and uninhibited, Patrick is trendy and affected; not in a grandiose sense but in the way that his unwavering hipster dress and demeanour – designed to look haphazard – seem to derive from a substantial amount of forethought. You wonder how differently Patrick might behave were he to follow his impulses: would he still pour the porridge oats out of the cardboard box and into a glass storage jar? Might he occasionally watch a rom-com or wear colour?

He works in digital marketing for a brand-design agency who all have photos of themselves as toddlers on the company website. He confesses he has little knowledge of theatre or the arts but is engaged when you speak and asks questions regarding your work. He's also pretty to look at, and although his thighs are smaller than yours and you suspect he weighs less than you, he's what you and Lillie refer to as 'a throwdown'; during sex he takes on a level of conviction he doesn't otherwise seem to possess.

Unlike Zach, who made his stance on relationships clear from the start, you don't know where Patrick stands.

'So . . . are you looking for anything official? Or just wanting to keep things casual,' you ask, two months into dating, angling yourself towards him on the sofa inside your living room.

Attempting indifference, you stretch your arms out to pluck the strings of the broken banjo beside you as you wait for his response. In the seven and a half years you've now been living here, the house has acquired further miscellaneous objects thanks to the stream of creative tenants passing through its doors, so that alongside the bath and banjo there is currently a giant papier-mâché head of Mr Blobby and half a table-tennis table propped against the wall (the explanation for which you're currently unsure of).

Patrick shrugs and reaches to top up his wine glass. 'If it turns into something more, then that's cool, but let's just have a thing and see what happens.'

This response had satisfied you that evening, but since then, another month has passed and there is no sense of growth or forward momentum; in reality, your 'thing' has not only plateaued but begun to decline.

Whereas at the beginning he'd been happy to schedule dates in advance, he is now increasingly slow to respond to your messages, leaving you wondering whether or not to factor him into your plans. The confusing thing for you is that he rarely says no to your suggestions, but it does feel as though he's waiting to see if a more appealing offer materializes before he accepts yours. You wonder if he is concurrently dating anyone else, or if his reluctance to commit midway through the week to seeing you on a Friday night is a general sense of not wanting to miss out on whatever his friends are up to. But if he liked you enough this wouldn't matter, would it? You have plenty of good friends you enjoy hanging out with, yet, at this age and stage of your life, the idea of prioritizing them over a man you're interested in is admittedly unlikely. You start to question whether he is using you for sex, and think the moment you have cause to even wonder this, it is probably happening.

One of his housemates invites you to her thirtieth birthday and you go along, can't work out how Patrick feels about the fact you're there, and so decide to introduce yourself to people you don't know rather than join in his conversations. You end up having fun and are pleased you've made a good impression when one of the group says to you at the end of the night, 'Fingers crossed we see you again, if Patrick manages not to fuck this up,' but also feel hurt that Patrick hasn't spoken to you the entire evening, only finally addressing you when he shuts the door to his room at three a.m.

You call Romily as you leave his house the following morning feeling hollow, as though you're a pumpkin whose flesh has been scooped out.

'Sorry, but this guy clearly isn't good enough for you,' she says in no uncertain terms and you suspect there's truth in this, but her relationship with Alec has been so unusually fast and committed that you don't feel it's fair to hold them up as a benchmark. Keen to deflect her attention, you ask, 'Have you told Mum and Dad yet? About the test results.'

'I've told Mum. I find it weird discussing my fertility with Dad.'

'Fair. And what did she say?'

'She's obviously delighted. Cares way more about the imminent prospect of becoming a grandmother than she does about my lost youth.'

'Thirty-three's not *that* young to try for a baby.'

'That's what I thought when I was twenty-nine but now I'm freaking out.'

'Why don't you wait a year or at least a couple more months, then?' A petulant part of you is now panicking at the prospect of Romily becoming pregnant. You have already felt your lives inching apart – the couple dinner parties and early-morning bike rides that have replaced the house parties and hungover brunches – but motherhood? This will seismically shift the terrain of your relationship.

'Well, no, that's exactly what we've been told we can't do. The top line is if we know we want them, which we do, it's now or never.'

'Christ. Just all of it. When did this thing that felt inevitable growing up become this daily source of angst?'

'I can't help feeling we're talking about you again.' Romily is right that you are projecting your own concerns on to her predicament and that, in addition to finding a partner, you now have twinges of anxiety regarding your fertility.

'Look,' she says. 'Not to use your own quotes back at you but you once told me to start dating guys I could imagine being dads. I'm just going to leave that hanging.'

Lillie takes a more diplomatic approach regarding Patrick when you sound her out in a cafe in Holborn around the corner from City Lit where she has just begun an eight-week film-making course.

'I agree it doesn't sound great, but remember it took a while before things properly got going with me and George,' she says, tearing open the cellophane wrapper of her baguette.

'A while? More like an age. I'll be thirty in a few months; my threshold for game-playing is pretty low at this point.'

'I'm not saying you need to game-play.' She removes a ring of red onion from the tuna filling before continuing. 'But you said yourself you've been playing it a bit cool as well, right?'

'Relatively. But I reckon my cool is probably his version of intense.'

'All the same. Maybe if you're holding your cards close to your chest then he might think you're not that into him either.'

'Do you actually think that or are you just saying it to make me feel better?'

'Bit of both. But it's possible, isn't it? That you're matching each other's vibe.'

'I guess,' you say, wanting – more than believing – her to be right.

The following week Patrick goes to Germany for a trade fair, is gone for six days and doesn't message you the entire time he's there. While he's away you consider that it was you who first messaged him on Tinder, you who first suggested meeting in person, you who's initiated almost every date since – resigning yourself to the fact that after a quarter of a year spent seeing him, it's definitively time to move on.

It would be satisfying to say that following this moment of clarity, you end things with him but, in fact, you do see him again, just one more time. The final thread is an invisible one that breaks not by anything he does that particular morning as he leaves your house, but by a series of threads that have been unravelling ever since the first night you stayed at his and didn't hear from him again until you messaged him three days later. As he delivers his ever-casual goodbye, a shrug and the line, 'See you soon, then,' something inside you snaps. 'See you,' you say curtly, knowing you won't message him again, and you don't.

It's after things finish with Patrick that you take pause, acknowledging that in your efforts to make it work with him, you've neglected your own friendships and interests. You start swimming in the local reservoir, go on a day-trip to Whitstable with Lillie and Ishani (where you once again try to enjoy the taste of oysters but get no further than indifference), call your old schoolfriends who you feel increasingly disconnected from as their lives branch off at ever growing distances to yours but who continue to care deeply about you, and vice versa.

One morning at the start of March, you set your alarm for five a.m. and catch the bus to Bank where you get on the DLR to Canary Wharf and walk from there to Billingsgate Market in the dark. Wren had told you about Billingsgate years ago and promised to take you there. Ever since, you'd always imagined doing the outing with a partner, in proof that you'd moved on – that your life was markedly different to how it was when he left you at twenty-two. But when you'd mentioned it to Oliver he'd objected to the early-morning start, and so you'd waited ever since, holding out to share the experience with someone of note, and, in doing so, represent evidence of progression (which your career choice has so far failed to provide).

You have come here today by yourself in acceptance that you will no longer wait for someone else to permit you certain experiences, to recognize that moments in life, such as visiting a covered fish market alone at dawn, are as much a part of living as traditional milestones, even if there is no greeting card to mark the occasion.

Inside the floodlit hall, the wet floor is slippery and thrilling beneath your trainers. You walk past rows of gaping-mouthed fish, unnerved by their tiny sharp teeth and shocked wide eyes, until you find a man selling octopi. You haggle with him, remembering the advice of your father in a Tunisian market you'd visited as a teenager, 'Never take their second price either,' and carry it home in a white plastic bag as the sun comes up above the city. You put it in the fridge and go back to sleep until midday.

Later that afternoon, you remove the octopus from its bag and hold it over the sink by its head, its tentacles dangling like wet grey tights. After you have boiled it, you begin chopping it into pieces; its pink flesh is soft and hot and makes you think of a foetus. This is the part you'd withdraw from if you had embarked on the process with a partner, but because you are alone and reason you cannot leave a partially dismembered mollusc inside your communal kitchen, you persist.

Romily calls halfway through the procedure and you put her on speaker.

'Can you talk?'

'Not hugely. I'm dissecting an octopus.'

'Random. Can you pause?'

'I kind of need to push on through if I'm going to finish.'

'OK, well I'll keep it brief. You're going to be an aunt.'

You feel adrenaline coursing through you as your face breaks into an involuntary beam. 'Oh my god, this is so good and so massive. It is good, right? I mean, you're happy?'

'I'm so happy. I'm also so relieved I'm so happy.' Curiously, Romily's comment articulates your own feelings – your relief that you are delighted by the news, rather than in any way resentful.

'What about the tests?' you ask, suddenly confused. 'I thought they said it would take ages.'

'I know. I'd call the clinic and complain if we weren't so fucking thrilled.'

'Rom, this is the best,' you say, feeling additionally reassured for your own fertility. 'What does Alec say?'

'He's bawling his eyes out but he says hi.'

'Tell him hi back and huge congrats.'

'I will do. I've got to go, Mum's calling.'

'Does she know already?'

'I literally just got off the phone to her.'

'She's probably done a quick google of schools with the best Ofsted in your catchment.'

'Like actually, though.'

Romily ends the call and you begin to cry with the bigness of your joy, but it is tinged with sadness – the knowledge that things are going to change, for better and for worse, with or without your choosing.

That night, you grill the octopus with lemon and paprika and lay it on a ceramic dish embedded with butterbean puree. Later, you will read about how clever they are, that their intelligence means they can solve puzzles – the kind you have no aptitude for – and will feel ashamed about eating such a creature. But tonight, you feel proud and grown up as you lay it on the table and hear the chorus of compliments from your housemates which subdues the voice inside your head saying, *Yes you have produced an octopus dinner but your sister has produced an embryo. These feats are not of equivalent value.*

So much of your yearning derives from comparison – although how much exactly, you're unsure. Presumably you would still want a partner and a thriving career even if nobody around you had either of these things, but by pitting yourself against Romily and Lillie you are not even giving yourself a chance at happiness. This obvious realization fills you with self-compassion. Unsure where to channel it, you press your hands together palm to palm, but the gesture feels too much like a prayer. 'Eat!' you announce instead.

11. Noah

In the subsequent months, you work on cultivating yourself without the aid of a man, beginning by subscribing to the *New Yorker* and *New Scientist*, realizing you can extract knowledge in areas that you and your friends aren't well versed in from sources other than the men you are sleeping with. As you consume the information in front of you and spend time walking alone with podcasts and your thoughts, you feel yourself growing, as though your sinews are being stretched. Sometimes the sensation is uncomfortable but it's a satisfying kind of discomfort, comparable to a workout session or being waxed. In truth, you would trade growth for happiness but will accept the currency that is presently on offer.

Reluctant to get into debt by taking a third show to Edinburgh, you conclude that the financial model of the Fringe is unsustainable; for a fraction of the cost you could hire a fringe theatre in London and focus on building a loyal audience following, rather than competing with thousands of other performers during the same three weeks of the year as you all stack up multiple credit cards in the hope of luring producers and commissioners through the door.

This change of direction precipitates your decision that, after almost a decade working as an usher, it is time to get a more lucrative source of income if you ever hope to obtain a mortgage or a pension – the desire for which had unoriginally arrived to coincide with your thirtieth birthday. Thanks to your transferrable communication skills, the recruiter you sign up with lands you a part-time sales job at an advertising firm who are looking for 'a dynamic and persuasive candidate' to join their new-business team three days a week. Based in Shoreditch, on the fifth floor of a converted warehouse, the office is brightly lit with exposed bulbs hanging from the ceiling on multicoloured wires. Its Crittall windows provide a sweeping view of the city that pleasingly makes you feel part of something, even if this 'something' has no obvious social, moral or artistic value. The company's co-founders – two public-school boys both called Harry – keenly refer to themselves and the business as 'quirky' and as a result are encouraging of your acting career, allowing you to take time off for castings, which although increasingly sparse, reliably arrive at ludicrously late notice.

It's probably no coincidence that now your attention is focused on other areas of your life, Noah enters the scene.

There's a new-writing night called Off the Record that you regularly go along to and occasionally perform at. It's produced by a friend of yours who has a monthly Sunday residency at a small studio theatre in Peckham. The night has garnered a cult following since its inception eighteen months ago, so that the black-box space is now often crammed and overheated with audience standing at the back; you don't mind the sweat of the other bodies, think it only adds to the atmosphere.

The premise of the night is that six playwrights each write a ten-minute piece inspired by a well-known music album, and that's how you know about Noah who's one of the show's core writers. His plays routinely make you laugh by catching you off-guard, the comedy firing in without warning rather than after an obvious set-up. They're not just funny, though; buried within them is always a sharply observed social commentary. The couple of times you've chatted to him in the bar after the show he's been friendly but reserved, almost formal, leaving you unsure whether he has any real interest in the conversation or is just being polite. In any case, you don't pursue him as you know he's involved with another actress in the company and therefore consider him to be off-limits.

But then two things coincide; you go along to watch that month's show inspired by Pink Floyd's *The Dark Side of the Moon* in which his play turns out to be your favourite, and later that night in the bar your friend mentions that he is no longer involved with this other actress, that things have been amicably over between them for a couple of months now. And so you wait until he is briefly unaccompanied before approaching and congratulating him on his piece in which two newly graduated unemployed friends break into an office to experience what it's like to have jobs, only to discover they're unable to leave because of an invisible force shutting them in. It had definitely been the most entertaining play of the night and had left you thinking about it after it had finished, so that you found yourself not really listening to the piece that directly followed it.

'Hey, so just between you and me, I thought yours was the best tonight.'

'Really? That's awesome.' It's endearing to you that he makes no attempt to flirt or respond with anything other than genuine surprise and pleasure. 'Thanks, Margot.'

Bolstered by the fact he's remembered your name, you add, 'It was dark but funny. Kind of reminded me of a Pinter play.'

'Pinter's my hero so that's the highest form of praise.'

You like how he doesn't doubt your judgement – think his ability to take a compliment at face value must be because he's Canadian and has therefore been taught self-belief rather than self-deprecation.

'The invisible force was a metaphor, right?'

'Sure.'

'So, what did it represent for you when you were writing it?'

'What did it represent for you when you were watching it?' he asks, smiling.

'Fair question,' you say with a laugh. 'I guess I've got three theories. Either money, status, or something like rungs on the career ladder. Basically all the things that keep people trapped in office jobs they want to get out of.'

'Totally. I mean, I think it's all and any of those things.'

'I liked that the ending was unpredictable, that it didn't go where I thought it was going to go.'

'Yeah, I've read a ton of books on structure but I get kinda bored watching classic narrative arcs. I write to keep myself interested, I guess.' You think the last part of his answer is sublime.

'So, what's the theatre scene like in Canada?'

'Erm, put it this way, can you name any Canadian play-wrights?'

'Robert Lepage?'

'Sure, apart from Lepage. Name me one other and I'll buy you a drink.'

'Um . . . Noah Belanger.'

'Ha! Very charming. What are you having?'

You stay and drink with him and the rest of the company until the bar closes. As you pile out on to the street and there's talk of going on to a cocktail bar up the road, you wait to see if he'll join – overhear him telling your friend that he has a brunch tomorrow morning with his mother who's flying in that night on a business trip from Montreal and that once he starts on the whiskey it'll be downhill from there. He comes over to say goodbye to you and this time seems to linger as if he doesn't want to leave your company. Reasoning that you have nothing to lose other than your pride, which has never yet been enough to stop you doing anything of importance, you say, 'You could take my number if you like?'

He laughs and says, 'I would like. Very much.'

Energized by his response, you end up going on to the cocktail bar and are surprised when you get a message from him while you're still there.

Regretting not staying for that nightcap

You send him a photo of your whiskey sour with the caption, *Not to rub it in but . . .*

I think you just did, he replies.

You end up messaging throughout the rest of the evening and keep up this same density of texting over the next couple of days, following which he says he'd like to take you out to dinner when his mother leaves town on Thursday, if you're keen and willing, which you absolutely are. You even enjoy the two further days of waiting time, think there's a romance and a properness to the lack of immediacy which would have ordinarily frustrated you; is your patience a result of ageing and maturity, you wonder, or just of having been messed around by Zach and Patrick, that you now welcome Noah's respectful approach?

The afternoon of the date, you shave your legs with uncustomary precision so as not to nick the grooves around your knees and ankles. Rubbing scented moisturizer into your calves and thighs, your skin looks thick and white like the layer of fat on a gammon. You undertake this procedure solely for your own benefit; you've already decided you're not going to sleep with him even if the moment presents itself. As much as you would like to believe that having sex on your first date will not minimize the likelihood of a relationship developing, you don't care to gamble your future happiness on proving this theory to be correct.

He asks you to meet him at a canalside restaurant in Haggerston and when you arrive he's there waiting at an outside table, dressed in an open-neck white shirt, sunglasses perched on his head. The luminescent sky is streaked with charcoal. You can't help assessing how of all the men you've been out with, you are physically most drawn to Noah. Six foot and perfectly proportioned, he has the ideal body for an actor: a blank template on which to imprint a character. Does he know his physique and good looks are wasted on being a playwright? His blond hair is woven with strands of grey which only add to its texture and his green eyes look intermittently hazel. When he sleeps he makes a fist with his hand and clutches the top of his head, looks like a Rodin statue, but of course you don't know this yet, don't yet know that this near-stranger is about to become the most significant man in your life to date.

Standing to greet you, he kisses you on the cheek, doesn't sit down again until you're seated. Although unversed in his background, you note the way he instinctively lays his napkin on his lap and says, 'Excuse me,' after he clears his throat, suggesting a level of etiquette superior to your own – but he's relaxed and loose to be around. At one point you get tahini on the underside of your arm while reaching across the table for more water; he takes hold of your elbow to lift up your arm and uses a piece of bread to remove it, saying, 'I might eat that later if we run out of dip,' making your insides feel like foam.

When you've finished the meal which he insists on paying for, promising he'll let you get the next one, you say, 'OK, you've shown me your haunt. How about I take you somewhere with whiskey and noise?' Your need to impress him feels both vital and silly.

'Lead the way.'

But after fifteen minutes of walking along the towpath towards Broadway Market, the now-black sky starts to pour. You take shelter under a tree for a few minutes, waiting to see if it will stop, until he turns to you and says, 'What do you reckon? Happy to make a run for it, if you are.'

You once read in an online article that the way someone deals with tangled Christmas lights is indicative of their broader personality. Similarly, you think Noah's light-hearted, gung-ho approach to the rain suggests an adventurous and positive temperament – something you keenly want from a partner.

By the time you make it to the bar, your clothes are stuck to your skin as though thin cotton wetsuits. Staring at each other, your panting and laughter give way to desire and he pulls you into his torso where you press yourself to him. Tucked in his arms under the red neon sign above your head, you feel delicate and compact like a succulent. As your lips break apart, you cup your hand in front of your mouth and hold it there.

'Damn, was it that bad?' he asks.

'I'm trying to stop smiling.'

'Why would you do that?'

'So . . . I can play it cool?'

'Hm. That's kinda problematic cause I really want to kiss you again.'

You take your hand away and he kisses your smile, making you feel you are being folded into origami.

Leaving the bar later that night, he asks if you'd like to come back to his place, doesn't ask again when you force yourself to smile and shake your head, only asks when he can next see you.

'I'm free next weekend?'

'Then let's do next weekend.'

'Great, which night?'

'All the nights.' You laugh and he says, 'What? I'm serious. Let's spend the weekend together.'

'Start with Friday and see how we go?'

'Friday to Monday it is. I'll see you then.'

You assume he's joking, discover he's sincere when he messages midweek, *You take care of Friday? I'll hatch a plan for Saturday and Sunday.* As you type *deal*, you wonder if you ought to remain cautious in order to protect yourself, but know you won't. There's probably lots about love you still don't understand but know by now that fear is pointless, that its only guarantee is loneliness. Besides, he gives you no reason to be anything other than trusting. He doesn't ask to reschedule or cancel, or become distant in his messages, and the fact that you have sex repeatedly that weekend changes nothing and everything. Nothing – in that he in no way gives you cause to think that sex is now his primary interest in you – and everything in that it completes and confirms your compatibility.

Three weeks into dating him you go on holiday with your parents, Romily and Alec. You speak every night on the phone – Noah from the study of his two-storey flat in Highgate, you from the roof terrace of an apartment in Puglia.

When your mother asks on the third morning who you've been speaking to, ordinarily you'd be vague but you surprise yourself.

'His name's Noah. We've only been seeing each other a few weeks but I don't know, it feels different to the times before.'

'Maybe I'll get to meet him at some point,' she says, failing to disguise her hopefulness as she turns back to her novel, her pursed lips twitching with restraint not to bombard you with questions.

For six days, the five of you go swimming in the mornings and read under rented parasols. When the sun gets too hot even in the shade, you come back to the cool-stoned apartment and eat thick plaits of braided mozzarella and sweet yellow bread that tastes like cake. Your father buys anchovies in oil from the market which are so salty they make your lips sting but it all feels so idyllic that you appreciate this semblance of pain. After lunch you sleep until the heat subsides, and at sunset put on sandals to walk to the cluster of restaurants in the square which serve fresh seafood and orecchiette with garlic and olive oil.

Nobody argues and nobody cries, leading your mother to conclude on the penultimate night that it's been the most successful family holiday in years.

'It ain't over till the fat lady sings,' says your father, sucking on the orange slice from his empty glass of Campari soda.

'That's fat-shaming,' says Romily, pressing her hand against the compact bump protruding from her slender frame. 'I don't care, I'm just telling you what's woke.'

'Thank you for educating me.'

'That's a first,' she says, turning to Alec who laughs and then smiles at your father, having mastered the art of appeasing them both.

'How about the contoured lady? Is that allowed?' asks your father, breaking into operatic song before your mother shushes him.

'Michael, the noise.'

'Anita, we're in Italy, it's all noise.' He kisses her across the table and she looks pleased that her attempt to quash his enthusiasm has been thwarted. It feels golden, the five of you all together – all in good health and at happy stages of your lives. You're struck by the preciousness of this, but resist the urge to comment on it, knowing your earnestness will be met with irony from the rest of your family. As you stare at Romily's bump, you feel an excitement as well as a responsibility towards your unborn nephew; placing your palm over her stomach, you make a silent promise never to undermine him and to always listen to him, to really listen. Not yet knowing anything about his character, this feels suitably broad as an offering.

Later that evening, you climb the four concrete steps up on to the roof to call Noah, and find your father positioned on the edge of the terrace, staring up at the lapis-blue sky. You stand next to him, feeling the hairs of your arms touching in the cool breeze.

'I hope you're not considering flying.'

'I thought I'd save that for tomorrow night.'

'You're drunk,' you say with surprise, observing his dilated pupils and forced precision of his speech. 'You always claim you can't get drunk.'

'I still maintain that,' he says, deliberately swaying and slurring his words, making you laugh. 'Your mother tells me you have a man on the scene.'

'I rarely *don't* have a man on the scene. But I think she's hoping this one's of note.'

He smiles, turning back to look out over the flat rooftops filled with silver satellite dishes.

Over the years you've found it easiest to converse with your father if you imagine him as a stranger at a dinner party who you are attempting to entertain, rather than to infiltrate the back catalogue of his joys and regrets.

'That's a pretty spectacular sky,' you say, gazing into the night as you exhale deeply.

'I've never understood that expression.'

'Do you need me to break it down for you?' You expect him to match your mocking tone but he continues with a rare openness.

'It's like when people say, "She's got spectacular eyes." Sure, there are varying degrees of beauty, but at baseline, aren't all skies spectacular?'

'Actually,' you say, turning to look at him, 'I don't disagree.'

'Still said with a double negative,' he says, smiling.

'I'm just appealing to my audience. I know he withers without combat.'

Your father laughs proudly, is always seemingly fondest of you in moments when you use wit to undermine him. The two of you stand in silence, and just as you are about to break it, he says, 'When you were a few weeks old, I took you out for a walk one evening around the block, just the two of us. It was maybe seven or eight o'clock, that shift between day and night. I looked up at this expanse of pink and orange and white and decided I wanted to hold you up to it. I don't know, it just seemed like the most obvious thing for you to be surrounded by this mass of coloured air and light. I took you out of your pram and dangled you up there. It must have been all you could see and feel, and you started to cry. Not a normal baby wail like you'd done before, but a howl that shook your whole tiny body like grief. I've never been able to disassociate the two things – you and the sky.'

'Are you trying to tell me I'm spectacular?' you ask, your throat pulsing as you fight not to cry. He stays looking up and out, frowning in contemplation as you mentally craft his desired response.

And so, of course when he says, 'I'd no longer presume to tell you anything about yourself,' the line feels anticlimactic because that's what happens when you script people's responses as if they are characters, but still you do it anyway.

The following afternoon you go directly from City airport to Noah's flat where he hoists you over his shoulder and begins carrying you up the stairs, stopping to catch his breath as you clutch the banister, heavy with laughter. Afterwards, you stay wrapped in a yellow sheet while Noah fetches a bottle of wine; your skin feels soft and fuzzy like a peach.

'Hey, so my old school buddy Conor called while you were away.' He pulls out the cork and tosses it into the air where it lands next to you on the bed. 'He's invited me to stay with him at his holiday home next month. Wanna come?'

The ease of his invitation makes you stretch out your arms languidly. 'Sure, where is it?'

'Northern Ireland, but like rural Northern Ireland.'

'Proper countryside? Fun.'

'Oh yeah, it's like full-on rainboot territory.'

'Great, I'll need to get some.'

'I'll get you some.'

'Why would you buy my shoes for me?'

'Because I want to.'

'Sweet, but I don't think that qualifies as a reason.'

'OK, I won't. On an unrelated note, what's your boot size?'

You throw the cork at him and try taking a swig of wine but your smile obstructs you.

That Sunday you host a lunch to introduce Noah to your friends, appeasing Romily who's staying with Alec's family in Aberdeen that weekend by promising her a separate dinner date later in the week.

'Cute,' says Lillie, examining the bowl of orecchiette you've brought back from Puglia. 'They look like mini tortoiseshells.'

'Apparently they're named after little ears.'

'Big ears get all the bad press but I reckon really small ones would look equally weird.'

'You could hide them better, though.'

'This is true,' she says, looking up at the clock next to the fridge. 'What time is he getting here?'

'I told him to come for one.'

'I can't believe you're not going to let me interrogate him before the others arrive.'

'I figured you were going to do that anyway, so I'd spare him a double round.'

Your doorbell rings and Lillie grins. 'I'll get it. Hopefully he's early.'

As you remove a tray of roasted pine nuts from the oven, you hear the sound of Ishani and Lillie cackling in the hallway, feeling a warmth for facilitating the occasion.

'I'm dying to meet the American boy,' says Ishani as she enters, presenting you with a bottle of wine.

'He's Canadian. And not far off forty.'

'Such a fiend for accuracy,' she says, stroking your vintage floral shirt in approval as Lillie's phone pings.

'George is held up at the storage unit. Says his ETA is more like one fifteen.'

'When do you guys move into your new place?' Ishani asks, removing the screw cap from the wine and pouring herself a glass.

'Six days and thirteen hours.'

'Not that you're counting or anything.'

'Not to sound ungracious but I seriously need out.'

'No caveat needed. I've been back at my parents' for four years now. It's wrong and unnatural.'

'But oh so sweetly cheap,' says Lillie, holding out her glass.

'Right. That's the bind.'

'Can you two stop complaining about your subsidized rent set-ups and lay the table, please?'

'Is she going to be this strict with us all lunch?'

'I don't know about you but rules make me want to misbehave.'

'Absolutely,' says Lillie, moving to open the cutlery drawer. 'How many are we total?'

'Six if Oliver comes, but I doubt he'll make it. He's moving out of Sophie's place this weekend.'

'I didn't know they'd broken up,' says Ishani. 'That's sad.'

'I still think it's amazing he ever moved in,' says Lillie.

'Hey, so if Oliver's not coming then presumably nothing's off-limits conversationally and we can really get stuck in,' says Ishani, eyebrows raised.

'Guys, don't make me regret this.'

'No, but this is actually great for you cause we can ask all the awkward questions you really want to know the answers to but don't want to ask.'

'Yeah, like why did you break up with your exes—'

'And how many people have you slept with—'

'And do you have unresolved issues with your mother, et cetera.'

The doorbell rings and the two of them look at each other before simultaneously running to get it.

As they re-enter, flanking Noah on either side, Lillie asks, 'So I hear you're taking Margot to stay with your friends next month. Based on first impressions, are we more or less fun than them?'

'Oh, resolutely more,' says Noah, not missing a beat.

'Off to a good start,' says Ishani, winking at you.

'Now for the crucial question. What's your opinion on dogs? Not just puppies, even old ill rescue dogs?'

'I'm a fan. The older and mangier the better.'

'Yep, he's a keeper,' says Lillie.

Noah catches your eye and says, 'That's good, cause I'm planning on sticking around.'

Conor's holiday home turns out to be a seventeenth-century castle with grey stone turrets set among sprawling grounds.

'Er, what school did you guys go to?' you ask Noah as you're shown to your room, furnished with an ornate four-poster bed, off to the side of it an en suite containing a freestanding cast-iron bath.

'Lakefield College in Ontario.' You look at him blankly and he adds, 'You know Toronto? It's about a ninety-minute drive east of there.'

'Sure, I meant what kind of school? I know you boarded but are we talking like along with royals and sons of sheikhs?'

'There were a few of those, but no, it's mainly popular with military families. Conor's dad was a colonel in the British Army based out in Alberta for a while.'

'Right.'

Three other couples are also staying at the castle, forming a group of ten adults including Conor and his wife, along with half a dozen children. Apart from Noah and a pale-skinned Ethiopian woman who's supremely calm and almost regal when she speaks, the other seven of them sound inherently British – all share the same tight 'o' vowel sound you associate with Conservative politicians, which makes sense when you learn that they were schooled at the most elite institutions across the country, unlike you who attended a co-educational comprehensive in Norwich.

Intrigued that Conor wears a tartan kilt to dinner – or rather 'supper' – every night, you ask if he considers himself to be Irish to which he replies, 'Anglo-Irish,' and goes on to tell you that the castle has been in his family for twelve generations – that, along with money, it takes effort and creativity to keep this sort of place going. And what a pharaonic place it is, the kind you have only ever entered on school trips or family outings to National Trust properties, so that you cannot quite believe you are residing there as a guest. At points throughout the stay, you look at Conor's five-year-old son, how at ease he is inside this castle he will presumably inherit, and realize that he will likely grow up thinking such things are normal.

Despite being a holiday, there is a daily schedule of activities which everyone is expected to throw themselves into; you do so willingly, bemused and open to all the new experiences on offer. Breakfast – an Ulster fry – is served at seven a.m., followed by a bracing swim in the lough, and 'snug time' which you mistakenly think will mean reading your book, but entails a raucous game of squashed sardines, after which the exhausted and exhilarated children are quickly fed lunch and put down for their naps.

When the adults have eaten and consumed liberal quantities of Sancerre, the children are woken and there is an afternoon boat trip back out on the lough – involving songs and chants you don't know but do your best to sing along with – or croquet on the lawn if it doesn't rain. The men play golf every other morning while the women stay and help the nannies entertain the children. Noah asks, concerned, if you mind him leaving you on these golfing mornings but you assure him you're happy playing with the children, chatting with the nannies and trying to make a good impression with the wives who regard you with warm curiosity.

The evening meal comprises several courses of food and wine prepared by the chef who lives in the local village, and often features the bream and pike caught on the boat that afternoon. Although there are lots of opinions shared around the dining table that you disagree with, you remind yourself that it would not only be rude but also hypocritical to rant against the inequalities of capitalism when you are being so generously hosted by strangers who have welcomed you into their home. And so you largely keep your views to yourself, choosing to speak out only on select occasions when it feels most appropriate or relevant and even then not with any particular force but with an intended wit and softness that you hope will be agreeable. You're not sure whether these moments of presenting the opposing viewpoint are for your own integrity or whether you genuinely think you might alter any of the group's opinions. On the final morning, the men go into a side room with panelled walls to collate tips for the staff while the women clear the breakfast table. As Conor's wife removes a teaspoon from the marmalade and places the jar on to a tray with an assortment of other spreads, she says in a tinkling voice, 'It's as though feminism never happened,' and you and the other wives all laugh but you're not sure why it constitutes a joke, rather than an accurate observation.

Although Noah shows no desire to replicate Conor's lifestyle, he doesn't appear to be daunted by it, making you wonder if perhaps his own upbringing was not so dissimilar, although of course a Canadian equivalent. You know Noah is wealthy – that he owns his flat in London thanks to shares in his late grandfather's global investment firm, of which his mother is a current director – but now you start to probe further, learning that the school he boarded at was the same one his father and father's father attended, and that while his family home is in a suburb of Montreal, most summers and Christmases were spent at their family's lakeside cabin in the Laurentian Mountains, skiing in Mont-Tremblant and water-skiing on Lac Mercier. Yes, he confirms in answer to your questions, he knows how to row and ride and sail. You are conscious of not wanting to sound either too impressed or intimidated by his answers, but privately feel as though you have been dropped into an alternative universe of yachts and summer houses, of couples in tennis whites and children on horseback.

Just as you are finalizing this image of his affluent childhood, you are offered the chance to view it for yourself. It's a fortnight after returning from Northern Ireland, and you are sitting at Noah's kitchen table, your legs stretched out on the chair in front of you as you circle the wine inside your glass with small movements of your wrist, watching him chopping a leek at speed.

'So, I spoke to my mom today about joining them at the lake cabin next month,' he says offhandedly. 'What do you reckon? Fancy it?'

You stop making your wine swirl and look up at him. 'Seriously?'

'Sure, why not?' he says, taking a steel saucepan from the set hanging above the hob.

'I mean . . . I'd love to, I just can't really afford to. Plus, I've used up all my holiday so I'd have to ask the Harrys for unpaid leave.'

'You don't need to worry about paying for anything,' he says over the hiss of melting butter. 'My mom's already insisted she'll take care of the flights and we'll just be staying at the cabin. No pressure, but if that changes anything then you could check if you can get the time off?'

'Erm. OK. I mean, wow, then yes. Yes please.'

It's all so easy and possible. Is this what it feels like to have such vast sums of money? Not only thrilling and liberating but, more than anything, enabling.

You've never flown business-class before, are too exhilarated by the experience to eat much of the food which is laid out on a white linen tablecloth with silver plane-shaped salt and pepper shakers. You allow the air steward to top up your wine glass before remembering you want to be alert on landing and so switch to sparkling water, even though you prefer still but want to be the kind of woman who drinks sparkling, who prefers black coffee to white, dark chocolate to milk, wonder if you can train your taste buds to cooperate.

Noah hires a car from the airport to drive the hour and a half from Montreal to Mont-Tremblant. It's so hot that you keep the windows shut and blast the air-con, but every twenty minutes or so lean your head outside to feel the wind and speed of the highway. Your cheeks stick to your face like suction pads as you whizz past fir trees, telegraph poles, green road signs in French.

At some point the highway merges with another, smaller one and the steel safety barriers disappear, so that the wide expanse of tarmac is bound only by the forest on either side.

'Not long now, just another couple of minutes,' says Noah, forking left on to a gravel track lined with feathery cedar trees, strips of blue lake visible through their branches. 'You nervous? Don't be, by the way; they'll really like you.'

You feel slightly queasy but attribute this to the two glasses of Chenin blanc on a near-empty stomach and the turbulence on landing, rather than the fact you're about to meet your new boyfriend's parents – having done this too many times before to get worked up by it.

As he pulls into the drive, the lake is right in front of you, glistening in the late-afternoon sun. As for the house itself, so much for a lakeside cabin: it looks like a luxury resort on water. Built on an open-plan layout over three floors, its high cathedral ceilings and panoramic windows emit a biblical quality of light so that as you enter you wonder if you're about to undergo some kind of physical transformation.

'Mom?' Noah calls as you survey the interior. Everywhere you look, there's plush furniture, elegant lamps, classy woven rugs on the wooden flooring. The double doors of the main room lead on to a decked veranda where further down the sloped expanse of grass, dotted with several kayaks and a fire pit, is a private beach opening out on to the lake with a vista of maple trees and cyan sky.

'Noah?' A short Hispanic woman with soft-looking wrinkled skin leans over the pine banister on the upstairs landing.

'Hey, Alma. Good to see you,' he says warmly.

'Your mother's gone to get bulgur wheat.'

'Sure. How are you? You're looking well.'

'I lost five pounds.'

'Hey, that's great.'

'You get taller?'

'Ha, no, I think just the same size as last time.'

'So tall to me!'

'Alma, this is my girlfriend, Margot.'

'Hi, nice to meet you,' you say, trying to match Noah's cordiality.

She peers down, as if only now noticing you, and wags her finger. 'You tell him to stop growing.'

'OK, I'll do that,' you say with a laugh. 'Who is that?' you ask Noah, as she disappears into one of the upstairs rooms.

'Our housekeeper. She's been with us since I was a kid.'

'Oh.' You yourself experienced various childminders growing up, as well as a fortnightly cleaner who had done her best to dust the cluttered surfaces of your parents' house, but nevertheless the word 'housekeeper' denotes the significant contrast between yours and Noah's childhoods.

'So, what do you fancy? A drink, a nap, a tour?'

'Tour sounds good.'

'Sure, I'll just get the bags.' You start to follow but he insists, 'No, it's fine. You hang here, I'll be back in a sec.'

When he's gone you permit yourself a whispered 'wow', as you take in the tastefully framed artwork above the stone fireplace, the bowl of fruit stacked in a pyramid formation in the centre of the granite kitchen island; you feel as though you have wandered into a magazine, had no idea people actually lived like this.

'Sorry about the lack of a welcome,' Noah says as he re-enters with the bags thrust over each shoulder.

'I don't mind. I don't mind at all.'

'My mom'll be back soon. I guess my dad's taken the boat out. Want to head upstairs?'

You nod and he hoists the bags further up on to his shoulders, again refusing your offer of assistance.

The bedroom, with its panorama of the lake and king-size mattress displaying descending scatter cushions, leaves you quietly stunned.

'It's all just so nice. I mean, that's like a totally obvious and inadequate statement, I just . . .'

'It's pretty sickening, right? My grandparents bought the plot of land back when my dad was little. Everything I have is basically owing to that generation's savviness and foresight.'

'Including your humility?'

'If you mean my accurate perception, sure.'

You smile at his self-deprecation and follow him along the landing, past four more double bedrooms each with their own colour scheme, and a children's nursery containing a row of bunk beds.

'That's where we slept when we were kids. My nephews use it now.'

'Did you used to ride on that?' you ask, pointing to a dappled rocking horse with a worn ruby saddle.

'Sirius. I only got to ride him when my sister let me. By the time I was big enough to stand up to her, I'd outgrown him.'

'Well, that's tragic.'

'Yeah, well as you can see, I had a pretty deprived childhood.' You laugh and he puts his arms around you, kissing your forehead. 'Hungry?'

'Actually starving.'

'Let's go and see what we can find. Alma's guacamole is off the chain.'

'Noah? Is that you?' A low female voice, rich with gravitas, travels up the stairs.

'Ready to meet the folks?' he asks, grinning.

You feel a surge of nervous excitement as you tap your fingers across the door handle, hoping to appear blasé.

'Might as well, since we've come all this way.'

Unlike your own mother, whose interlocutory approach is to target people with facts and questions, Noah's mother has an indirect way of involving you in the conversation without requiring your input.

'I had an aunt called Margot,' she says, greeting you with a light touch on your shoulder and kissing you on the cheek. 'She was terribly attractive and terribly rich. Also wise enough to never marry.' Her poise and distaste for pleasantries leave you curiously shy and unsure how to respond.

'I've asked Alma to do roasted cod,' she says to Noah, hugging him with a gentle pat. The exchange feels oddly formal yet casual, as though they are acquaintances who recently left each other's company, rather than mother and son reunited after several months.

When you find yourself alone with her inside the kitchen the following morning, you ask if they come here often to the lake cabin. She turns from the sink where she's washing grapes in a colander, dressed in white linen trousers and an aqua silk scarf loosely knotted around her neck.

'Oh, usually a month in the summer and a week at Christmas and Thanksgiving,' she says, placing the colander on the draining board as she touches the base of her palm to her coiffed silvery-blonde hair.

'I was just thinking you could rent it out and make a fortune all the other weeks of the year you aren't using it.'

Her pale green eyes look briefly surprised before regaining their astute gaze.

'Why, yes, I suppose we could. That's a shrewd idea.' And you realize that they have no need to; they are wealthy enough to let this multimillion-pound staffed house sit empty for the majority of the year in order to avoid the faff of having strangers in their home, but Noah's mother is too couth to say this outright.

Despite her charm, she possesses an underlying steeliness you witness that lunchtime in her staunch support of a free-market economy and her vocal opposition to a wealth tax, arguing with Noah that it will drive business off Canadian soil. Watching him concede under her sharp reminder that this is 'her industry and not his', you are reminded that she sits on the board of an

international investment firm – a detail you might have otherwise forgotten.

'I think I thought your parents would be more pressuring
than they are,' you say to Noah late in the afternoon as the two
of you swim out to the square wooden raft on the lake, squint-
ing at the sunlight bouncing off the water.

'How do you mean?'

'Professionally. I guess I thought maybe they wouldn't support you being a writer cause, well, it doesn't exactly lend itself
to success, at least not in the traditional sense.'

'Ouch.'

'Hey, no, I didn't mean it like that.'

'No, it's cool, I get it.' While Noah is by no means unsuccess-
ful as a writer – has had commissions from the National Youth
Theatre as well as full-length runs of his plays at several fringe
theatres in London – he is still yet to write for an established theatre or make the move into television, a level of prestige he feels
would validate his chosen career path.

'There's not pressure, but there's an expectation,' he says,
frowning as he steps up the steel ladder and on to the raft, droplets of water sticking to his brown thighs. 'I mean, how could
there not be after all the money they've spent raising me? Sure,
I can pick my own field of interest, but I'm meant to succeed in
it. It's not an upbringing that sets you up to fail or even be aver-
age. Sorry, it sounds so dumb and self-pitying.'

'No it doesn't, it just sounds difficult.' You pull yourself up
the ladder and stand next to him, your toes curling around the
edge of the wood.

'Thanks, but I don't think the privileged have a right to
suffering.'

'Not to be glib, but don't the privileged have a right to
everything?'

He pushes you playfully and you grab his hand, the symmetry of your splashes as you land like porpoises jumping above water.

Noah's sister and her two children – six- and eight-year-old boys who look as though they have been plucked from an outdoor-pursuits clothing catalogue – arrive midway through the week, allowing you to observe conversation rather than having to constantly partake in it.

The following afternoon she walks out on to the decking in a halter navy swimming costume and matching Alice band, her blonde hair parted on either shoulder.

'I like your headband,' you say, looking up from your book as you try not to stare at her long, slender legs.

'Oh. Thanks.'

You hope she might ask what you're reading or comment on an item of your clothing in return, but her phone rings – a motif of the four days you spend with her – and she turns to answer her husband's call with a curtness that appears customary.

Noah's nephews are polite but largely uninterested in you. You predominantly see them at mealtimes; otherwise they seem to be permanently positioned inside the basement games room, their small fingers frighteningly adept at navigating the bends of a Grand Prix racetrack, until they're summoned to go for a daily swim or boat ride by one of their grandparents.

On the final night, Alma cooks a lobster supper which you eat around the fire pit looking out on to the lake. Although still on guest behaviour, after a week with Noah's family, you are comfortable enough to sit in silence with his father as the two of you watch Noah down on the sand hoisting a nephew under each arm and threatening to throw them into the water.

'Those two are a handful. A lovely handful.'

'Was Noah like them when he was young?'

'He was quieter, more inquisitive. He'd spend hours interviewing us and writing down our answers in his journal. He had a whole stash of them, they filled half his bookshelf.'

'I guess it helped he grew up before the PlayStation was invented.'

'I don't like to be that dinosaur who says it was better before but . . .'

'It was better before?'

'What do I know?'

'More than I know. But probably less than your wife knows.'

He turns to look at you and you wonder if you have been too familiar, overstepped the mark, but then he does a rasping laugh in the back of his throat and says, 'Well observed.'

When the embers have finished burning and everyone else has gone inside, you and Noah walk down to the stretch of sand overlooking the moonlit water. The two of you are laughing as you take it in turns to list the best worst RnB lyrics, and then – unprovoked by anything in particular, just in the way that a piece of music changes cadence without warning – he stops laughing and says, 'I know this is early days still so don't freak out, but how do you feel about marriage and kids? Not right now. But, you know, not a million miles away either.'

You find it incredible that you have met someone who is not afraid to ask this question outright. While you are too rational to marry and reproduce with a man you have known all of eight weeks, the suggestion that he wants these things in the future doesn't frighten you in the slightest; it reassures you.

'Um, yeah. I've always imagined doing both of those things. The kid thing especially.'

'Good. That's good. I guess it's being here, where I spent so much time when I was little, or maybe hanging out with my nephews, anyhow it gets me thinking, reminds me I thought I'd be a dad by now.'

'That makes sense,' you say, taking hold of his hand and stroking your thumb across the top of his palm.

'You're really important to me already. I just want to check we want the same things cause I don't want to get into something and then find out we don't, you know?'

'Noah, I think you're amazing. And it's weirdly soon to admit this, but I feel like this could be it for me now, in terms of being with you.'

'But . . .' he says, smiling nervously.

'There's no but. Well, it's not really a but—'

'But.'

'All I'm saying is, I want those things but just not right now.'

He slants his head and looks concerned. 'And by not right now, you mean how long?'

'What, like, specifically?'

'Or at least approximately.'

'OK . . . well, I guess I always assumed I'd live with someone for at least a couple of years before getting married or anything.'

'Huh,' he says, his confusion surprising you.

'Just cause otherwise it's still the honeymoon phase, right? And that doesn't feel like enough of a basis for a lifelong commitment.'

'Sure, I guess not. But I don't think the honeymoon phase lasts two years, does it?'

'It doesn't have to be exactly two years. I just mean not anything crazy like a couple of months.'

'Right. And kids?' he asks, letting go of your hand and scratching the side of his head.

'There's still so much I want to do. I've only just turned thirty.'

'Thirty's not exactly twenty.'

'It's still eight years less living than you've had.'

'I get that, I do,' he says, taking hold of your hand again. 'I just . . .'

'Can you trust me that I absolutely one hundred per cent do want them? Just not yet.'

He breathes in deeply, closing his mouth as he exhales so that the air is funnelled through the small gap between his lips.

'Look, I'll be honest, my timeframe is pretty different to yours.'

'So then . . . ?' You're suddenly alarmed by the implication of your discussion. What if it reaches a conclusion you don't desire and have not prepared yourself for?

'So, then I guess the snag for me is . . . I think you're worth waiting for.'

The release of tension breaks your face into a beam.

'Ow. That was painfully sweet.'

'Oh, don't get me wrong, you're still a massive inconvenience.'

'A total glitch to your system.'

'A massive fucking spark.'

'How completely annoying.'

'I'm going to kiss you now.'

'Even though I'm an irritant?'

'More like an absolute menace.' As he leans in to kiss you, you register the cognitive dissonance that will allow you to simultaneously hold the knowledge that this is now the fourth time you have fallen in love, as well as the belief that this time will be the last.

'Shall we go inside and eat ice cream?' he asks, lifting you out of your thoughts. You nod and he leads you into the kitchen. The ice cream is vanilla and has been churned inside a barrel. Its coldness is a pleasurable ache in your forehead.

On the flight home, following the captain's announcement that the plane is beginning its descent, Noah asks you to move in with him. 'That's unless you have a two-year timeframe for that too,' he adds.

You smile and laugh as you shake your head. 'No. That's no to the timeframe, yes to moving in.'

'I've timed this badly in terms of us toasting,' he says, touching his empty Coke can to your half-finished cup of water as you return the tray table to its upright position.

'Champagne's overrated. I mean, it's not, it's the best, but this is somehow better.'

When you land you call Lillie from baggage claim, who expresses with delighted mockery that 'of course your wealthy-yet-socialist, assertive and emotionally open boyfriend is also committed to a shared future'. You try to rebuke the comment but it contains too much truth to deny it with any conviction, and so allow yourself to bask in her description, watching Noah from the other side of the hall as he lifts your luggage off the conveyor belt and places it on to a silver trolley. You think of landing at Gatwick with Nathanael, of meeting Wren at Heathrow, of returning from New York with Oliver, and of all the men since, to have arrived at this moment, as though it has been your intended destination all along.

'I've got news too,' says Lillie, bringing you back into the present. 'You know that film application I submitted? Well, I found out yesterday I've got funding to write the script.'

'Lils, congrats! That's amazing.'

'Yeah, I'm not even going to downplay it, it's freaking cool. And I sent another idea, a short I've written, to this hotshot DOP on the off-chance she's up for shooting it and she's just come back saying she loves it. Finally something's happening for me, like finally.'

Although thrilled for Lillie, you're disturbed that her career appears to be launching at a time when yours is stagnating, but this concern is soon overridden as you observe Noah smiling as he steers his way towards you. There will be time to prioritize work again, but for now, haven't you earned this time to give in fully to love?

And so you move into Noah's flat and over the next few months enter a new stage of your relationship in which your infatuation settles into something more independent of each other. While the two of you enjoy watching French cinema and *Seinfeld* together, walking hand in hand on Hampstead Heath, staying up late with a bottle of wine and inventing ridiculous games, you are not reliant on one another for your moment-to-moment fulfilment. The several hours you spend apart in different rooms, absorbed in your own projects, mean that the occasions you convene in the kitchen to share lunch or decide to stroll around Waterlow Park always feel like a choice; the lack of routine and expectation that you will do these ordinary everyday activities as a couple makes doing them together feel unique and gratifying.

As the relationship deepens, the more you come to understand him, but think one of the things that both excites and slightly concerns you is that you feel you could never fully know him. Part of this is presumably due to the age at which you met – how formed you each already are – but also how differently your brains are wired so that you find it hard to predict his response to things. His spontaneous thoughts make him charismatic and instinctive, the kind of person who excels in a crisis or moment of boredom, whereas your structured mind is adept at making informed decisions – able to work backwards from a larger goal and mark out the smaller steps it will take to achieve it. In this respect you complement each other perfectly, although you think if he could see inside your head, all the arrows and boxes leading to various outcomes like the flowcharts in the magazines you used to read as a teenager, it would unnerve him.

★

That November, Romily goes into labour. Forty-eight hours later you sit on her sofa, cradling your nephew – this tiny, bleating, incapable human – and cannot contain your love for him, like dropping a spool of cloth and watching it roll out in front of you before you can catch it.

'Sorry, I think I'm getting him wet,' you say, twitching your face and tilting your head back, too terrified to take even one finger away from holding him. You have loved fiercely up to this point in your life but having always been the youngest – as a daughter, sister and partner – have never loved with a protectiveness that now overcomes you.

'What about you guys, then?' asks Alec. 'Got any plans to give Toby a cousin anytime soon?'

'How about it?' says Noah. 'I've got a window tomorrow around midday?'

You smile and shake your head, secure in the knowledge that the moment you are ready, the day you say the word, you too will become a parent. That's not to say you're immune to fertility concerns; occasionally you are gripped by the belief that you will be incapable of conceiving – a notion which stems not from any biological diagnosis but from a fatalistic and malevolent fear that you will somehow be denied this thing that you have always known you want. However, the finding of a willing partner to start a family with and watch it grow together, this you believe you no longer have cause to question, and so you make the mistake of thinking you are safe. But when is anyone ever safe in a relationship which involves two continually evolving people who might be slowly moving out of each other's orbit without even realizing?

You have to go back to fill in this part of the story, back to the moment of you stalling Noah's vision of the future on the final night of your stay at the lake cabin – a memory you'll compulsively return to like picking at a scab, always wondering if you'd reacted differently whether you'd still be together now. Because, while you assume your love will only grow into something stronger and more nuanced and in doing so make you ready to commit to marriage and children with him, you have no idea that his attitude towards these things will go in the opposite direction – that for him, when the impulsive initial stage of your relationship comes to an end, although he still loves you, the impetus to marry and start a family begins to leave him.

It's a strange but familiar pattern – how such a defining change can't be attributed to a specific moment, but rather a subtle shifting of unarticulated feelings, so that when two and a half years in, you bring up marriage, jokingly saying, 'Anytime from now, by the way!' he laughs hesitantly and changes the subject. When six months later he takes you to Venice for your three-year anniversary and you admit on return that you thought he was going to propose, he sits down on the opposite end of the sofa, rubbing his fingers over his temples, and looks concerned.

You are not traditional, would have yourself initiated getting married by now had he not told you a year into the relationship (precipitated by watching a woman going down on one knee outside Kenwood House) that a proposal is something he's imagined doing since he was young, saying he'd feel slightly cheated if he was denied the opportunity, and so ever since, you had discarded the thought.

'It's not that I love you any less, it's totally not that. I just don't know if I want all that stuff . . . marriage, kids, holiday newsletters.'

'I don't get it, though. You used to want that stuff, so what happened?' You tuck your knees into your chest, feeling vulnerable and bird-like.

'I don't know if anything happened. I'm not sure I've ever wanted those things.'

'But you did. You told me that night by the lake. And

incidentally,' you add with disdain, 'I don't have any intention of doing holiday newsletters.'

'Sure. Listen, this is hard for me to articulate . . .'

'It's also hard for me to hear.'

'I know that and I'm sorry. It isn't that I definitely don't want them, I'm still trying to work it out.'

'I just don't understand what changed.'

'I think . . . I think maybe when I met you, I was still holding on to this image of myself where by the time I was forty I'd be married with kids and making a living from writing.'

'OK.'

'But, well, because those things didn't happen, I've had to reassess that idea I had of myself. You know, ask whether these were things I ever really wanted or if they were just things other people expected of me. And that's not something I've ever really stopped to question until now.'

'So, what's the answer?' you ask, picking at the tassels on the throw next to you, the small fibres of wool sticking to your fingertips.

'I don't know yet, but I think it's worth me continuing to investigate. For both our sakes.'

You can't not agree with this and so you say, 'OK. You waited for me, you gave me time and so I'll give you time. But let me know as soon as you know.'

'I will, of course I will.'

That afternoon you let go of the idea of a romantic proposal and big white wedding – an image you'd only briefly entertained since meeting him, and even then felt as though there'd be something fraudulent about yourself in a long white dress with six bridesmaids at the rear. Before Noah, anytime you'd thought about marriage over the last decade you'd imagined a small ceremony taking place in a registry office with a handful of friends and family just as your parents had done.

The next time the conversation comes up, triggered by yet another friend announcing their engagement, you tell him that a conventional wedding isn't important to you, that it's the marriage vows themselves and the legality of it that appeals.

'We could do it with just the two of us and a couple of witnesses,' you say, rubbing night cream on to your neck inside the bathroom as you glance at the plants on the wooden ladder-shelf in the corner, at the framed narwhal print you'd simultaneously gravitated towards inside the Natural History Museum gift shop. *So, this is what it means to build a life with someone. Not so much shared values, as shared stuff.*

He enters the bathroom and stands behind you so that his eyes meet yours through the circular mirror above the basin. 'You know, in Quebec, a couple who have lived together for three years are considered to be spouses under common law, by which standard we'd already be legally tied to each other.'

'Well, exactly,' you say, confused that both of you see this fact as endorsing your own point of view.

You wonder whether your affair with Wren is to blame for your antiquated desire to get married rather than continuing to live together as partners, whether the experience has given a sanctity to the title of 'wife' that you otherwise might have been indifferent to.

But over the next few months you force yourself to decide what's really important to you, so important that you would risk losing Noah, and, having made up your mind, tell him, 'Listen, I've dropped the idea of marriage, but I can't relent on children.' This bit of your narrative is fixed, and not because motherhood is something you've always imagined for yourself and therefore cannot let go of out of principle, but because at thirty-three and a half, you now actively ache to experience it. Yes, you can continue to embrace being an aunt – but it is in no way comparable to being a mother. The impenetrable bond between Romily and Toby is proof and painful reminder of this. It is Romily who Toby is soothed by when he's crying and Romily who his face lights up for when she enters the room. You, and even Alec, exist outside of what the two of them share.

'Is it that you're afraid?' you ask him. 'Cause I'm frightened too, I have doubts.'

'You do?'

'Well, of course but I think that's normal, isn't it? With something as big and unknown as becoming parents. Surely it requires a bit of blind faith or else I'm guessing no one would have them.'

'Maybe. I don't know.'

'What about it frightens you? Is it specific things or just the fact it's, you know, forever.'

'All of it, I guess. Fear of losing my freedom, fear of regretting it. Fear I'm not capable of being a dad.'

You are stunned by this last admission. To your mind, he has every suitable resource and characteristic required for parenthood – unlike you who have no assets, are inconsolable watching Pixar films, cannot drive, or even blow up a balloon. If either of you is ill-equipped to take care of another human, you point out it is definitely not him.

'Then what makes you so certain you want them?' he asks cautiously, presumably unsure whether he's permitted to ask this question.

'I just . . . do.' There it is: the fact articulated with grave inadequacy.

You try explaining that ever since your early twenties you'd walk the streets of North London at dusk when lamps inside living rooms had been turned on but curtains and blinds not yet drawn, would see the families inside and miss the warmth and complete safety of your own childhood which, although underscored by your father's idiosyncrasies, had never once felt under threat. 'I guess I want to recreate that feeling as an adult.'

'You know it won't feel the same, though, right? This time around you won't be the kid.'

'I know that, I do, but it's still family. I mean, that's the only way it keeps going, isn't it?'

'That really is the most important thing to you. Family.'

You wish you could say it wasn't, that your thirst for adventure or drive for professional recognition was stronger, but what is the point in lying? You have spent your twenties exploring both physically and emotionally, and now you are hungry to put down roots, disappointingly unoriginal though this is. As for your career, you have accepted at this stage that your theatre shows are unlikely to generate a sudden 'break' – the kind that would enable you to make substantial-enough income to live off. And while you appreciate the two-line TV roles you occasionally land, this is largely due to the money they yield and the novelty of being on set rather than deriving any fulfilment from the fleeting parts themselves. You wonder if this waning in ambition is due to your biological clock, or a self-protective mechanism which will not allow you to feel the same appetite for success as you felt in your twenties because obtaining it no longer feels possible, and hurt without hope is just hurt.

'Look, I've laid down my hand, you know what I want. You need to let me know what you want. I can't just go on waiting.'

'I know you can't, and I really don't like myself for putting you through this. I'm going to take until the end of the month and let you know. Is that OK? I mean, obviously not OK as in good, but as in an acceptable amount of time.'

You shrug, inured to his indecision. 'That seems liveable.'

The next two weeks are weird. You try to behave normally but feel continually sick when you think about what will happen if his answer is no. It frustrates you that the situation is not only painful but conforms you to gender stereotypes so that it feels like a combined insult: that Noah is unsure about wanting children with you, and that in wanting them you have become a cliché. You think how preferable it would be not to care, wondering if you can manipulate yourself out of wanting them, but how perverse – to deliberately go against your biological impulse to procreate. You try to determine whether you have been brainwashed by the value that society places on motherhood, but it's impossible for you to work this out, and even if you could, this knowledge wouldn't make you want it any less. The 'damage' has already been done.

'Rom, I'm terrified. What if he doesn't want them?' You are sitting inside her kitchen watching Toby select a purple marker pen and draw jagged lines over a mass of green scribbles. The chaos of his drawing makes you feel momentarily calmer by comparison.

'He will, he's just having a wobble. Here, have a banana,' she says, attempting to roll one towards you across the table. 'I'd offer you a biscuit but you'll have to go into the bathroom to eat it.'

'Biscuit,' says Toby, looking up at Romily.

'No biscuits, just bananas,' she says firmly. 'At least you don't have to hide in the toilet if you want to eat processed sugar. Seriously, though, you look thin.'

'You just mean in relation to how I looked before. I'm not actually thin-thin.'

'I have zero interest in weight as a topic of conversation but fine, yes, "proportionally to your normal body-type" you look thin and I feel it's my sisterly duty to point it out.'

'I'm not trying to be, I just feel permanently anxious.'

Toby holds up his picture and you admire it enthusiastically, grateful for the requirement to smile.

'I like it! What is it?'

'It's my bedroom and it's under the sea.'

'Oh that's very cool.'

'And the shark is allowed in my bed but it's not allowed to eat any toys or people.'

'That sounds like a good arrangement.'

Toby nods and then gets off his chair and runs out of the room.

'Should I get Alec to talk to him?' asks Romily, bending to retrieve marker-pen lids from the floor. 'Do you think that might help?'

'No, I think that might freak him out. Alec's so into fatherhood, it's kind of intimidating.'

'You're telling me,' she says, rolling her eyes.

'Don't.'

'What?'

'Do that thing parents do where they make out they regret becoming parents even though everyone can see they get a total kick out of it.'

'I don't regret it. It's hugely awful but it's more hugely brilliant,' she says, wincing in the knowledge that this will hurt. 'Only slightly but it's still a favourable ratio.'

'Why can't Noah see that?'

She looks sad but, more alarmingly for you, genuinely concerned.

'I don't know,' she says, stroking your arm as Toby re-enters holding out a Pritt stick.

'This is for you.'

'For me?'

He nods and then looks very serious as he asks, 'Do you already have one?'

'No, not for years,' you say, trying hard to sound earnest. 'Thank you.'

'You can stick things on your drawings like Cheerios and

leaves but you have to put the lid back on or else my teacher gets cross.'

You pull him into a hug and say over the back of his shoulder, 'It might help if you trained your son to be less adorable.'

'Feel free to join us at the dentist's on Tuesday.'

You and Noah don't actually get to the end of the month because you crack before then, blurt out halfway through scouring a casserole pan that you can't stand the countdown, before crumpling over the sink like an overly tired child. It's then that Noah takes you in his arms and says, 'It's all right, I've realized I probably do want them. Kids.'

'Only probably, though?' You press your face into his jumper so that your words come out muffled.

'I'm definitely leaning more towards wanting them than not. Don't get me wrong, I'm still nervous about being a dad but I definitely see my future with you and children in it.'

'Really?'

'Yeah.'

You look up at him, embarrassed by the bigness of your smile. 'So, when? I mean, when should we start trying?'

'I . . . don't know.'

'I'll be thirty-four in May so how about then?'

'May's only a few months away,' he says, surprised.

'It could take months to get pregnant, though, maybe a year or even years . . . we just don't know. I don't really see why we'd be waiting at this point. I mean, there's no real reason to delay, is there?'

'No, I guess not.'

'So, is that decided, then?'

'OK,' he says, nodding.

But before May arrives there's a day in April where you look out of his study window, at a vermilion Frisbee stuck in the branches of a tree, and say, 'I guess this would become the baby's room, wouldn't it?'

You feel the energy in the room become thick and charged, turn to see his shoulders contracting, panic setting across his face.

'What? What is it?' you ask, already knowing the answer.

'May just seems so soon.'

He tells you he's been counting down with dread and apprehension, struggling to write and concentrate, doesn't think a baby is meant to be conceived under these conditions. He'd let himself be talked into the idea during the last conversation because he finds the notion of making you unhappy and of losing you intolerable, but can't lie to himself or you any longer.

You say nothing, have depleted all your arguments, have no energy left to fight. Or is it that you know fighting is futile because even if you could convince him momentarily to change his mind, it would never feel right knowing you'd persuaded him, rather than having entered into it, excited and apprehensive, but at least together?

'Margot? Say something, please.'

'Is it that you don't feel ready to start trying next month or that you won't ever feel ready?'

'I don't know. I want to want them, I really do, I just . . .' It's strange and sickening to you that this man, who had presented such confidence and clarity at the start of your relationship, could now be faltering and crumbling to the extent he is standing in front of you unable to even finish his sentence. You feel duped, as though he has stupendously mis-sold himself to you.

'Let's give it three more months,' you say, turning to leave the room. He takes hold of your fingers as you pass and squeezes them. You don't reciprocate with any movement. Your hands feel dead as if they belong to someone else, the way they get when they go white and numb from the cold.

You wonder how you're going to get through the next twelve weeks. You hadn't even made it through fourteen days last time, but know it's crucial you give him the allotted space to think. The stakes feel pivotal this time around because there is no doubt in either of your minds that this next stage of waiting is the final one. Three months from now a decision will be made in either direction: you will stay together and start trying for a baby or you will break up; either way, this period of stasis will end.

Couples talk about the life-altering arrival of a child, but it's odd to think that yours and Noah's joint existence might be abruptly terminated by the absence of one. And you realize that in the same way that you'd resent him if you never got to be a mother, what if you choose to have a child over him and end up resenting it for having lost him? It feels as though there is no favourable option, that you cannot win from either outcome of your choosing, only by him deciding he wants children. And this is what makes the situation deplorable – that for the next twelve weeks all you can do is wait.

At least when you are sad Noah is able to comfort you. The times when you are seething, rich with purple rage, you see his trepidation around you and feel a distance being forged. Aware that you are in danger of destroying the relationship regardless of the outcome of his decision, you do your best to bury your anger but feel it fossilizing inside you.

On days when hiding it is impossible, when you feel fury pushing upwards towards your surface, spitting and steaming like the geysers you once visited in the Atacama Desert, you take yourself off for long walks, fuming down the phone to Lillie or Romily if they pick up, or to the skeleton of a leaf if they don't. How dare he? How dare he have made declarations of marriage and children only to have been silently retreating ever since without signalling this to you? Doesn't he realize that as a woman every year from thirty onwards is critical? No, of course he doesn't because he has the luxury of being a man. And now he has the audacity to make you wait further while he deliberates, does not even have the capacity to decide, to set you free either way. You consider how he's even desirable to you after the anguish he's caused but, because he is, conclude there's little point analysing why.

As the end of three months approaches, you resist your impulse to bring up the topic, trusting he will initiate it when the day arrives that marks twelve weeks on from your conversation inside the study. All that morning and afternoon you look for signs in him that he is preparing to deliver his verdict, but the day goes on as normal, or rather this new version of normal which doesn't feel normal at all. You wonder if he is waiting until evening to broach the subject but, as you enter the kitchen and begin unloading the dishwasher, he finishes cooking to a soundtrack of electronica rather than discussion of children.

'So, guess what I found out today,' he says, placing a bowl of squid-ink spaghetti on to the table. 'The largest waterfall on earth is actually under the sea, called the Denmark Strait. Do you know about this?'

You shake your head as Noah spoons mounds of black strands on to your plate that look like a pile of baby grass snakes.

'Apparently it's caused by the difference in water temperature of two separate currents when they meet. Because the cold water's denser, it sinks below the warmer water and flows over this massive drop in the ocean floor. And get this, the amount of water dropping per second is the equivalent of basically two thousand Niagara Falls. That's insane, right?'

You want to shout, *so what?!* but steel yourself as you ask, 'Is there video footage of it?'

Yes, the world's biggest waterfall is astounding, and so much more noteworthy than anything concerning your own two small lives, but you have lost your ability to see outwards, to care about waterfalls and natural phenomena, only care whether the man you love wants children with you, and if that makes you small-minded, you don't care about that either.

It's only after you've finished eating and together cleared the table, only when he then stretches out on to the sofa and picks up the TV remote, that you take it from his hand, and say, 'Noah. I can't wait any longer.'

You think that if he looks confused, or claims not to understand what you are talking about, you will actually scream.

'I know you can't. Please don't hate me.'

You're not immediately sure if he's asking you not to hate him for leaving you in suspense, or for the answer he's about to give.

'I can't keep asking you to wait for me to want something I might never want, can I.'

You feel oddly calm and weightless as though you are floating above your body, watching this scene play out that you have imagined so many times but which always featured you crying inconsolably, not this surprising detachment that now suffuses you.

'I just can't imagine not waking up with you and getting to hang out and go to bed with you. It seems so crazy and pointless, like there has to be another option.'

'I know,' you say, agreeing utterly. 'But there isn't.'

You watch him press his wrists into the corners of his eyes, and then you do cry because witnessing him attempt and fail to hide his pain is somehow so much more distressing than watching him fall apart. It makes you think of something one of your acting tutors once said, 'Empathy is determined not by emotion itself but by the energy required to suppress it,' which was basically another way of saying, *If you want the audience to feel your character's pain, you have to resist showing it to them.*

In boy-like fashion, Noah pulls down the sleeves of his jumper and wipes his eyes. 'I want to set you up, financially I mean. I at least owe you that.'

'No you don't.' Your voice is soft but decisive. 'You owe me nothing and, anyway, you've already given me so much.' It's thanks to his refusal to let you pay rent these last four years that you've been able to put a portion of your income into a savings account each month. You now regret not having set aside as much as you could have, but haven't been irresponsible either; while you are by no means in a position to afford a deposit on a property, you nevertheless have a relatively substantial nest egg to support yourself.

Six days later, he hires a small van and drives you and all your stuff to your new rental place you've found on Gumtree. It's a studio flat in Haringey belonging to a retired Greek Cypriot couple who inform you they built the property at the bottom of their garden for the woman's elderly mother to live in before she died, and that by the end she had eaten only lemon mousse. You offer your condolences and compliment the jasmine plant growing on the patio inside a terracotta pot. The interior is hot and airless, full of dark wooden furniture which is not to your taste, but it feels preferable to communal living at this stage, and you can always buy a fan.

Noah's concerned expression as he surveys the room makes you even more determined to be positive.

'It's lovely,' you tell the woman as she hands you the key and walks back towards the house.

When you and Noah have finished carrying the final bags and boxes in from the van, he hesitates by the door, stooping under the low ceiling. Touching your shoulder, he says again, 'I'm so sorry.' But you don't know if he's sorry about unintentionally misleading you, or losing you. You don't discuss long-term goals like friendship; contemplating staying in each other's lives is too painful and, to be honest, too irrelevant compared to the task that now lies ahead of you.

At thirty-four you are tired. It has been seventeen years of both brief and substantial encounters with the opposite sex, and you had grown comfortable with the idea that you had found your life partner – that the search was over. The thought of starting again exhausts you. Is there even time for that? To embark on the process of meeting someone when they too might change their mind about wanting children, even if they assured you they did at the start. Besides, it's always taken time to find men who you really connect to – there were whole years between Oliver and Noah – and this is time you don't necessarily have any more.

You've never forgotten an embryologist friend of your parents coming to dinner when you were a teenager, how he'd talked about the black market in eggs sourced from aborted female foetuses, making your mother grimace.

'Just imagine it. Your biological mother never having been born herself.'

'But wait,' you'd asked him. 'Are you saying a female baby is born with their eggs?' Until now you'd just assumed that they arrived at puberty, along with periods.

'Their entire lifetime's supply. Other cells in the body regenerate but the ovarian reserve is non-renewable.' *Non-renewable.* He'd used that exact phrase and ever since it had made you think of a wheelbarrow full of eggs being poured into a coal pit and set alight each month. What a waste, all those eggs being available when you didn't want them, the pointless amount of pain and discomfort you've gone through bleeding each month, preparing your body to do something you hadn't been in any way – aside from biologically – ready to do. How many are left inside you now? You have no idea but know that after hundreds of menstrual cycles it can't be anywhere near as many as you started with.

As much as you would like to avoid an audit into your depleting egg supply, you recognize its benefit in enabling you to make an informed decision about your next move. Overwhelmed by the quantity of Google search results, you book a fertility test at a clinic in St Paul's which you choose on account of its location, median price and the fact they don't refer to it as an 'MOT', unlike many of the other clinics.

You wait tentatively in the week between the test and the follow-up appointment to discuss your results, try to avoid assuming the worst-case scenario – that you are infertile – although acknowledge that this deep loss would avoid you having to make this next hard and irreversible decision.

On the afternoon following your consultation with a brusque but not uncompassionate gynaecologist, you go for a walk with Lillie around Leyton Flats near the terraced house that she and George have recently bought with financial assistance from his parents. You're not sure why, in all the heterosexual couples you know, it is the man who possesses family wealth, consider it either a coincidence or that all the women in your life (yourself included) are subconsciously looking for economic security when they select their partners.

'So . . . ?' asks Lillie, as you walk a woodland trail littered with beech leaves. Thick tree roots protrude on to the path so that you have to keep looking down to prevent tripping over. 'Are you going to tell me if you're barren or just leave me hanging?'

'Tactfully put. And no, I'm fine, all "normal" down there.'

'Phew, that's a relief.'

'At least everything looks normal. Normal uterus, normal endometrial thickness, a healthy number of follicles. My AMH level's a bit low—'

'What's that?'

'The hormone they use to assess your ovarian reserve, basically your egg count. Mine's within the normal range but on the lower side so she suggested not leaving it until my late thirties and I don't want to wait that long anyway.'

'Even so, that's reassuring, right? It means you can afford to wait a bit.'

'The tests aren't always accurate, though. Romy got told to get a move on cause she'd struggle to conceive and she was pregnant within, what, three months?'

'I still think you should freeze your eggs,' says Lillie, stopping to photograph a swan fanning its wings. 'That way you buy yourself some time but also take precaution.'

'There's no guarantee they'd even survive the process. It would almost feel like the same gamble as holding out to meet someone. I mean, what would be the point in losing Noah if I also missed out on being a mother? I just . . .'

'What?'

'Badly want to be doing this with him.'

'I badly want that for you too.' She smiles weakly but looks pained by your hurt.

'I still can't get my head around it—' Lillie's phone interrupts you with the sound of an email notification.

'Sorry, one sec. I'm still waiting to hear back on that BFI feature funding.'

As she opens the message you arch your neck back, remembering the existence of the sky.

'Damn, doesn't matter, it's just their newsletter. What were you saying?'

'Nothing you haven't already heard.'

'It's fine, say it again. I'll find some nuance.'

'It's just the total waste of it, us not being together. It's so maddening.'

'God, I feel for him.'

'For him?' you ask, assuming you've misheard her.

'Obviously I feel for you more. But at least you know what you want. You always have done.'

'Sure,' you say reluctantly. 'But wanting a child doesn't stop me wanting him.'

'Of course not.' As she strokes your arm in an uncharacteristic show of tenderness, it strikes you that through all of these men (bar Elliot and Joe) Lillie has been there as this constant, and that really what you feel towards her now is a deep kind of love.

'Hypothetically, if you did do it, how would you do it? I guess you could just go on a night out and meet someone.'

'Yeah, and have more chance of getting an STD than of getting pregnant. No, I'd use a donor.'

'Hey, you could ask Oliver.'

'Oliver's nervous about bodily fluids as it is. Add the prospect of it resulting in his offspring and he'd definitely freak out.'

'He wouldn't have to be involved as a father, though, would he.'

'I just think it'd be weird. I'd rather he was godfather to it than an absent dad-figure who's only around once a month.'

'Yeah, fair.'

'Also, he's what, forty-four now? If I want to give myself the best shot, I might as well use young sperm.'

You emerge from the covered woods to take in a large pond in front of you, an island of thin trees reflected in the water.

'What about Frank?' she says, her pupils glinting at the prospect.

'I reckon the baby would come out with a fag in its mouth asking what lagers I've got on tap.'

'Lol but also true.'

'Plus, I haven't seen him for years. He's probably married and got a kid of his own.'

'I reckon he'd do it for you anyway, if you messaged him and asked.'

'I'm categorically not going to do that.'

'So, listen, if Oliver's godfather—'

'Hang on, it's not an official thing. I have no idea if I'm even going ahead with it.'

'Sure, but if you do then I'm godmother, right?'

'Obviously. So long as you promise to be secular and fabulous.'

'Oh please, when have I ever not been both of those things?' She pirouettes and a young girl who's passing stops and stares, pulls on her father's sleeve as she points and says, 'Daddy, look at that lady.'

Aware that she has an audience, the natural performer in Lillie means she can't resist following this with an entrechat and an arabesque which subsequently encourages you to join in with a grand plié. Despite the lack of time you've spent employed as actors, you're grateful to your drama-school training for making you unselfconscious and playful even as adults – the value of which has increased the older you've become.

'Seriously, though, what do you reckon?' you ask, as the girl is reluctantly led away by her father who looks embarrassed and unsure how to engage with either of you. 'Am I crazy to even contemplate it?'

'Honestly?' A magpie lands on a branch above your heads, screeching in front of a mound of messy twigs. 'We should keep walking, that's probably its nest.'

Once out of the magpie's territory, Lillie turns to you, looking you up and down as if considering what you are made of.

'OK – and this isn't me telling you what I'd do. I mean, George is broody as hell, and I'm like, "Babe, I can't *have* a child when I still feel I *am* a child." But if you know for certain you want to be a mother—'

'I do.'

'And you can feasibly afford to do it, then yeah. It's definitely something to consider, isn't it.' After another moment, she adds, 'I think it would be incredibly hard but not necessarily something you'd regret.'

'That's what I think.'

You take her hand and your fingers grip hold, not wanting or even able to let go, but then a cyclist approaches at speed, severing you apart.

12.

You step off the Euston Road and through the revolving doors of the Wellcome Collection. Inside the cafe the sounds of screaming children and talking adults bleed into each other like a watercolour. You're not sure why you've suggested this as a meeting point; the place holds no particular relevance. The two of you once went to a free exhibition here about the psychology of magic which had been interesting enough, although – ironically for magic – unremarkable, but perhaps that's the point: the situation is emotionally loaded without the added weight of nostalgia.

Passing the steel canteen-top lined with bowls of salads and rows of cakes, you spot Noah on his Kindle at a table by the window. As he swipes his index finger across the screen, you wonder what he's reading; your ignorance, through no fault of your own, offends you.

He looks up before you get to the table, which means there are whole seconds of just staring at each other before you're in speaking range, but apart from when he says, 'Margot,' neither of you say anything anyway, just stand in silence holding each other. His back is warm and vast, reminds you of the flank of a horse. As you suspected, the passing of four months has not lessened your love, has only injected it with longing.

'How are you?'

You give the obligatory, 'I'm OK,' which leaves room to suggest you are both hurting and surviving without specifying which of these you are doing more of. 'You?'

'Same, I guess.' As you break apart he looks tired and frayed, the skin around his eyes crinkled and dark. 'I'll get us drinks. What would you like?'

'I'll have an Earl Grey. Thanks.'

'Cake?'

'Um. Sure.'

'What kind?'

'Maybe orange or lemon if they have it?'

It feels ludicrous to be talking about tea and cake, given the enormity of what you are about to tell him, but you acknowledge you can't sit here without buying anything. Similarly, when he returns carrying a tray of thick-rimmed cups and plates you are obliged to make small talk because it would be farcical to launch straight in with the reason why you've asked him here today. There's a rhythm and a pattern that's expected and would require more effort to break than to conform to, and so you ask after his family, whether the showerhead has leaked through the ceiling again, and if he has seen the latest series of a Spanish Netflix show you used to watch together.

You hope his responses will infuriate you, that he'll say something that will allow you to hate him, but he skilfully navigates the conversation, toeing the line between humour and sincerity so that you're unable to silently accuse him of being either unfeeling or indulgent. You're particularly conscious of the tops of his hands, their broad expanse, but chiefly the fact you're no longer allowed to touch them. Your right to his body has been removed, making you question whether you ever had any right to it in the first place.

At some point – you have no idea how long the two of you have been sitting there – the lightness of the exchange starts to feel superficial and you understand this is your cue to tell him why he's here.

'There isn't really an undramatic way of saying this so I'm just going to say it, OK?'

He twirls the teaspoon in his fingers like a miniature majorette baton before gripping it in his fist and nodding.

'I'm planning to go ahead and have a baby.' He's so still for a couple of seconds that you can't see him breathing.

'You mean you've . . .' he says, exhaling through his teeth. 'You've met someone already?'

'No. But I've researched my options and this just feels like the . . .' What? *Best? Only?* 'Most suitable.' How absurdly businesslike.

'So, it's . . . it's IVF or something, is it?'

'IUI.' He looks blank and you add, 'Artificial insemination. It's cheaper than IVF and less invasive.'

'And the . . . what about the . . .'

'Sperm?' You're surprised, disappointed even, to discover you get no satisfaction from his discomfort.

'Is it someone you know?'

'It'll be an anonymous donor, from a bank.'

'You haven't chosen it already, then?'

'Not yet.'

He doesn't say anything for quite a long time, and then he says, 'I don't know what to say,' which feels superfluous. 'I mean, I guess you've thought everything through and you're sure?'

You nod, not attempting to explain that however much you researched – despite the discussions and blogs you read online, the books you bought about solo-parenting and networks you joined for 'single mothers by choice', however many hours you stayed awake during the night thinking about it – you could never be sure, or at least not certain. Because who ever is? You don't say that because you are single you have felt the need to interrogate your desire to become a mother more than you would be expected to were you with a partner, that it feels as though you are not permitted to have doubts, that your motive

248

must be pure and entirely void of ego – unlike couples who are allowed to be hesitant and gamble on becoming parents together even if part of the reason is wanting to see their genes passed on and have a go at creating the perfect person who will have none of their vices and all of their virtues. You don't ask him why he thinks this is, you already know why: because it will be so much harder for you, because you will not have anyone to voice your concerns to in the small hours, who will be able to reassure you that you've made the right decision when invariably at times it will feel as though you haven't.

'When? When might you do it?'

'My planning consultation's on Monday morning. That's when I'll sign the consent forms and make the payment. After that it could be anytime from four weeks that I start the treatment.'

'So, you could be pregnant within, what, a month?'

'It's unlikely to work first time. Even with a three-cycle package the chances are only around fifty per cent.'

'Huh.' He looks unimpressed with the odds – a sentiment you agree with, to the extent that at times it had felt ridiculous how much thinking and planning had gone into making a decision that only had a fifty–fifty chance of materializing even if you went ahead with it. You'd lost count of the number of hours you'd spent these last four months working through practical details: sorting out your finances, researching subsidized childcare, checking your company's maternity policy in your contract, even broaching the subject with your landlords who'd assured you they had no plans to ask you to move out – the woman keenly offering to babysit, lamenting the fact her own grandchildren lived in Cyprus. Most women avoided announcing their pregnancy until after their twelve-week scan, and here you were having to discuss and think through the post-birth scenario of a non-existent child with your boss and landlords before you'd even made the decision to go ahead and attempt to get pregnant.

'Do you want me to be there, to . . .' He tails off, glancing out of the window.

You fight the impulse that tells you to grab hold of his offer, that to have him in any capacity is preferable to not having him at all. Is it pride or pain that makes you reply, 'I don't think that makes sense, not unless you're offering to, you know, continue being there.'

You drink your tea which is now tepid and pick at the cake with your fork. Suddenly you feel like celebrating but there's nothing to celebrate.

'I wish,' says Noah.

'What?'

'It doesn't matter, it's not relevant.'

'Say it anyway.'

'I don't think it's helpful but sometimes I wish it had just happened by accident, you know?'

You do know, had thought the same countless times yourself, wished you could have been reckless or careless or just 'unlucky' to have avoided actively making the decision, but the two of you were none of these things. You know his sense of duty means he'd never abandon you with his child – that if you'd become pregnant he would of course have stood up and assumed the role of partner and father, and, you suspect, been pleasantly surprised to discover it wasn't the end of his life, but the beginning of a new one.

'How is that different to choosing to do it now, though?'

He opens his mouth as if to answer but then closes it again and begins assembling a pile of crumbs on the inner ring of his plate.

You need to move, to not be sitting at this table with him any more. The realization is like cramp, jolting through your legs.

'I'm going to look inside the gift shop.'

'I'll join you,' he says quickly. 'I mean, if that's OK?' You nod and the two of you stand.

Walking around, absorbing the cards and stationery and limited-edition prints, you remember the first time you went to a museum of your own free will rather than being dragged there by one of your parents, realizing that you could visit the shop before the exhibition, your delight in this discovery. Today the experience doesn't evoke its usual pleasure but the neatly stacked books and clinical white walls cauterize your nerves, alleviating the pain.

'I want to get you something. Anything. What do you want?' Noah asks, holding up a soft-toy microbe so that you infer he means from inside the shop. If only it would be permissible to answer, *you*.

'Nothing, I don't need anything.' He doesn't push the matter, is presumably cautious of buying your affection, not that he needs to; he has it for free. You continue walking, trying to work out what you are to each other now. Pausing in front of a plastic skull, you consider that there is a risibly thin line between a partner who you cannot imagine living without, and someone you used to live with.

As you exit on to the street, the November air permeates the space between your skin and your clothes, making your backbone judder; you don't question why or how it is that almost an entire season has occurred since you last saw him. That first October after Wren left, you raged against the sight of golden leaves but are now experienced enough at heartache to no longer resist the passing of time without someone but to accept it as inevitable.

'I'm heading this way. How about you?' you ask, tightening the fabric around the collar of your coat with your fist.

'Hang on, wait a second.'

Will he object to your plan? Tell you not to go ahead with it – that he wants to do it with you instead? You have tried not to hope for this outcome, but why else have you asked him here today, if not to give him a final chance to choose you and a child instead of neither?

'I'm here for you. You know that, don't you?'

So that's his answer. And of course it is. He'd already made his choice by not making it, back when the two of you were together. You feel shamed by the persistence of your hope.

'Sure.' You will not cry, not here in front of him. Your nails digging into your flesh are in prevention of this.

'No, I mean it. I know it's not the same, but I still want to be there – a bit, or a lot, or however much you want.'

'Thanks, but you don't have to be.' And he won't be. Or rather, he'll be there as a friend perhaps, but friends aren't there at three a.m. and five a.m. and six a.m. when the baby is crying, or there when you find out it's got mild autism or severe dyslexia and is being bullied at school or is bullying another child. You wonder which would be worse. Do you really have what it takes to do this?

'I know that. But I want to be.'

'The appointment's on Monday morning. I'll just be—' Don't say *waiting*. Don't say *hoping*. 'Around until then.'

On your way to the Tube, you pass Euston Travelodge, and think of the one on Greenwich High Road you went to with Wren. Eva and Cai would be teenagers by now. Presumably the two of you would have a baby or young child of your own. Is there some malign interplay between your current childless state and Wren having come close to leaving his children for you? Perhaps this is a form of punishment, although you don't really believe in karma. You wish you did; it would be easier to explain how you've ended up here, comforting to have something to blame, even if it is yourself.

You have tried and failed over the years to come to any form of neat conclusion regarding your affair. At the time, Wren had seemed so much older and wiser and more grown up than you, but now from your vantage point of thirty-four, you are surprised by how often you reflect on his behaviour as fanciful and ultimately deluded. But still there is something disingenuous and lacking in nuance about this interpretation. It would be easy to dismiss your love as the cliché of an impressionable younger woman and opportunistic older man, and you don't deny the existence of these real and true factors. But what is harder to accept and prove is that your love had also existed – had been real and true – in spite of these factors.

As you reach the station and descend the escalator, hot air blows in your face. You consider the universe, first as an invisible force and then as physical matter: stars and galaxies, black holes.

Letting yourself into your sister's house, you are greeted by Toby, running towards you holding a piece of chopped apple. His smallness but completeness as a person always makes you want to laugh but you suppress the urge; not taking him seriously would be the deepest betrayal.

'I'm not speaking to Daddy but I am speaking to Mummy.'

'Lucky Mummy.' You scoop him up and plant a kiss on his nose before he wriggles free and charges into the living room accompanied by cartoon explosions coming from the television.

'Are you sure you're up for this?' Alec asks as he enters the hallway and points to the whiteboard next to the shoe-rack, displaying *I hate daddy* in Toby's four-year-old scrawl.

'What was the crime?'

'I ate the last of his birthday chocolate.'

'That's pretty bad, to be fair.'

'I know,' he says, holding up his hands in submission.

'We've agreed it's a just punishment,' announces Romily, clutching the banister and stepping her stiletto ankle boots at a diagonal as she comes down the stairs. She squeezes you in a hug, smelling sweet and woody in her signature perfume.

'So,' she says, still holding your arms. 'It's technically awkward if you cancel now cause we've spent nearly two hundred quid on the tickets, but you know we can one hundred per cent sack off the play and just get into our pyjamas and drink wine if you'd understandably rather not look after our child tonight.'

'You really don't want to go, do you.'

'Nobody wants to go to the theatre, you just do it to feel good afterwards, like cleaning or going to the gym.'

'At least you get to wear your new boots. Nice, by the way.'

'Thanks, I can't massively walk in them, but they'll be my theatre–cinema boots. Right, have we got time for a wine?'

'Nope,' says Alec, holding out her coat. 'Actively running late now.'

'Damn. OK, call if you need anything, eat and drink whatever you like—'

'At your own peril,' Alec interjects, flicking his thumb towards the whiteboard.

'And let's have a chat when we get back. I want to check you're still, you know, all set.'

'I am. Stop stalling and go and say goodbye to your son.'

You watch Toby launch himself at your sister, smothering her in kisses before shooting at his father with an imaginary machine gun so that Alec staggers backwards, miming convulsions.

'We'll be back about elevenish. Love you.'

As they shut the door, you feel the emptiness of the corridor without them but it's a relief more than a loneliness. You adore them both but right now can do without the perfection of their family. You imagine Romily rebuking your definition, 'Er, hello, did you see the trolling on the whiteboard?' but what she won't have considered, because in fairness to her she hasn't ever had to, is that Toby has the luxury of temporarily turning against one parent because the other parent is still available to meet his needs. And that she and Alec have each other to share in the amusement and annoyance of their son's moods, which they are likely discussing on their way to the theatre at this very moment.

'Is it your birthday?' Toby asks, as you sit down next to him on the sofa, running your fingers through his curls until he shakes you off.

'No. Why do you think that?'

'Mummy said to be extra specially good tonight.'

'Did she?'

'Yes and Daddy ate my chocolate.'

'Yeah, I heard about that. That wasn't great of him.'

'It was very bad,' he says, engrossed in a fluorescent jellyfish that's appeared on the television. You envy his ability to be entirely absorbed in what's in front of him. Unable to resist the urge, you check your phone hoping to see a missed message or call from Noah sent in the hour and a half since you left him.

'Do you want to play a game?' you ask. 'Maybe the one where everything we walk on turns to lava.' You could do with the distraction of a make-believe world, where cushions are lumps of molten rock, spewing orange liquid.

'After my show.'

'Sure.'

As an afterthought, he adds, 'Please.'

Despite Romily's intention that Toby should make tonight's babysitting experience as easy as possible, through no fault of his own he has a heavy nosebleed which happens inside the bath so that while it avoids staining his clothes, the carmine-tinted water looks unnervingly severe. Thankfully you're not squeamish and calmly instruct him to pinch the soft part of his nose and tilt his head forwards as you google to confirm you've remembered this correctly.

You give him a dinosaur sticker for being brave, pressing it on to his planet pyjamas overlapping Saturn's ring, and then award yourself one for passing the test you've just been given. Toby smooths the stegosaurus on to the neck of your jumper, stroking your collar bone so gently it tickles. Lying on his bed, you read him a story about two brothers who find treasure which only one of them keeps and as a result their lives go in very different directions.

'They're not friends any more because Herbert has all the money,' says Toby, turning the final page of the book.

'That's sad, isn't it.'

'I don't have a brother,' he says with indifference.

'No, but if you did I suspect you'd share the treasure with him.'

'I would share it but only three pounds.'

'Maybe that's something to think about while you fall asleep.'

'I can't because I'm going to be thinking about trucks.'

'Fair enough.'

As you kiss his forehead and turn out the light, your pelvis hammers with love for him.

On your way back downstairs, your phone rings and you run to answer it but it is only your mother wanting to check in regarding Monday's appointment.

You'd first broached the subject with her and your father inside a Greek restaurant in Southwark following their quarterly outing to the Tate. Their response had been almost offensively accepting, even offering to pay towards the three rounds of treatment.

'We'd probably have ended up contributing the same sum

towards a wedding,' your mother said, glancing at the gold band on the finger of the waiter as he placed a meze on the table, as if to rule out his eligibility.

'And your mother deems the creation of a second grandchild a worthier expense,' your father added without stating his own preference, while forking a stuffed vine leaf from the oval ceramic plate and putting it whole into his mouth.

'Well, of course I do. A dress she'd wear once and a converted barn for her and a hundred people to get drunk in. It's a no-brainer.'

You'd briefly thought about refusing their offer as proof of your independence before quickly acknowledging that you are in no position to turn down financial support, that you'll need every bit of your savings for if and when the baby is born or if the treatment doesn't work and you need to consider other options.

'Thanks, guys,' you'd said, reaching for the water jug to refill your glass even though it was almost still full; their brilliance, not only as parents but as people, left you feeling profoundly inadequate.

You put your mother on speakerphone while you place five fish fingers on to a baking tray inside the oven and open a bottle of wine that looks suitably expensive but not as though it's being saved for a special occasion.

Your mother goes through either a mental or literal checklist of last-minute considerations, wanting assurance that you've addressed these factors (all of which you have) before she and your father can recommence with the Venezuelan documentary they have currently paused.

'Oh and Grandma rang earlier and told me to tell you there was a single mother by choice speaking on *Woman's Hour* yesterday and that she only caught half the programme but she transcribed what she could and she'll post it to you.'

'Completely charming but did you tell her I can just listen on BBC Sounds?'

'You know she's dubious when it comes to technology. She also said to tell you that SMC sounds too much like STD so if it's all right by you she won't be using the acronym.'

'You can tell her that's fine.'

Satisfied that the two of you have covered every eventuality, your mother concludes, 'I'm very proud of you, you know. We all are.' You feel your throat swell and become hot as she puts the phone down.

A panel show is now playing on your sister's television, the bright colours and formulaic jokes soothingly predictable. As you eat the fish fingers and drink a second small glass of wine, you consider the treasure in Toby's storybook – how the brother who gets the gold ends up rich and alone on top of a mountain, his long grey beard draped over the treasure chest he guards throughout the night, while the other brother grows old, smiling in a large armchair surrounded by grandchildren. Why is it that children's stories show people having either money or love, when in the real world those you know who are happiest have both?

The next morning you cycle down Green Lanes inside a sauna of exhaust fumes, picturing your lungs as an outline in pencil, smudging and filling up with grey. Turning left off the main road, you lock your bike to the thin green railings overrun with ivy while the branches of a willow tree brush the top of your helmet.

At the other end of the car park, the still enclave of the reservoir greets you like an old friend who you've never fallen out with or had even one hostile thought about – unheard of in terms of your actual friendships. Swimming here always feels like cheating, as though you ought not to be allowed to share this pool of water with its inhabitants of birds and fish and plants, while simultaneously getting to live within six miles of the West End.

The temperature that was refreshingly cool even in the height of August is now bitingly sharp and verging on torturous but you enjoy testing your body, seeing how much pain it can withstand as if conducting your own human experiment. It feels sentimental to make the link between cold-water swimming and your capability to be a single parent, but you make it anyway, reassuring yourself of your mental and physical tenacity as you front-crawl between the marked-out orange buoys, joined briefly by a duck on your right-hand side. The strong wind is making sizeable waves so that it feels as though you're in the sea, despite the wild grassy bank and high-rise buildings encircling you.

When you're no longer able to feel your hands and feet, you stumble up the slanted wooden ramp attempting to steady yourself on the algae which is silky and slippery between your toes. Your body convulses while you dress, as though your limbs are a stubborn child resisting your efforts to clothe it. As you stand in a small circle of sun cupping the steaming lid of your Thermos flask, you try to work out at what age you became grateful for simple things, for water and light; definitely not before thirty. At some point nature became extraordinary to you, in the same way as Artificial Intelligence or Space.

You are aware that outings such as this morning's swim will become an impossibility or at least an anomaly if you go ahead with single motherhood, but oddly you're OK with this. You no longer want to be this free, not if the cost of freedom is being unattached, of things continually ending and starting again, of relentless possibility which you used to find thrilling but now find limiting – not so much the broadening of a horizon but the narrowing of one.

As heat returns to your core, you reach inside the pocket of your rucksack, your part-white part-pink fingers reminiscent of the Drumstick lollies you consumed in your adolescence. Checking your phone, you try to quash hope of seeing Noah's name and instead see a missed call from Ishani who's 'finally met the one' after more than a decade of singledom. Although you dislike your lack of generosity, Ishani's happiness stings with a sharpness that makes you flinch as though pressing on an open wound. You can't bear the weight of her lightness or stand to hear the undisguised doubt in her voice about your decision.

'You're joking, right?' she'd said when you first confided in her, not even looking up as she scraped chopped garlic into a frying pan inside her newly purchased shared-ownership flat in Wood Green.

'No, actually,' you'd replied, rocking back on the chrome barstool. 'But the question suggests you think I should be.'

At this point she'd left the frying pan unattended as she leant forward over the laminate countertop and stared at you.

'That's kind of extreme. I mean, you could totally still meet someone.'

'Yeah, and I could also not meet someone,' you'd said calmly, determined to retain composure.

'Sure, but that's just part of love. It's a gamble, isn't it.'

'Well, I'm done gambling, hence the new plan.'

'You know it's not a game of poker where you can just fold, right? Like, this is pretty massive just to throw out there.'

'Look, I get that for you this is new news—'

'Tautology.'

'Fine, new information, but it's not exactly an overnight decision for me, and your reaction's kind of implying it is.' You hear the rising defiance in your voice, annoyed she has provoked your defensiveness.

'Listen, obviously I'll back whatever you decide. I just think if you're going to do it at least do it for the right reason.'

'I'd be doing it to not miss out on being a mother. What part of that sounds not right to you?'

'Nothing, but that's only part of your reason. The other part is you trying to hold on to your weird belief that you can plan out what happens to you. Fuck, the garlic's burning.'

This last comment had struck a nerve you didn't want to acknowledge and so you'd segued into her bold interior-design choice to paint the walls navy and gold – a gamble which had admittedly paid off.

She'd since tried to be supportive, had told you repeatedly that you were 'brave', a word that had become tiresome to hear, but she couldn't hide the fact she wanted you to hold out for love. For Ishani, who shirked at even the prospect of online dating, selecting a sperm donor based on a profile of attributes was tantamount to sacrilege. Instead of calling her back, you sit on the raised concrete changing area and cradle your arms while listening to a podcast about architecture which you find relaxingly irrelevant to your own predicament. You learn that in Utah the roads are so wide that there are buckets of flags attached to the traffic-light poles that people wave when they cross because there isn't always time to make it to the other side before the light goes green again.

'He might still call,' says Lillie, later that night, pressing the tips of her fingers on to the edge of her pine kitchen table. 'He's still got twenty-four hours.'

George gets up to clear the plates and you mouth, 'Thanks,' unsure why no sound was attached to the word.

'I just hate that I even want him to.'

'OK, but that's like hating being human,' she says, swigging from her glass to punctuate the point. Her stained lips look striking; maybe she should start wearing lipstick.

'Loads of stuff I've read talks about it being a really positive and empowering decision, so why can't I feel that way?' The lasagne and red wine have made you feel sedate but unsettled. You dislike the petulance in your voice but don't know how to get rid of it.

'If you're still hoping he'll say he wants to do it with you, do you think maybe you don't want to go ahead without him?' She twiddles her hair as though to casualize the question.

'I don't know if it's even possible for me to feel good about doing it alone; it just is the situation.'

'It just feels like you're holding on to doing it with him.'

'That's cause I am.' You pick up a burnt piece of ciabatta for something to hold rather than eat.

You know Lillie's cross-examination stems from wanting the best for you, but are tired of having to endorse your decision alone – are exhausted with defending your position, would like to let go but are afraid that if you do you will smash and not be able to reassemble again.

'I'm going to meet Ewan for a drink,' says George, hovering by the door. You smile at him; it's testament to how at ease you are in his company that you speak so openly in front of him.

'What, and forgo this wild Saturday-night chat?'

He laughs, removing his coat from the banister. 'Hey, you're always good company.'

'Deeply untrue, but thanks.'

'Come over anytime, yeah?'

'Remember we're putting up the shelves tomorrow,' Lillie shouts, seconds before the front door closes with a thud. 'I don't know, maybe you should just wait a bit longer, see how you feel a month from now. I mean, nothing's official yet, you haven't signed the forms or made the payment.'

'I'll have sunk three hundred and sixty quid for the

appointment and have a month of folic acid in my system, but sure, it's not that. It just doesn't feel like more time is going to make any difference.'

'It might, though.'

'How, though? It's not going to change the fact I want to be a mother.'

'True.'

'Or that biologically the chance of that happening is only going to get smaller.' Hearing it aloud, rationally it makes sense.

'So then you should do it, right?' You study Lillie's face, unsure if she's performing reverse psychology or expressing her genuine opinion.

'I just resent that I have to. I mean, *when I grow up I want to be a single mother with help from an anonymous sperm donor* isn't exactly the future I imagined for myself.' For a moment, you see versions of yourself as a child and a teenager and a twenty-year-old, want to apologize and protect them for landing them here, but they are busy collectively trying to save a bumblebee which is drowning in an inflatable paddling pool; you feel left out that they are all together in the past, strong and hopeful, while you are alone in your present, unable to join them.

'Is it that you don't want to do it without a partner or that it looks different to how you imagined?'

'Both. It feels as though I'd have failed and be losing at the same time.'

'I get that.' There's a beat before she winces. 'Sorry, mate, desperate for a wee.'

Leaving the bathroom door open, she continues the conversation out of eyeshot, the trickling sound of liquid hitting the toilet bowl.

'And all the stuff online says you should go for it, right?'

'Don't get me wrong, people are honest about it being the hardest thing they've ever done but also the best. No one's said they regret it, but then I guess you wouldn't once you had it, would you?'

'I don't know about that. I've had two people admit to me drunk that they wish they'd never become parents. And they're both in relationships.' You wait until the sound of the flush has stopped before replying.

'Yeah, well maybe their partners are shit, or maybe all the solo parents are just in denial cause they can't afford to be honest with themselves.'

'Or maybe they just want it more,' says Lillie, buttoning her jeans as she re-enters the kitchen. 'I mean you'd have to, right? To get to the point of doing it alone.'

'That's the thing, I know I'll want it so much once it's born, and even once I find out it's alive inside me. It's just, until then, I can't pretend to be . . .'

'What?'

'Happy about doing it this way.'

'I don't think you have to be happy about it, but I do think you need to have accepted it.'

'I have accepted it.'

'No, I thought you had but you haven't.' You open your mouth to object before realizing Lillie is right.

'Do you want to try George's sloe gin?' she asks, taking a bottle of cardinal-red liquid off the shelf, the floating berries like preserved specimens inside formaldehyde.

'I think I'm done on the booze front.'

'In that case . . .' She picks up your wine and pours the rest of it into her glass before raising it out in a toast. 'Here's to you, whatever you end up doing. You'll be fine either way; you always make strong choices.'

Is fine the aim, though? you wonder, holding up your glass of spidery dregs.

★

Waking at ten, your body feels thick and concentrated. You drink the pint of water next to you and then refill it from the bathroom which is adjacent to your bed even though your landlords have explained that this tap is connected to a storage tank which means the water is stagnant and maybe also has small particles of lead in it; when hungover you make allowances for such things.

You turn on your laptop and watch three episodes of *Real Housewives of New York,* feeling better about your life because the women in the show possess too much money and not enough self-awareness to induce genuine envy. As you shower and get dressed, your body feels like a soft-boiled egg, runny on the inside, held together by a thin hard shell; it occurs to you how strange it is that as an adult you're expected to be both vulnerable and self-sufficient – that it's simply assumed you're capable of existing in this contradictory state.

Your stomach feels empty and full at the same time, as though it's a newly pumped tyre with a hole where the air keeps escaping. The fridge has seeded bread, feta and half a brown avocado in it but eating on a Sunday always feels as though it ought to be an event and so you decide to go out to get lunch. You don't have a place in mind, your only requirement that it's in keeping with your new weekly budget.

It's a cold but sunny afternoon, making you content to keep walking without a fixed destination. You walk all the way down Green Lanes and on to Newington Green, through Canonbury and on to Upper Street. As you pass rows of idyllic Islington townhouses and imagine their owners, you challenge yourself to imbue their idealized lives with complexity, inserting fictitious obstacles in their path: the law-firm partner who yearns to be a writer but is trapped by her children's private-school fees, a cross-dressing househusband who wants to transition but fears it will be the end of his marriage, the esteemed academic whose work and identity are bound by her homosexuality, fantasizing of late about penile penetration.

Inside Pho, you sit at a table by the window facing out on to the street. You don't have a problem eating alone, have never felt the presumed self-pity attached to solitary dining. You've read multiple online forums in which single mothers by choice recount the judgement of other parents, steeling yourself for the inevitable remarks – considering what you'll say when asked about 'the father', both by your child and near-strangers. You intend to be honest from the off about the fact there isn't one, at least not by any definition you'd recognize as being entitled to the term. Your child will legally be able to find out its donor's identity when it reaches eighteen and you won't discourage it from doing so but, at least until then, you will refer to them as a donor, not a dad.

You do question your right to consciously deny your off-spring a father, when your own – in spite of his emotional absence – was physically present and dutiful throughout your childhood: painstakingly parting the back of your hair every morning during your phase of wearing bunches, and later in your teenage years tirelessly striving to purchase the right kind of tampons when you and Romily and your mother wrote them on the supermarket shopping list. At this age, you are accepting of your father's quirks and foibles – have made peace with his stubborn refusal to converse and behave in a 'fatherly' manner. What does it matter, given there is no shortage of love?

Your reservations are not gender-related. You would have no qualms whatsoever about two mothers raising a child together, or two fathers; what concerns you specifically is that there is only one of you. That said, your child will have no shortage of care-giving adults in its life. You're ashamed to admit that you want a partner as much as you want a second parent for your presently unconceived child because, while you are prepared for and can tolerate the social stigma, the bit you dread and fear is the private loneliness.

As you pay the bill, you decide spontaneously to go to the cinema, chiefly for the fact it will force you to turn your phone on silent and stop looking to see if Noah has messaged, which now feels like an established tic in the way that you absent-mindedly dig the nail of your index finger into the skin of your thumb.

The neon lights inside the foyer and oversized drink options bolster you with their confidence. You watch as two teenage girls select sweets from the pick 'n' mix stand, one pointing while the other scoops; sometimes they change their minds and retract the contents back into the colourful drawers as if you are rewinding them. You choose a film about a woman suffering from Alzheimer's because you want to connect to something on a meaningful level without being able to relate to it personally, but there turns out to be a subplot involving the woman's daughter and her young child who looks vacant and distressed through-out. Still, you enjoy sitting in the warm dark and having the company of strangers without having to make conversation. You find comfort in the smell of hot maize and scratching sound of the couple eating popcorn in the row behind you; so much stuff changes that it feels important to hold on to small constants.

Pleasingly, you are not triggered by the actors onscreen suc-cessfully doing the job you once so aspired to. You still intend to write and perform in the future, but refuse to allow your career to deprive you of the chance of becoming a parent – especially when you feel it has already deprived you of a stable income and, at times, your sense of self-worth.

The moment the credits start to roll, you feel for your phone and then stop yourself, resolving to exercise self-restraint at least until you exit the cinema, but your temperance is not rewarded. You have a text message from Vodafone about increased tariffs and a WhatsApp photo from Romily showcasing her newly blistered feet with the caption, *I repeat. These boots aren't made for walking.*

On the bus home a toddler screams the entire way. You spend half the journey gritting it out, wanting to test your levels of tolerance, before giving up and putting your headphones in. Turning the volume up high, you listen to Fleetwood Mac, 'Go Your Own Way'. On the seat in front of you a woman eats chicken from a box and drops the bones on the floor.

It's not until you get off the bus and instinctively reach inside your pocket to run your thumb along the serrated edge of your key that you discover it isn't there. In your hungover state you'd uncharacteristically put it back inside your puffer coat after letting yourself in last night and are now wearing your Sherpa-lined denim jacket. Initially you panic – not because the act of calling a locksmith is anything more than irritating, and money you could do without spending – but because it makes you question your competence which in turn makes you doubt your decision to embark on becoming responsible for another human.

Stepping back from the middle of the pavement, you tuck yourself into the fluorescent light of the corner shop next to a sagging crate of red and yellow bell peppers. As you type *Haringey locksmiths* into Google, you reassure yourself that being a mother doesn't equate to infallibility, remembering the time your own accidentally enabled you to overdose on vitamin tablets as a toddler, or absent-mindedly left a steel doorknob on the parcel shelf of the car so that when she hit the brakes you got concussion – not to mention Romily's benign admission that twice now she's forgotten to pick Toby up from school. The fact that both your mother and sister having partners didn't prevent these incidents from occurring is mollifying.

The locksmith is loud and jovial on the phone as if your error is an achievement. You give him the address and he says he will be at your flat within the next half hour, that he will call when he is outside. As you hang up, you wonder if it was safe to tell an unknown man where you live, a stranger who will arrive in the dark and who you will simply have to trust because what's the alternative? Your landlords are in Milton Keynes for their niece's wedding, and you have not, until tonight, considered keeping a spare key with a neighbour.

On the opposite side of the street, the warmly lit booths of the Kurdish restaurant look inviting and draw you to cross the road. It's early evening, the scent of charcoaled lamb and sweet apple shisha pervades the air; neither smell is unpleasant. Whatever day of the week, whatever the time, this particular stretch of North London is always animated, a reminder that your own existence is part of a wider network of lives and that even though you don't know these other capillaries branching off at various angles, you function as part of a collective. At times you find your own insignificance distressing but tonight it's consoling.

Inside the restaurant you order tea which comes in a small oval glass with a gold rim; it tastes floral and bitter. As you stir in a sugar cube, watching it dissolve to leave a thin layer at the bottom like sediment on the seabed, you hear your phone ring and feel the rising of hope before seeing it is Lillie. At the table opposite, a little girl in a chequered pinafore dress and gold hoop earrings is staring admiringly at you, her dark eyes large and doll-like. You press your phone to your ear to hear Lillie over the noise of the restaurant.

'I maybe definitely shouldn't ask this,' she says.

/

Looking around the room, you see the girl is now gripping her cutlery and sticking her tongue in and out as a plate of heaped meat and piled rice arrives at the table. You glance out of the window, at the road filled with gridlocked traffic, hear cars honking, as you watch a figure stepping out of a taxi, and then sit forwards with a jolt when you realize it is Noah.

You lean closer to the glass, convinced you're mistaken, but no. There he is, crossing the road towards you, hands in the pockets of his olive-green jacket, eyes focused on the traffic so that he hasn't noticed you inside the restaurant. Is he here by coincidence or has he come to find you? You grip the padding of the seat, your palms clammy against the leather.

As he gets nearer, you press your hand to the window as though you're trapped inside a tank. For a moment you think he's going to walk right past; then what will you do? Shout and hammer against the glass? Just as you're wondering whether it could withstand the force, he glances down to where you're sitting and stops.

His expression is one of confusion, as surprised to see you as you are to see him. You stare at each other for several seconds before he turns and walks in the opposite direction; whatever he's come for, he must have changed his mind. You feel the blood draining from your arm but still don't take your hand away, clinging to hope.

'Is it OK if I sit?' You turn to see him standing at your table, his cheeks pink from outside. Something yanks inside your torso making it hard to breathe.

You nod, too afraid to speak in case it makes him disappear. As he slides into the seat across from you, cold air radiates off him.

'That's handy you spotted me. I was on my way to your place but the traffic's so bad, I just decided to get out and walk.'

'I got locked out.'

'That's unlike you.'

'I thought the same thing but maybe I've changed.'

'Have you?'

'I don't know.'

He pauses, as if trying to come up with the answer to this, before asking, 'Do you want me to have a go at breaking in?'

'Thanks but I've called a locksmith.'

'That's probably preferable. I'd end up smashing a window.'

You smile even though you disagree; knowing Noah, he'd expertly navigate his way inside – no doubt another skill in his repertoire. You look at each other in silence until his gaze is too intimate and you have to look away.

'Margot—'

'So, wh—'

'Sorry—'

'No, you go.' Your words overlap the way your bodies used to.

'OK. Well,' his voice is calm, his eye contact steady. 'I've been doing some thinking, too much thinking, and I want us to have a kid together. I really do.' You say nothing. All the muscles in your face are focused on preventing you from falling apart. 'I'm just really hoping it's not too late, that you still want that too.'

You nod, still don't speak, convinced that if you open your mouth out of it will come a wail or a sob. You think of how in Egyptian times they shaved their eyebrows when their cats died as a sign of grief. Then again, some widows wear black for eternity; at least eyebrows grow back eventually. Why are you having these morbid thoughts?

'I'm just so sorry it's taken me this long to figure it out. When you told me you were going ahead without me, I just . . . I couldn't work out why we weren't doing it together.'

You see yourself dressed in yellow, sprouting hair all over your face in proof that you were wrong: he is not gone. He is here, in front of you, taking your arm across the table the way he did on your first date, squeezing your hand, kissing the circumference of your palm like a row of stitches.

'I've been properly, sensationally dumb. Totally moronic.'

'I don't care,' and it's true, you don't.

'No, but I have been and that's it now. No more discussion, no more potential start dates, I'm here fully, one hundred per cent on board.'

'You can be less than a hundred,' you laugh, allowing your tears to fall freely. 'You can still be, you know, human.'

'Sure, I'll be like ninety-two per cent or whatever's optimum. Basically I'm saying I won't be changing my mind. So you can stop crying if you like,' he adds, smiling.

You wipe your face with the thin paper napkin on the saucer, suddenly feel shy as though you've exposed yourself in front of a stranger. You want to hold on to the details of this moment – Noah's trimmed nails, the gelled quiff of the waiter walking past, the men in tight T-shirts with goose-pimpled arms being led to their table – imagine telling this anecdote to your future child of how it almost didn't come into existence, from the safe place of its weight in your lap.

'What do you reckon?' asks Noah. 'Shall I take you home?'

'I'm locked out, remember.'

'Oh. I meant our home.' He looks embarrassed to have caused a scenario in which this ever needed clarifying. 'We can come back for your stuff tomorrow.'

You nod and slip out of the booth. He cups your face in his palms and kisses you, his lips firm and soft, the perfect equilibrium. When you break apart you see the little girl in the pinafore dress watching. *It starts as young as this*, you think. *The fairy tale where the prince comes to the rescue.* You want to apologize to her for reaffirming the fantasy of romantic love. But what would you say? 'Not everyone gets a happy ending.'

You did, the girl would think, and on the narrative goes.

You sit on top facing him, your legs hooked around the curve of his hips. His hair hangs in sheets over his forehead covering the tops of his eyes so that it feels as though you are looking through a waterfall. There is no resistance or hesitation as you take his penis and brush it against your opening, no rubber to separate your cells from his as you slide him into you, the feeling of wet clay. Your hands splay across his back, the pressure of your grip like a starfish sticking to a rock. Where do you end and he begin? You like that the answer is currently unknowable. What is he thinking? Is he thinking at all? His face is so unreadable. You are crying again, can taste the burning saltiness of your tears as he gasps and comes inside you like a humid sky breaking.

Still wrapped around him, you cling on tightly, your head draped over his shoulder the way you once saw a baby orang-utan clasp its mother in the Sumatran jungle. *I would stay like this forever*, you think as you unhook your legs and slowly release him. There is something mournful yet mesmerizing about the birthmark on his thigh – that you might never have got to see it again/that you are now getting to see it again. His body is both a salve and a wound to you.

Lying down, he holds you from behind, your head moulded into the crook of his shoulder as if you were purpose-built to fit into each other, that such a design could not be unintentional. You feel his heartbeat on your back, the tacky cushioning of his chest like the crocodile inflatable you used to float on as a child. You want to laugh or weep; the difference between the two feels negligible.

Inside the kitchen, still with the stickiness of sex on you, he cracks eggs into a frying pan as you picture his sperm swimming up through your womb, resisting the barriers your body has unhelpfully put up, only the strongest and fastest surviving.

'Everything's still the same,' you say, looking around the room – at the vintage maps you'd jointly chosen from Portobello Market, the Swiss cheese plant you'd picked out together on a trip to the garden centre one midweek morning in January;

even the photograph of the two of you inside a gondola from your trip to Venice still hangs on the wall.

'What did you think I'd do, redecorate?' You don't tell him *yes*, that as you lay alone inside your flat at night, you'd imagined another woman moving in and making subtle changes, unnoticeable at first until finally there would be little left that you recognized. You don't tell him that along with the agony of losing him there was the frustration and petty loss of having helped build and curate your home, only for you to have to leave it because it wasn't your home; it's his. You say none of this. Trivialities are for those who have been cheated, and you have just won.

That night you have sex again; it feels so effortless now there is none of the halting awkwardness of him reaching into the drawer for a condom, unwrapping and peeling it down himself while you watch or look away, unsure of your role in the procedure. Lying there afterwards, he doesn't shy away from discussion of children. You don't fixate on the subject but he doesn't seize up or avoid it either, speaks with the same ease and dynamism about fatherhood as he does about hockey or politics or theatre. Yes, he's taken time but he's got here in the end; that's all that matters now.

You wish you could stop crying. It's getting absurd, as if he's died or disappeared, rather than come back to you. A thirst and a homesickness surge inside you. Clutching him like a raft, you hold on helplessly as if your survival – or at least the point in surviving – depends on not letting go.

In ten days' time you wake early, and with a full bladder walk to the local pharmacy where you buy three pregnancy tests and a box of Lemsip. Your limbs are taut and you are sore between your legs from all the sex you've been having but your body feels soft and blonde like caramel.

You know it's unlikely, but nevertheless have an inkling as you sit on the toilet seat, the stick flat on the vanity top beside you. The idea that a creature might be alive inside you at this very moment astounds you; is there anything as miraculous and simultaneously commonplace? To your mind, the process of reproduction is as remarkable as the migration of the Serengeti or a solar eclipse but because it is happening every split second around the world it's become akin to growing tomato plants or baking sourdough.

Three minutes later, your instincts are proved wrong; you are not pregnant. As you come out of the bathroom and on to the landing, you shake your head, stick in hand. Noah strokes your hair and assures you that it doesn't matter, that the two of you will keep trying until you are. You discover you have too much trust to cry. That night he cooks kedgeree and kneads your feet with his palms, his fingers stained yellow with turmeric. Oddly, it doesn't tickle where before it always used to. The smell of curry powder permeates the room, sweet and thick and sharp.

Eight more months pass until one day in July your body starts to change in slight but perceptible ways: the firmness of your breasts, the queasiness that arrives without explanation, your sudden aversion to morning coffee replaced by a thirst for orange juice with pulp, and then, finally, the omission of a rusty stain on your underwear. Taking a test feels redundant; you know you are, and yes. A million wildebeest cross the Mara River, the moon moves between the earth and the sun, the two of you have made a person.

As you walk into the bedroom and hold out the test to him, his smile obliterates any memory of his earlier doubt. Wrapping his arms around you, together you face the full-length mirror looking back at yourselves. He spreads his palm across your stomach and tilts his fingers slowly across your torso like a crab crawling over a mound of warm sand. You did it: you got your ending.

/

Someone's phone is ringing; it sounds like your own. As it gets louder, the mirror fades, the stone walls of the restaurant come back into view, the small girl is staring again. You look down at your screen, wondering for a second if it's Noah calling to say he's changed his mind, but it is only the locksmith informing you that he's outside your flat – sounding less jovial than before to discover you aren't there.

Assuring him you're only two minutes away, you place a five-pound note on the table and slide out of the booth, dazed and intensely present. As you stand, you can't quite believe the emptiness of your breasts, the absence of Noah's hands across your stomach; it had felt so real.

Outside, the cold air dries your tears, making your cheeks waxy and tight. The grief of it aches, not just the loss of him but of what you thought your story would look like, but for the first time you feel a lightness at having let go of both.

As you turn off the main road and on to your street, you see the figure of the locksmith in the distance outside your flat. Quickening your walk into a slow jog, you look up at the sky. The moon is gold and moreish like a coin; spectacular.

13. Margot

The receptionist calls your name from behind the magenta desk and gestures in the direction of a lilac corridor lined with potted orchids. Presumably all the purple is meant to signify quality, to confirm that this premium service warrants the thousands of pounds you're about to spend.

You stare at the interlaced hands of the freckled woman and her partner sitting opposite, count eight rings between them. You had declined both Romily and Lillie's offers of coming with you today – despite their multiple attempts to persuade you otherwise – assuring them that you have every intention of involving them in the lead-up to the birth (and in the weeks and months and years that follow) but had felt the need to come to this first appointment on your own.

Besides, you're not the only one here alone. An older woman in a salmon trouser suit is sitting a few seats away, flicking through the *Financial Times*. Across from her, a woman who looks as though she's in her mid-twenties is crocheting with headphones in. Perhaps she's here to freeze her eggs; you've read about the trend in younger women doing this.

As you stand you look down at your phone, at the message from Noah sent earlier this morning. *Thinking of you today. Call me if you need or want to xx*. Need and want. How compatible are those two things? Oliver had once told you that in order for a character to get what they need, they often have to let go of the thing they want. But as you walk along the corridor, towards the smiling nurse waiting for you outside the partially open door, it feels as though what you need might finally be what you also now want.

The nurse beckons you inside, tells you her name is Joelle and asks you to take a seat. You pause before you sit, aware that the next time you stand you may be one step closer to motherhood. Then what will happen? You have only a vague idea. Acknowledging this makes you inhale sharply.

Posters of multiracial children and same-sex couples line the walls, *Helping You Create the Family You Imagine*. It is comforting to think that you are building a family, that in time your child will hopefully be able to not just take love but also give it. Of course, there are no guarantees.

Joelle looks up from the paperwork she's studying and smiles again; her teeth are big and cylindrical with gaps between them.

'So, you're here today to move forward with your treatment plan. Three cycles of IUI with donor sperm, is that right?' Hearing it aloud confirms that it does, for the first time, feel right.

The rungs of light through the slats in the blind form the shadow of a staircase on the ceiling. Excitement twitches inside you like a flickering bulb.

Acknowledgements

The people who have influenced me and inputted into this book, either directly or indirectly, are too numerous to list by name, but I'm particularly indebted to the following:

Cara Lee Simpson for your enthusiasm, shrewdness and composure throughout this process; I'm wildly fortunate to have you as my agent.

Helen Garnons-Williams and Ella Harold for your brilliantly intelligent and perceptive editorial notes and for delivering them with such tact; you've elevated this book far beyond what I could have hoped it to be.

Sarah-Jane Forder and Natalie Wall for your rigorous and sensitive copyedit and editorial management.

Alexia Thomaidis, Kayla Fuller, Anna Ridley, Rosie Safaty, Karishma Jobanputra, Charlotte Daniels, Alice Chandler, Autumn Evans, Samantha Fanaken, Laura Ricchetti, Eleanor Rhodes-Davies, Alison Pearce, Rachel Myers, Georgia Taylor, Zoe Coxon, and everyone at Fig Tree/Penguin General who has championed this book; I'm so grateful to all of you.

Fiona Mitchell, Katy Mack, Léa Rose Emery, Emilie Sheehan and Frances Merivale for providing such astute and encouraging feedback on early drafts. Rowan Lawton for generously giving up your time to meet me and read the manuscript (twice!); your comments were so compassionate and insightful.

Josie Dunn, Lucy Palmer, Keiran Goddard, Roger Lee, Don Harold and Charlie Clarke for ensuring the accuracy of my research (any inaccuracies are my own or intended to be fictional).

Cas Donald and Alison McManus for generously opening up your houses for me to write in, and Fiona Lesley Bennett for nurturing these connections.

Abigail Butler for being my first reader and for your host of contributions leading up to publication; your friendship and opinions are invaluable to me.

Alys Metcalf for your feedback on a very early draft, and for, well, fifteen years of creative and emotional companionship and inspiration; neither this version of the book (or of me) would exist without my knowing you.

Ed Caruana, Jay Bennett, James O'Brien, Sarah Wikeley, Charlotte Benning, Lucy Palmer, Harriet Roberts, Emilie Sheehan, Natalie Orringe, Josie Dunn, Adam Buchanan, Clara and Andrew Whatton, George and Jeni Marshall, Katy Mack, Ted Wilkes, Phil Hughes, Patrick Wray and last, but far from least, Jim Burke: my thanks to you all for your unwavering support during the writing and lead-up to publication of this book (and many of you, for long before it).

Finally – to my parents, Ceri and David Dunn, and my sister, Gemma Dunn, for your radical constancy. You three are arguably my greatest loves.